BONES OF EMPIRE

BOOK ONE OF
THE RELICANT
CHRONICLES

STEVEN SAVILE &
AARON ROSENBERG

PROLOGUE

"Unacceptable!" Emperor Hibikitsu's handsome young features contorted into something macabre. The planes of bone shifted beneath his skin, transforming his usual benign smile into a grimace every bit as horrific as the demonic war masks that hung on the wall behind his throne. The masks were vivid, garishly painted with the single purpose of striking terror into the heart of the enemy, but that momentary flash of The Echo of Victory's anger was far, far more frightening to behold. The oiled topknot peeking above his jeweled crown quivered. The movement was barely perceptible, but those who served him had come to learn the telltale signs of his temper.

Hibikitsu straightened to his full height and leaned forward. His brow furrowed, the shadows deepening around his jade-green eyes. His nostrils flared as his breath became harsher with each exhalation.

The last remnants of sunlight streamed in through the streaked glass high above, colored beams crisscrossing the marble floor. Dust motes twisted and trembled, trapped within the radiance.

The emeralds, garnets and tourmalines studding Hibikitsu's silken sleeve caught and glittered the dusty light as his hand came slashing down through it and struck the small table set beside his throne. The impact shattered the delicate antique. Hibikitsu raised his hand and studied the flakes of lacquer now clinging to his palm. He brushed them away. The flakes fluttered like wind-tossed flowers as the emperor's rage bubbled forth, no longer contained. Now, in this moment, was when Hibikitsu was at his most dangerous. Now was when reason escaped him and he was at his most volatile.

Beneath the dais, the emperor's faithful account managers cowered and fawned and silently prayed that he would not call upon them. None of them wished to hear their name touch his lips while Hibikitsu's temper raged. They prostrated themselves before him, foreheads pressed to the polished marble floor, arms stretched in a vee above their heads, palms pressed flat to the cold stone. The only sound in the entire chamber was the subtle chorus of panicked breath. Every man was recognizable by the way fear shifted his breathing. Hibikitsu knew this. He had studied those he surrounded himself with well enough to recognize them in the dark by sound and scent alone. One did not live long as emperor if one did not know his enemies and his lackeys both. And though he had held the throne only three years, Hibikitsu intended to retain it for many more years to come.

"How can this be so? Tell me in words of one syllable. Explain it to me," Hibikitsu demanded, calmer this time, mastering his temper. He focused on the air flowing in and out of his lungs. Slowly, deliberately, he pushed the shattered table aside and rose from his throne. Lacquer crunched beneath the supple leather soles of his hand-stitched boots.

He leaped down from the dais and landed among his account managers with all the grace of a mountain cat. They shrank back, recognizing the predator now stalking among them.

Mirisai whimpered. He was one of Hibikitsu's Dojo Kuge, the minor nobles entrusted with the day-to-day administration of his bountiful empire. The man had no balls to speak of, literal or metaphorical—he had been gelded as a boy as punishment for his father's many transgressions. Mirisai would be the last of his family's line. There was no greater punishment. He, more than anyone, knew better than to make the mistake of replying to the Echo of Victory's rhetorical question. Anyone foolish enough to make a sound would become the focus of the emperor's ire, but to ignore a direct question was to defy their ruler. He was doomed in either case.

"We have checked and double-checked the tallies, your majesty." Mirisai chewed on his lower lip, staring at the patch of fog his breath left on the stone tiles just an inch from his nose. "I regret there is no mistake."

"You regret? You regret? You would willingly be wrong?" Hibikitsu's face twisted as he wrestled with his fury. "You would willingly fail me, Mirisai? It is for the great good that your line will soon come to an end, I think, for only a fool surrounds himself with people who would willingly fail him. But praise be to Segei Genbinken, you have your wish, there is a mistake." The emperor's voice sank from the roaring of rage to a quieter and more deadly calm. His footsteps echoed hollowly off the stone tiles as he strode over to the wretched account manager. "Are you curious to know the nature of the mistake you were incapable of deducing, Mirisai?"

The Dojo Kuge pushed his face down against the tiles. He felt each of them pressing into his cheek, the rough edges where one abutted the next abrading his skin. He barely dared breathe but somehow found the strength to voice a single word. "Yes." And quickly added, "Your Imperial Majesty" after that, lest he be found to be insubordinate as well as whatever other faults the Emperor chose to heap upon him.

Hibikitsu smiled down at him. Despite the disparity in their ages, anyone with the temerity to look upon him then might have mistaken the emperor for a kindly father looking down upon his wayward son. "The mistake was in allowing this empire to continue, when it should have been razed to the ground. From the detritus of a nation we could have built anew. There is honor in the phoenix. The great bird knows when its time is over and chooses to burn that it might be born again to rise from the ashes in glory. There is no honor here, Mirisai. Even dirt clods and lean-to huts would be better than this."

The smile was gone from Hibikitsu's face. There was nothing fatherly about his expression now as he glared down at the back of the Dojo Kuge's head. In that moment he yearned for nothing more than to draw his sword, Kosshiki, "the Bone Spirit," the legendary blade wielded by the first Relicant Emperor more than two hundred years ago. It was a beautiful blade, still mirror-bright and razor-sharp. In his mind's eye he unsheathed Kosshiki, gripped its braided handle tight, and then slashed downward so speedily the air itself screamed as the Bone Spirit's edge separated the cowering man's head from his shoulders. He breathed deeply, savoring the thought of Mirisai's head rolling free of his miserable shoulders as his feeble body toppled sideways.

Yet, even as his hand tightened on the sword, Hibikitsu knew he would not draw Kosshiki from its scabbard. As much as it pained him, the emperor knew this crisis was not the Dojo Kuge's fault. And even in rage Hibikitsu was not the sort of man to punish another for something beyond his control.

Yet his fury continued unabated, burning inside him like the mythical bird so close to immolating itself. He needed to destroy something.

The emperor knew his own mind. Anger this great must be vented, or it would swallow him whole. The table, no matter how beautiful its lacquered surface, was not enough to sate his need for violence. He looked down at the miserable Mirisai, mastering the sudden urge to deliver a devastating blow to the man's curved spine. That was, of course, assuming the man had a spine at all.

No, it would not do. Hibikitsu glanced quickly around the chamber, his eye sliding past the beautifully detailed carvings on the wide columns that supporting the arched ceiling, and settled instead upon a tall, intricately hand-painted vase that stood against one of the columns. It was old beyond counting, a relic from the days before the Schism, and as such was irreplaceable. Perfect. A dozen quick strides brought him within arm's reach of the antique vase. Only then did Hibikitsu allow his rage to slip its leash.

He drew Kosshiki free of its scabbard in one smooth motion and whipped it though a glittering arc. The blade was so sharp it sliced cleanly through the vase's neck instead of shattering it. A whisper-thin ceramic ring flew sideways to shatter upon the floor. But the damage was too clean. Sometimes a kiss with a fist was what was required by the moment, not the grace of a blade. Something more intimate, more explosive. More satisfying. The vase wobbled on its plinth but did not fall, robbing him of even that small satisfaction. There was not so much as a crack in the glaze following its sudden decapitation.

A snarl escaped Hibikitsu's clenched teeth. Kosshiki still in hand, he spun on his left heel. His right leg lashed out with blinding speed. His boot smashed through the delicate ceramic. What remained of the antique vase shattered into a thousand tiny fragments, becoming a cloud of ceramic dust. Several of those minute shards stung his cheeks as they detonated from the point of impact.

Hibikitsu remained locked in that pose for a long second after the blow, leg still fully extended, the sole of his boot pressed flat against the broad pillar that had so recently sheltered the now-destroyed vase. He exhaled. Better. Then, finally, he lowered his leg until both feet rested solidly on the ground once more. He resheathed his blade, wiping it clean between his fingers as he did.

"Explain to me," he demanded, his words still soft, but clearly only a mask over the steel behind them, "how is it that we find ourselves in such a wretched state?" Hibikitsu did not glance behind him, though he could hear the Jigi Kuge, the lesser bureaucrats of his stumbling empire, shifting as they turned to study his back. "How is it that our noble empire has fallen so low? How can it be that our coffers echo with silence, such is their emptiness? How," he went on without pausing for a breath, "is it that our lands suffer such famine, and our borders shrink in on themselves like withered blooms? This is Rimbaku!" He ground ceramic shards beneath his feet. The sharp cracks of them disintegrating against the stone tiles echoed through the vast chamber. "We are an ancient and powerful nation! Tell me, Mirisai, how could we have fallen so far?"

"Your majesty," Mirisai began, looking for the words the emperor wanted to hear, but Hibikitsu held up a hand and the Dojo Kuge lapsed quickly back into silence. It was a small mercy. There was nothing the man could have said.

"Leave me," Hibikitsu ordered after more uncomfortable silence, and the bureaucrats obeyed at once, rising quickly and noisily to their feet, grateful to flee the room.

When the doors at the far end of the throne room finally closed behind them, Hibikitsu turned to survey what felt like the limits of his domain—the long, ornate chamber, with its sumptuous decorations and detailed carvings, its rich banners and delicate inlays—but he barely registered what he saw. Instead his mind quested outwards, to the real empire beyond these walls.

The Relicant Empire.

His empire.

This land, Rimbaku, had been under his family's protection for longer than that doomed vase had rested in its embrasure. A dozen generations. Once, it had been strong, powerful, feared. Now it faltered. That was the way of all flesh. The young were strong and vital, the old withered and decrepit. If he could not find a way to cheat that natural order, Rimbaku would fall.

His name meant "Echo of Victory" but he heard no echoes here. Only the hollow clatter of encroaching defeat. And soon that echo would become so distant that none would ever recall the original sounds of triumph.

But what could he do? The bureaucrats had done their job only too well, painting an all-too-clear portrait of the ailing nation in his mind. The blight had taken firm hold. Their crops had been failing for years, since before his reign began, and such a simple thing, sustenance, was now almost beyond them. There was so little money to be made because there was so little they could afford to sell. What food could be grown in their blasted soil went to keeping the people alive, and only the most prosperous could claim to be well-fed. Their armies were weak, not solely from ill nourishment but also from lack of skill and lack of supplies. They were bested time and again by the neighboring nations, and each defeat weakened their borders still further. Soon those nations would not be content merely to test their defenses—they would march through them and claim the outlying regions as their own. Rimbaku would shrink, losing land and people. It would dwindle and fade like a dying candle.

Hibikitsu lashed out with his fist this time, driving it into the uncompromising stone of the pillar. The pain was almost a relief. It gave him something else to think about for a moment, but that moment was too short.

The land was still strong deep within, but the people were weak. That was the crux of it. That was the rot at the heart of his empire. The people that should have been the lifeblood of it were dull and lazy and stupid. They were uninspired. They were useless.

A low growl escaped him.

The nobles, his warriors, his commanders and counsel—fools, the lot of them. Lazy, predictable, selfish fools.

How could he be expected to restore the glory of Taido Segei's empire—his empire—when he was surrounded by so much weakness?

Hibikitsu shook his head. The only echo here was the hollow, mocking laughter of defeat closing in on all sides.

He would not surrender. Not while there was blood in his body and breathe in his lungs. He was the Relicant Emperor. He would find a way to reinvigorate his land and his people.

But how? That mocking laughter again. It haunted his every waking moment. How could he stave off the final death rattle of his dying land? The truth was that soon only his capital, Awaihinshi, would remain, and eventually even the City of Polished Light would fall if he could not find an answer to that one simple question. Then all that would be left of Rimbaku would be the dirt itself, and everything that had been the Relicant Empire would vanish into the dull annals of history.

We must become like the phoenix, he thought again, imagining the fires consuming his palace and burning away the blighted soil. We must rise up out of the ashes in glory.

But how? that mocking voice demanded, bitter laughter ringing the question round.

How?

CHAPTER ONE

Noniki really didn't want to go over the wall, but he couldn't live without what was on the other side.

Above him, the moon offered the merest sliver of itself to the night, casting a silvery crescent that was more shadow than light onto the sloping red clay of the rooftops below. The roots of stubborn weeds worried their way into cracks in the mausoleums, climbing all over the huge tombs of the graveyard. The weeds were the only signs of life for miles around. For a moment, beneath the sickle moon, it looked as though the earth itself was reaching out to reclaim the old bones and draw succor from their marrow.

Noniki shivered despite himself.

Shadows moved in the graveyard, the low-hanging leaves of the weeping maples rustling as they dragged across the dirt.

Not for the first time Noniki wished he had even half his elder brother's common sense. Instead of skulking in the graveyard shadows, Kagiri was curled up under one of the tables in the Happoa Kappua, huddling beneath a thin blanket and no doubt dreaming of ample-breasted girls with welcoming smiles and outstretched arms while Noniki froze his backside off.

He shifted from side to side, flexing the muscles in his calves, thighs, and buttocks to keep his blood circulating. His entire body was numb with the cold.

He had felt a pang of guilt when it came to stealing from his brother, even though technically it was both their money his light fingers had appropriated. But he knew Giri would forgive him, especially if he returned bearing bounty.

Noniki hunkered down, pressing his back up against the cold stone wall, and listened to the sounds of the town at night. It was anything but silent. His own breathing formed a cocoon around him, loud enough that he almost didn't hear the bannin's footsteps as the guard approached. Fortunately Noniki's old clothes were faded to the color of mourning, which, given his surroundings, was every bit as useful as it was appropriate.

This was his fourth night studying the guards while they walked the cemetery wall.

His stomach growled, the grumbling surely loud enough to be heard on the other side of the wall. It had been hours since his last meal, a bowl of the same stew and a hunk of the same stale bread Taki fed to the tavern's guests. The food was filling, Noniki had to admit, but not particularly good. And he was tired of surviving on the same fare day after day. That would change soon, though. It had to. He closed his eyes, praying to Taido Segei, the First Emperor, to thicken the shadows and deepen the silence so that together they might hide him all the more thoroughly.

He didn't dare move.

His heart hammered against his breastbone. He could feel the inner tumult all the way up in his throat.

The guards were disciplined and organized. At first Noniki had mistakenly thought breaching the graveyard's wall would be a simple case of memorizing the pattern of their rounds, picking his moment, and scaling the wall without being seen. But there was no discernible pattern to their movement. Sometimes it took them a fifty-seven count to cross paths, sometimes a ninety count, and other times one-hundred-and-thirty. They would cross from the right, they would cross from the left. For all the world he couldn't see a way to predict which way they would come from next, nor how long he would have before they appeared. All he could do was watch from the shadows, frustrated. It wasn't carelessness, either—on the contrary, what he was seeing took incredible discipline. So for the last three nights he had gone back to the Happoa Kappua tavern empty handed. But not tonight. Tonight when he returned he'd be rich with old bones.

If, he amended. If he returned to the Foamy Cup.

Noniki looked down at the ground. He'd been sure by now his dragging feet must have worn a furrow in the dirt with his constant pacing from hovel to hovel. It didn't matter where he watched from, the patrol was every bit as irregular and every bit as frustrating. And for good reason.

The graveyard occupied the very heart of Ginzai; a long-dead and silent heart, but curiously vital just the same. The perimeter wall stretched more than a half-mile in all directions, spanning districts. Less than five hundred feet from his hiding place the road widened and finally opened up to become the market square. The wall formed one side of the marketplace. Built of sturdy bone-white stone, the wall stood five feet high, and sprouted an ironwork grille that rose another five feet beyond that, exploding outward into a confusion of sharp spikes. The graveyard wall was the only protective wall in all of Ginzai. Its craftsmanship and strength spoke to the reverence they gave their ancestors' graves, and even more so to the value society placed upon the bones—the aishone—housed within.

The shadows crept along the graveyard wall as the moon traversed the night sky. Beyond the wall, row upon row of mausoleums held wealth beyond imagining. The death houses were purely functional in form, lacking any kind of ornamentation. There was no sign of love for the dead, which only made the graveyard more oppressive. Noniki eased himself to his feet and ghosted from his hiding place, running across the no man's land between the houses and the cemetery wall, back into the deeper shadow at its foot. He rose up on his toes and grasped the iron bars, peering through.

The mists would come soon and last for a few hours. Every night it was the same: as the moon reached its azimuth, the mists began to rise off the river and drift toward the mountains that formed a natural north wall to the town. The curtain of rock loomed over the black ribbon of water that bisected the streets, creating a natural division that went all the way through the graveyard. The mists were merely cold, damp air from the river being carried by the early morning breeze toward the bare rock of the mountain, but that did nothing to diminish its eeriness—nor its usefulness to a would-be grave robber.

Noniki edged around the wall, keeping his body pressed flat against it.

He could see the first curls of mist rising from the water.

He smiled, feeling his nerves begin to settle. He was committed to his course of action. There was no turning back now.

The mist transformed the streets into shrouded otherworldly avenues, and within it Noniki's imagination ran wild, turning the bannin into crude-faced demons and angry devils as they prowled the graveyard. It was a valuable lesson, that even knowing did not prevent such wild notions.

Ginzai was full of lessons, for the curious and the careless alike.

The first lesson Noniki had learned during his months in Ginzai was that people here were more reverent of the mists than they were the dead. It had not taken him long to realize that it wasn't reverence but simple fear, which worked just as well for him.

Everything about Ginzai was intimidating to Noniki, from the heights of the jagged peaks sheltering it to the hundreds of buildings and narrow streets, to the dyed clothes of the merchants and the wares in their market stalls, to the mounds of fresh fruit, stacks of wine casks, cuts of meat and strings of sausage laid out to entice the hungry—everything, that was, apart from the river itself, which ought to have been the lifeblood of the place. This close to its source it emerged from the mountains as little more than a babbling brook, and bore little comparison to the frothing beast it became downriver as the ground shifted from hard rock to softer marshland and the water cut a wider and wider course.

Noniki had briefly considered using the river to break into the necropolis. Growing up in a fishing village meant water was every bit as natural a habitat for him and Giri as dry land—all he needed was a reed for a breathing pipe and he'd be able to swim just below the surface all the way into the heart of the graveyard. The wall's architecture had quickly put paid to that idea. While the stone might have stopped at the riverbanks, a quick, wet, reconnoiter revealed that the ironworks sank deep into the riverbed, allowing the river to rush through it while keeping unwanted flotsam and jetsam—or, in this case, a would-be bone thief—out. He had spent the remainder of that night shivering in wet clothes and seeking other ways in. Ways that did not involve coinage.

Another lesson Noniki had learned since arriving was that, in Ginzai, even being someone's child did not entitle you to their bones. The notion was utterly alien to him. The very most that birth assured you was the right of first refusal if you had the coin to purchase them. Nothing more. The town itself claimed ownership of all aishone in exchange for burial and grave protection. It kept the graveyard under lock and key, and patrolled from dusk 'til dawn. Those with coin enough could legitimately purchase all the aishone their hearts desired from the graveyard merchants during the day. They could pay their respects, too, but that rarely happened. In Ginzai, the dead were a source of wealth and knowledge, not a subject of veneration—that was another lesson he had learned. It was all commerce. And business was one thing the town took very seriously indeed. The punishment for what he was about to do was terrifying in its finality and barbaric in its cruelty: if they caught him, Noniki would be boiled alive, then the flesh would be stripped clean and his skeleton broken to create more aishone—though why anyone would want to buy the bones of a thief unskilled enough to get caught was beyond him.

It was all so different from the village they'd left behind, but that was no longer a surprise to him. It was another world. Ginzai was full of strangers, where the village had been full of friends. There was no intimacy to these streets. Even surrounded by so many people, without Kagiri around Noniki felt utterly and completely alone in a way he never had before. Ginzai was the loneliest place he had ever been, lonelier by far than the wide, empty plain the brothers had crossed to get here. People ceased to matter in any way Noniki could understand. Back home the living were the heart and soul of the village, and when they returned to the earth, sprinkled over the dirt as ash to nurture the crops, they became the lifeblood of the land. It wasn't so here. Here in Ginzai it was as though the graveyard wall created more than just a physical barrier between the living and the dead. The bones of their ancestors became mere commodities to be traded, their souls simply forgotten. Not so in the village. It wasn't that the villagers shunned the Relicant Way—far from it. Like everywhere else in the empire, the village's survival centered on aishone. Without drawing on the relic bones, all of Rimbaku would have crumbled and fallen long ago. But where Noniki came from aishone were not goods to be bought and sold so callously, they were the dead's legacy, one last gift to their children and their children's children. The people of Ginzai seemed to be in a hurry to forget who had come before them and transform the trials and triumphs of their lives into mere merchandise. The fact that the graveyard itself handled the sale of the old bones turned his stomach. It was wrong. These people were soulless.

It wasn't so long ago that Noniki couldn't remember every last detail of what it had been like watching his mother burn on the funeral pyre. Even now, he could still feel the ghost of the flames' warmth against his cheeks when he closed his eyes. Some things he remembered better, more vividly, than others, like his brother's need to stare morbidly at the rice paper-wrapped corpse as it charred and burned. Mama Teryin wasn't in there. She wasn't trapped within her earthly flesh. She had risen into the hands of Taido Segei and found peace. He had faith. He believed. Did any here in Ginzai believe? he wondered, watching again as the bannin crossed. Their tanned leather cuirasses were only a few shades off the color of their skin, creating the illusion that they walked naked through the mists.

The old witch-woman, Obasan, had paid well for his mother's aishone—five small bronze coins. It had seemed like a fortune at the time, but the simple necessity of living had seen it spent all too quickly. Now, thanks to his light fingers, when Kagiri woke he would know that the brothers didn't have so much as two brass to rub together. There was no money to buy aishone, and without it they were husks, as soulless and disconnected as everyone else in Ginzai. Nor was that likely to change while they worked at the Foaming Cup, mopping the floor and clearing away the dishes. Taki did not pay enough for them to save any money, but it had been the only job available to two strangers who lacked aishone of their own and at least it kept them fed and housed. That was why Noniki had decided to go over the wall. Desperate times called for desperate measures. He longed to feel a connection with the ancestors, to touch their lives and experience all that they had, to feel skill and talent thrum through his veins once more.

Without it, he felt hollow. Without it, he was hollow. Hollow and useless.

The nature of the aishone was such that a person could tap the residual skills and knowledge of the deceased—be that a man's talent for fishing, for mending nets, for building walls or fashioning wood into furniture, practical gifts on which society was built or more esoteric ones like the keen eye and deft brush needed to create the wondrous art that made life so much richer. Tap them and absorb them. It could make artisans and artists out of anyone, allowing them to work with all the skill of the ancestors while the aishone lasted. In that way an aspect of the dead would live on, but only as a remnant. The connection did not grant the living a way to commune with the dead—it was purely parasitic.

Consuming her bones would not bring his mother back.

It was people's aitachi, their Relicant Touch, that allowed them to absorb the talent of the bones. No two men possessed the same degree of talent, nor wielded it in quite the same way.

Noniki was Suponichi. Like the sponge, he could absorb skills quickly from the bones. But, also like a sponge, those skills leaked out even as he drank them down. He simply could not hold onto the trace talents, no matter how desperately he tried. In that he was Tokimichi, a flutter touch, meaning his appetite for the bones was rapacious and unquenchable. He had to absorb the same skills over and over again, needing more and more aishone simply to maintain his grasp on the gift.

His brother, on the other hand, was Chosinichi—like a reservoir, Giri was capable of drinking in and storing skills for months upon end. But there was a hammer's bluntness to his touch—he lacked finesse, and that meant Giri needed vastly more aishone to absorb even the slightest trace from the old bones. In that he was Sokuichi, a crude touch.

In that way the brothers shared their sorrow, for their father's aishone that Kagiri carried over his heart was so worn down it was useless to either of them, and they had sold their mother's for the coin they needed to escape. Together, though, they were a perfect whole, like two aspects of the same soul that had been splintered at birth. Only a Jubanichi—someone capable of using their perfect touch to absorb quickly and hold the skill for a long time—was stronger, and the Jubanichi were mere myths, not real people at all.

Still, it didn't matter how strong they were, together or alone. Without relic bones to leech from they might as well have been Mukanichi, one of the accursed Untouched, cast out and cast aside. Which was why Noniki had snuck out in the middle of the night, leaving his brother to sleep on, blissfully oblivious. It had pained him to do so, for the two had always been inseparable. But this time had to be different. Knowing the consequences of failure, Kagiri would have tried to stop him.

Noniki crept along the wall, watching through the iron latticework as two of the bannin crossed paths. They nodded to each other once, neither one lowering their eyes, and took the time to check the heavy padlocks and bolts to be sure the gate was still secure. Both of the bannin were large, powerful men, a head taller than Kagiri and wider than Noniki, but for all their obvious strength age was creeping up on them, and their guts strained at the sturdy leather jackets where the bannin were turning to fat. Not that the extra pounds would make any substantive difference to the outcome if he was caught—they would still be more than capable of throwing him up against the nearest building and beating him bloody until the magistrates arrived to boil his bones.

The bannin were armed, as well—spears and clubs, common weapons, crude but no less lethal in the hands of a skilled warrior. At least neither man carried a nihono. Noniki had only seen such a weapon once, when one of Emperor Hibikitsu's elite soldiers had cut through the village on his way to the border, but even that brief glimpse was unforgettable. There was something absolutely compelling about the long, curve-bladed sword resting against the warrior's thigh. It was a thing of contradictions, beautiful and ugly at once, thrilling and utterly terrifying at the same time. Death had walked with him that day. The brothers had badgered the warrior to show them the blade, but he had refused, saying simply that if he drew it the nihono would need to quench its blood thirst before he could sheath it again. Noniki had offered his, but the warrior had said he could not spill innocent blood. The encounter was carved into Noniki's mind now every bit as indelibly as if the blade's gleaming tip had engraved it there. He shivered again, but not because of the cold this time.

Enough idle thought and memory, though. Now was a time for action.

Noniki turned his back on the main gate and rushed along the line of the perimeter wall, crouching low and running hard. His old village rags whispered furiously as he ran. Shy of the gates, Noniki dropped to the ground, breathing hard. The mist had thickened around the river now to mask any wandering spirits or restless dead that might have risen with the night. It seemed almost to be alive itself. The faint breeze caused tatters of white to eddy out and slowly contract in on themselves again and again in ever-expanding waves. It gave the disturbing impression that the mist was somehow breathing. In and out, in and out. It was little wonder the mists inspired such dread and superstition. Noniki licked his lips, then chewed on the flesh of the lower one. It was hard to imagine the people of the village being so unnerved by something so natural; mist and marsh fog was nothing more than a simple fact of life. It was as though, by surrounding their ancestors with walls of stone, the inhabitants of Ginzai had somehow cut themselves off from nature itself and transformed something of beauty into a hiding place for the restless ones fallen from Taido Segei's embrace.

The mists could not gather swiftly enough for Noniki's liking. No matter what his brother said, there was nothing virtuous in patience. More of the white wraiths corkscrewed up from the shallow river, thickening as they drifted across the canted rooftops.

He turned his attention back to the graveyard.

There were other bannin beyond the wall, though the combination of mist and darkness made it impossible to tell if two, four, ten, or forty prowled among the mausoleums.

Noniki stuffed his hand into his pocket and closed his fist around the firecracker he'd bought with the last of their money.

He'd insisted it have a long fuse, longer than the few seconds children usually wanted for their flash-bangs. He needed the fuse to be slow enough that he could plant it and hide, so when it erupted, whistling like a damned spirit and showering the graveyard gate with sparks, he'd be far enough away to take full advantage of the distraction.

Impetuous, yes. Stupid, no.

Noniki watched again as two bannin strode to the gates, crossed, and headed back toward the paths between the mausoleums. In the distance he saw thicker smoke that had nothing to do with the morning mist rising out of a chimney. It was one of the funeral fires. He drew three fingers sharply across his chest, making the sign of Taido Segei over his heart, and wished the dead safe passage into the First Emperor's embrace.

When the next pair of bannin crossed in front of the gates, Noniki began counting. It was three minutes before the next bannin came into view. He carried on counting out the seconds. Four more minutes until the next pair crossed before the gates, and two minutes before the next. There was never less than two minutes between them, but that did not mean no one was watching the gate or the perimeter wall. Still, the mists were thick enough now that visibility was reduced to two dozen paces, no more, which would buy him all the time he needed to plant the firecracker, light the fuse, and run. After that his fate rested in the hands of whatever spirits watched over graverobbers in the dead of night. He fervently prayed they were feeling benevolent, or at least admired his daring, because he had no wish to have his bones stripped and sold to the highest bidder.

It all came down to timing now. Timing and luck. He scurried forward, keeping low and giving the sliver of moon as little as possible of his body to conjure shadows from, dug a small pockmark in the dirt for the firecracker, and set it down. There was a tarry coating on the fuse that the apothecary had assured him meant it didn't need a naked flame to ignite it. All he had to do was roll the fuse between thumb and forefinger, just as the old man had shown him. The friction separated the two parts of the fuse, causing something in the tar to spark and catch.

The fuse began to smolder.

Noniki didn't stay to watch it burn. Even with the slow fuse he knew he had less than a minute to reach the stretch of wall he intended to scale, and he had to do so without being seen.

He ran hard, arms and legs pumping furiously as he drove himself on, counting out the seconds in his head.

The firecracker exploded before he reached the count of twenty. It sounded like all the underworld were breaking loose, snapping and cackling and tearing at the earth as the black powder burned.

He was far too close to the gates for comfort, but it was now or never.

Noniki cast one last desperate glance toward the mausoleums, catching sight of four bannin running toward the firecracker as it sputtered out. He couldn't see any more, and he could only hope that they could not see him either. He threw himself at the wall, grasping the iron railings as close to the spikes as he could, and hauled himself up, kicking at the stones for purchase as he scrabbled upwards.

Noniki had always been blessed with a powerful upper body— it came from years of dragging the fishing nets out of the river. Hauling barrels up from the Happoa Kappua's cellar for Taka had kept him in shape. He grasped the top of the railing and heaved himself up until his chin was level with the iron spikes. Now all he had to do was negotiate them without impaling himself in the process. And without getting caught. He couldn't hear the firecracker anymore, meaning the only thing he had in his favor now was the mist.

Gritting his teeth, he forced himself higher, until his wrists and the top of the railings were level with his chest, and then he leaned back, letting his weight act as a counterbalance until his elbows locked. He rocked gently in place, once, twice, three times, then surged upwards. Every second spent on the wall increased the chances of the bannin spotting him, or hearing him as he scuffled down on the other side.

Noniki's entire body levered up over the spikes, the iron digging into his stomach as his wrists trembled under the strain of holding him in place. He brought his leg up, wedging his foot between two of the iron spikes, and then he didn't know what to do. His entire body perched precariously on the iron railings, half in, half out of the cemetery, his arms trembling violently from the strain of holding him there. He couldn't bring himself to let go of the railing and he couldn't bring his other foot up. All he could think to do was cant slowly forward until his weight became too much for his arms to bear and gravity dragged him clear. It wasn't graceful, but worse than that, it wasn't quiet.

He came down hard, grunting as he landed, and lay there looking up at the few stars he could still see through the thickening mist. He couldn't hold back the grin. He'd made it. All he had to do now was get the aishone and get out. He lay there, taking the time to get his breathing under control.

The crunch of footsteps suddenly sounded against the crushed gravel. Close. Too, too close.

Instinctively, Noniki rolled over, pressing his body up against the base of the perimeter wall. He held his breath, willing himself absolutely motionless.

The footsteps grew louder, grit scuffing under soft leather soles.

He closed his eyes and struggled not to cry, waiting for a shout of alarm or the impact of a spear in his gut, whichever came first.

"You're really not very good at this sort of thing, are you?"

CHAPTER TWO

Something—a noise that shouldn't have been there—penetrated Kagiri's sleep. He rolled over. All things considered, it was not the wisest course of action. He had been sleeping wedged in between various table and chair legs, with very little room to spare on either side. Rolling over, he fetched the side of his head up against one of the many wooden legs tangled around him. Hard. The shock of it woke Kagiri and left him cradling his face.

He moaned with the pain as he felt around the softness of his bruised cheek. The skin was tender from just below his left eye all the way down to his jawline. Kagiri already wore the bruises of night after night spent sleeping on the tavern floor. He had lost count of the times he had been bested in a fight with the furniture while he slept—many more than he had won, though, judging by the state of his face.

But freedom was ingrained into his muscle memory; all of his life he'd had room to stretch out while he slept. He was used to tossing and turning—living out his dreams, his mother used to call it when he kicked off his blankets or tangled them around his legs like chains. It had never felt like a luxury before. So when he slept he thrashed and wriggled and writhed. What he didn't do was lie still, and on the floor of Taki's tavern that meant he risked concussion nightly.

Noniki had it easier on two counts: he was half a head shorter than Giri, and twice as thick-headed. If he cracked his head on a table he was likely to splinter the wood, not his skull.

Kagiri eased himself up into a sitting position. Night played with the landscape of the tavern, transforming every angle and shape into something curious and alien. It took him a full minute of scanning the darkness to realize that something was wrong with the night world—

Noniki's bedroll was under a nearby table, but Kagiri's brother himself was nowhere to be seen.

The darkness in the taproom was absolute. The windows were firmly shuttered, though a few errant chinks of moonlight managed to slither between the slats. Those glimmers meant he could make out the table leg that had just beaten him so mercilessly, and the vague outline of the next set of legs beyond that. But that was where the world ended, at least until his vision adjusted to the darkness. His brother could have been ten feet away and he never would have known.

Except that Noniki wasn't exactly known for being quiet.

"Niki?" Kagiri whispered, expecting his brother to answer.

He didn't.

Which raised the obvious question: what was the noise that had woken him? Because there had been a noise, of that he was certain. Something out of place enough to bleed through into his dreams and startle him awake. But what?

"Niki?" he whispered again, a little louder this time.

Still there was no answer.

Kagiri cursed his younger brother as he struggled to his feet. He gripped the edge of the table for support. Moonlight cast a handful of silvery coins across the tavern floor, as lovely as they were illusory, and his eyes finally adjusted enough for him to scan the room. There was no sign of his brother.

Kagiri listened to the darkness. It took him a moment to realize he could hear someone moving about the taproom, with heavy breathing and the shuffle of feet on the hardwood floor. "Niki?" He called out, louder now, knowing even as he did that it wasn't his brother prowling restlessly around the tavern like some sort of caged animal looking for trouble. Noniki would have had no reason to remain silent, unless he was caught in the middle of some empty-headed scheme—which would have been just like Noniki, he knew.

But Taki wasn't stupid enough to leave the lockbox with the day's takings downstairs. She took it up to her chamber every night and slept with it beneath her bed. So if Noniki was up to something, it wasn't stealing money. What, then? There was food to be had, but it was the same stew that bubbled almost dry over the fire every day, the same soup they ate freely, which made a mockery out of the idea of sneaking around in the dark to steal a bowl. Rice wine? Taki was a wily old fox and knew exactly how much there was in each bottle, right down to the smallest measure. She'd happily let them drink their fill and dock any discrepancy from their pay. With the solitary bronze coin they earned each week barely enough for a single cup of the weakest, foulest bottle, they'd be working off the debt from a single hangover for months.

As he discounted one harebrained schemes after another, Kagiri found himself drawing the only reasonable conclusion: it wasn't his brother sneaking about in the dark.

He heard a muffled thunk, and, right behind it, a low grunt. The sounds sent chills through him. Until then the idea of someone in the dark with him had been nebulous, and nothing more dangerous than his imagination running wild. With that single grunt, the danger became very, very real.

Because he knew the sound had not come from Noniki.

Kagiri froze, rooted to the spot. His mouth dried up. His heart rate rose rapidly, beating so hard he felt it high in his throat. Sweat peppered his brow.

His next thought was Taki, but he knew the old woman's rancid smell; it wasn't her. Besides, Taki wouldn't fumble around in the dark, she'd bring a lantern down with her. Which meant it was someone else—someone who had no business being in the Happoa Kappua in the dead of night.

The noise came again. Kagiri tried to match the sounds to images in his head as he imagined the layout of the tavern. The sound had come from the front door. The locked and barred front door.

He crept quietly across the floor, the wooden timbers groaning beneath his weight, feeling his way in the dark until he reached the tavern door. It was crafted from sturdy timber and bound with heavy iron ties, with a thick wooden brace beam that lay across it for added security. But Kagiri's right foot brushed against something, and by squinting he could just make it out— the brace beam, laying on the floor.

Even as he considered the implications of his discovery, and of his brother's absence, Kagiri heard the thunk again. Someone—or something—was on the other side of the door. And they were trying to get in.

There was a crescent moon out tonight, its dim light still bright against the darkness of the tavern. As his eyes began to adjust, Kagiri could make out more and more of the dark contours of the door, curiously giving the shadows at its base more depth and solidity. Then, slowly, he comprehended the error in his thinking. It wasn't that his eyes were adjusting. The thin gleam surrounding the door was only broken by the two hinges on the one side and the latch on the other, but even as he studied it Kagiri saw that there was more light streaming in from the upper left corner than the lower one, and more leaking through at the bottom right than the left. When the grunt came again, the illusion of the dark so perfect the intruder might have been standing by his shoulder rather than on the other side of the door, Kagiri understood what the uneven light meant: the door was hanging askew. And even as the thought struck him there was another crack, this one like bone breaking.

Moonlight streamed though unbroken all along the upper edge of the door as one of the leather hinges snapped.

No, Kagiri realized sickly, it hadn't snapped. It had been cut.

Someone was trying to break into the taproom.

But their trying to break in meant that, at least for now, they were still safely on the other side of the door and didn't know he was waiting for them inside.

Kagiri's mind raced, but curiously his breathing slowed, as did his heart, a surprising sense of calm settling over him. Why would anyone break in? What did they stand to gain? There was barely enough coin to make it worth robbing the place. Taki's most valuable asset was the rice wine, and anyone looking to sell that on the black market would have to answer the obvious questions of where it came from, given that every bottle had Taki's stamp on it and everyone knew the malodorous little tavern-keeper. Some people even claimed to like her. Which meant that any would-be thieves would have to sell their ill-gotten gains well outside Ginzai.

For a moment he wondered if the lurker at the threshold could simply be Noniki coming home. The grate of the blade on the leather of the second hinge disabused him of that notion.

Thinking quickly, Kagiri rushed back across the dark room, shoved open the door at the far end, and stepped into the pitch black of the kitchen beyond. He moved by instinct and memory. The cook's implements hung from hooks along the farthest wall, but without light to guide him Kagiri stumbled about like a blind man, reaching out for something to hold onto as he worked his way around the room. He barked his shin against something and cursed as he cracked his hip on one of the sharp edges hidden in the dark. He briefly considered the cleaver but knew if you brought a knife to a fight you had best be prepared to use it, and be prepared for it to be used on you in return. He had no wish to escalate whatever was about to happen to the point of breaking bones and hacking flesh. Besides, the meat cleaver was unwieldy and awkward. Kagiri had grown up scuffling with his brother and their friends, and figured he could handle himself in a brawl, but his skill with a blade was limited to boning fish and splicing rope for nets. Instead he opted for something big and solid and most definitely blunt, lifting down one of the reassuringly heavy cast-iron woks. Hammered against the side of an unsuspecting head, it would rattle any intruder.

Praying fervently that it wouldn't come to that, Kagiri crept back into the taproom just as the leather of the lower hinge sheered through and the entire door lurched within its frame. It was now held in place by the latch alone. A single sharp shove and it would topple inwards.

But instead of forcing it, whoever was on the other side seemed intent upon easing the door open, using the latch to take the door's weight as though it were a hinge. The perilous arrangement threatened to come crashing down as the makeshift hinge groaned pitifully against the strain, and then, as the door passed its point of balance, the latch howled like the banshee of legend, twisting out of true before finally giving completely.

The door fell, striking the floor with a noise akin to a blackpowder cannon detonating. Dust billowed up from the hardwood. Kagiri blinked to clear his eyes, then gaped as a towering silhouette loomed in the gaping hole where the door had been. The shadowy figure clutched a wickedly curved knife in one huge fist. The blade glinted silver in the moonlight.

CHAPTER THREE

The accusation came out of nowhere.

Instinctively Noniki scrambled back, but there was nowhere to go. His eyes darted left and right, scouring the mist for signs of his accuser. For a moment the shadow of a crooked tree standing naked in the narrow alleys between the dead houses had him fooled. Forgetting where he was—and the danger he was in—Noniki almost challenged the voice but bit down on the cry before it could escape his mouth. In that endless second Noniki's mind raced, his panicked thoughts like wandering spirits lost in the mist.

The voice hadn't been harsh or abrasive like he had imagined the bannin would sound; on the contrary, it was honeyed, its tone gently mocking, as though him lying there on his back by the boneyard wall was the funniest thing the guard had ever seen.

There was more to it than that, though—something not quite right about the voice. It wasn't merely honeyed, he realized. In four nights he hadn't seen a single female bannin guarding the graveyard. In fact, he hadn't seen a single female bannin in all of Ginzai. But despite the slight muffled quality to the words, there was no mistaking the fact that the voice belonged to a woman.

For the longest time Noniki didn't dare move. Every sense heightened. He could hear the blood pounding through his temples. He could feel every blade of damp grass tickle his skin, and the sudden chill of the mist as it curled around him. He could smell the sweat dripping from his face, and the chalky taste of long-dead things all around. He waited, breath quickening in his throat, drawing his legs up instinctively trying to protect himself, expecting the beating to rain down on him. But the pain didn't come.

The woman stayed silent.

The mists had thickened into a miasmic veil. He could barely make out the soft edges of the mausoleums as they blurred beneath the shroud of white. She was out there, somewhere. But where?

"You're no bannin," he said, barely risking a whisper.

She laughed at him, a low, throaty chuckle. "If you were any sharper you'd cut yourself."

"Who's there? Show yourself!" Noniki angled himself up onto one elbow but kept his back pressed against the wall. His feet dug into the dry, hard dirt.

"Why on earth would I want to do that," she replied, "after I went to all this trouble to hide?" But a moment later she appeared out of the mists, a slim form that seemed almost ethereal itself as she walked toward him without a sound. "It's a miracle they didn't catch you," she continued, offering Noniki a hand up. She wore a low cowl and a silken scarf to hide her features, but as he rose the dim moonlight revealed the delicate oval of her face and sketched the line of a pert nose. Noniki barely registered any of that, however. He stared into the girl's dark, almond-shaped eyes instead, and lost whatever it was he'd been about to say.

"You made enough noise to raise every damned atakai from here to Awaihinshi when you fell from the wall," she continued, gesturing to ward off the malevolent ancestral spirits as he heaved himself to his feet.

"And I suppose you move with the grace of the west wind?"

"Did you have any doubt?" She laughed at him again. "You had no idea I was there until I decided to introduce myself."

She had a point.

"So what are you doing here? Let me guess—something stupid. It's got to be something stupid." She jabbed her forefinger into his chest. Noniki caught the faintest hint of jasmine and lotus that clung to her skin. He wasn't used to the confusion the girl's perfume and proximity stirred, but the question brought him back to his task.

"None of your business," he snapped. Hardly the most scathing reply but it was short and to the point and he didn't have time to think up a more cutting retort. And then it hit him—he'd stopped counting. How long had he been in the graveyard? He looked about frantically.

"Relax," she said, reading his sudden panic. "They won't be back around for another minute yet."

Now it was his turn to eye her. He knew he was staring. In that one line she'd revealed more about herself than a dozen questions might have. For all the apparent randomness of the bannin's patrols, she knew their pattern. That meant she'd been studying them far longer than he had. Why? "So why are you here? Come to pay your respects?"

Her eyes crinkled from the smile he couldn't see beneath her scarf. "Not exactly, but you're right about one thing—we're running out of time. Stay behind me, keep your mouth shut, and try not to get in my way. Think you can manage that?" She didn't wait for his answer. Her cowl rippled in the wind as, soundlessly, she spun on her heel and set off deeper into the cemetery.

She was swallowed by the mist before she reached the first row of graves.

"Wait!" Noniki called after her, then covered his mouth as he realized just how loud his cry had been. The word was out—he couldn't haul it back. All he could do was hope that the guards were far enough away not to have heard it. In a few short minutes this girl had turned him into a bumbling backwater buffoon. Cursing his newfound stupidity, Noniki hurried to catch up before she disappeared into the mists forever.

Not ten steps in, he stubbed his toe on a carelessly discarded shovel. He kicked it away, and then as an afterthought scrabbled about to retrieve the offending tool. It would make digging up bones a lot easier. He couldn't believe he hadn't thought to bring one.

He scurried to catch up.

He caught sight of the young woman—the way she moved, the way she talked, everything about her save her disconcerting confidence suggested they were of an age, making her more of a young woman than a girl—as she slipped through a narrow crack in one of the crypt entrances. He darted after her, barely squeezing through the door before she pulled it almost closed. The thinnest sliver of moonlight slashed through the dark crypt. It was enough to illuminate row after row of bodies in various stages of decomposition, some in open caskets, others just left to rot on the stone shelves like forgotten produce. The smell was not something Noniki had expected. For some reason he had assumed the bodies would have been stripped of vital organs and soft meat so only the bones remained. Leaving them to rot down to their relic bones like this was nothing short of barbaric. The dead were afforded considerably more dignity in the village.

He edged his way deeper into the darkness. He couldn't see her, but he could hear her breathing. And then he couldn't. The crypt was absolutely silent. Instinctively, Noniki held his breath.

On the other side of the stone door, footsteps approached and then slowly receded.

"Who are you?" he whispered, finally able to breathe again.

"Seikoku. You?"

"Noniki."

"Well, my newfound friend Noniki, tell me—is this your first time?" she asked playfully. Then she answered her own question: "Of course it is—you've clearly never been here before."

"Have you?" he shot back. There was no way he could read her expression in the darkness, but her silence told Noniki everything he needed to know. "You have! You're koshitsu!"

"Seems to me you're in no position to talk, given you've obviously come here to steal bones." There was nothing playful in her tone this time.

Noniki shook his head. It was a pitiful denial. He had been planning to steal aishone from the graveyard, yes, but somehow in his own mind he'd rationalized it as a crime of necessity. To brand himself a koshitsu? A graverobber? It was as though a claw reached into his chest and closed around his heart, sinking its talons deep into that still-beating organ. The koshitsus' vile reputation had reached the village. The graverobbers were craven thieves who stole bones from the ground for their own nefarious purposes.

And this captivating young woman was one of them?

"I don't understand," he admitted quietly. "Why?" It was such a huge question he tried to fasten on something he could understand, and the only thing that made any sense to him was his own desperation. "Are they forcing you?" he asked, hoping against hope she would utter that one word, "yes," and somehow he would be able to save her. Not that he could save himself, Noniki thought bitterly.

Seikoku stepped forward into what little light there was. She drew the cowl back and tugged down the scarf so that he could see her face properly for the first time. Her raven-black hair was pulled back in a tight bun and held in place by two long wooden rods, Noniki realized, seeing the faintest suggestion of a pattern carved into their shafts. "Is who forcing me?"

"The other koshitsu."

She stared at him a second longer, her forehead furrowing as she scrutinized the earnest young man in front of her, and then she broke out into giggles. She shook her head. "Where have you been hiding all my life, Noniki? The other koshitsu." Seikoku couldn't hide her smile, which left Noniki feeling six inches tall. "You do know the word's a curse, not a guild, don't you?"

He stared. The koshitsu were a clandestine group of men—villains, thieves, charlatans, and murderers—gifted with unnatural powers, capable of moving among the dead. Some could even walk through walls. Everyone knew that. So why was she laughing at him?

And then it hit him—they were surrounded on all sides by walls. Were they being watched now? Was that why she was laughing? Was she trying to protect him from her paymasters, or throw him off their scent? He stepped in close, urging Seikoku to be quiet, but she couldn't stop laughing. Her laughter seemed so loud in the confines of the crypt. Surely it would reach the bannin? He clamped a hand across her mouth, masking those bow-shaped lips. She bit him. Noniki yanked his hand away, about to yell, when he heard a too-close shout beyond the stone door. "Fumati? That you?"

Noniki closed his eyes, willing himself invisible. He had no such gift. Neither could he melt away into the walls. In practice it seemed he made a rather poor koshitsu, but perhaps that was no bad thing. Assuming he actually got out of this mess.

"Not me." The bannin sounded so close—close enough to reach out and place the flat of his hand against the cold stone of the crypt's door. Noniki didn't dare move so much as a muscle. "But I heard it."

Noniki saw the realization reach Seikoku's eyes, and suddenly the silence between them seemed even more eerie. She drew away from him, pulling her cowl and scarf up to cover her face once more, and stepped back into the shadows. An unseen fleck of grit ground beneath her foot. The crunch of it was loud as a firecracker in their enclosed space. Both of them froze.

Then sound exploded outside the crypt:

"Halt!"

"Who's there?"

"Show yourself!"

Both bannin began hollering orders at once. Noniki stood rooted to the spot. Seikoku grabbed him by the arm and pulled him away from the chink of light.

"I will not be caught," she hissed. He could feel her fear in the trembling of her hand, but she sounded so sure of herself. "You do as I say or you're on your own. Make up your mind. Now."

"Tell me what to do."

"Follow me." Seikoku retreated another step deeper into the crypt, and then another. Noniki didn't realize what she had in mind until it was too late to turn back. She crouched down and crawled onto one of the lowest shelves, sharing it with the bones of a dead man. Seikoku wedged herself against the wall of the mausoleum, completely invisible to him. "What are you waiting for?" her disembodied voice drifted up to fill the darkness.

Noniki swallowed his disgust and moved quickly, finding a low shelf for himself. He reached in, easing the body aside. It still bore flesh, which suited his needs if not his stomach. He clambered in to the shelf, face pressed uncomfortably close to the mottled cheeks and blue lips of the corpse. There was barely enough room to wriggle across the dead man. The drawstring of his pants caught on the dead man's clothes. For a sickening moment he thought he was stuck—then the cloth tore and he was free. Noniki pressed himself up against the stone wall, doing everything he could to hide behind the rag-clothed corpse and praying to the king of all the dead that it was going to be enough to save him.

"What's this? This crypt's open! Fumati, get over here!"

Stone grated upon stone, and a moment later the chink of light widened into a huge slash, like a grin cutting through the dark.

Two bannin stepped into the light.

Chapter Four

"Ah!" The gasp escaped Kagiri's lips unintended, a visceral reaction to the sight of the hulking shadow before him. He backed away from the fallen door, wok raised defensively in front of him, the heavy pan shaking despite his using both hands to prop it up. "Go away," he managed to utter, the warning little more than a whisper. Then he licked his lips and tried again. "Go away!"

"Huh?" The stranger seemed to pause for a second, then shook his shaggy head and stumbled forward instead. Large, heavy feet clad in thick, sturdy boots stomped onto the door, pressing it deeper into the dirt floor as he stalked into the tavern proper, that large knife still clutched in one meaty hand. "Whozzat?" the man demanded, his voice as thick as the rest of him. "Taki, you little pustule, that you?"

"N-no, sir," Kagiri managed to stutter out, staring up in horror as the man came closer. By the Bones, he was enormous, a veritable giant! Then a glint of moonlight broke across the newcomer's broad, ungainly features, and Kagiri only just managed to resist gasping again. He recognized him!

The man's name was—oh, what was it? Kagiri tried to wrack his brains, but the series of shocks had rattled him so much he could barely think. Finally, though, a name surfaced from the depths, wriggling up like a starved fish after a plump worm. Batsu! That was it! No sooner had he recalled the name than Kagiri barked it out, striving to regain the tone he had employed so often when Noniki was up to something foolish and forbidden and potentially dangerous:

"Batsu!" he snapped, pleased that his voice did not stutter or crack this time. "Stop this at once! What are you thinking, coming here like this?"

The big man—a laborer at the mill, Kagiri remembered now—squinted down at him. "Huh? What? Who the devils are you?" he demanded.

"I am the one telling you to leave here right now, before you get yourself in big trouble!" Kagiri warned. "Look, just go and we'll forget this ever happened, all right?"

"Forget?" Batsu peered at him from under brows like great rocky overhangs. "Forget?" Those brows lowered even further, leaving only the faintest glimmer of his beady little eyes still visible. "Forget, like when Taki somehow forgets to refill my glass even though I've already coughed up good coin?" the man growled, his voice gaining volume with each word. "Forget, like the way her servers forget not to water down my rice wine? Forget, the way she forgets what a good and loyal customer I am, and ejects me just because someone else can't hold his liquor—or his tongue?" He leaned in, so close Kagiri could smell the sour waft of old wine and older sweat from the man's skin and clothes. "No, I don't think I will forget, little man. But you go right ahead. Forget I was ever here." And, with a hand the size of a plump hen, the laborer reached out and pushed Kagiri aside, none too gently.

Kagiri stumbled backward and reflexively raised the wok as he did, swatting the big man's hand aside. "You don't want to do this," he said softly, trying to quell the shaking in his hands and in his legs.

Batsu laughed, the saw-toothed sound as harsh and guttural as a saw splintering green wood. "Don't I?" he asked. "What is it I don't want to do, exactly?" He reached out and poked Kagiri in the shoulder with an index finger that felt as thick as some men's wrists, shoving Kagiri back another step. "Drink the rice wine Taki owes me?" Poke. "Shatter her tables and chairs to remind her to stay on my good side?" Poke. "Set fire to this hovel, to make it clear what happens when I'm turned away?" Poke. "Tear her little underling limb from limb for daring to get in my way?" He sneered, rotted teeth visible as broken stalactites and stalagmites in the blackened cave of his wide mouth. "Oh, I think I do."

Kagiri sighed, then gulped in air. "Fine." And, without giving himself any more time to think on it, he took a step—but forward this time, not back.

And swung the wok with both hands.

Batsu saw the ungainly makeshift weapon begin its arc and snarled. He was too close to get out of the way, but the big man threw up both arms, shielding his head from impact.

Whang!

The wok struck the big man's forearms with a loud clang, and even as the skillet rebounded the laborer howled in pain.

And dropped his knife, which struck the dirt floor with a dull clatter.

"I'll kill you for that," Batsu growled, rubbing his arms and glaring down at Kagiri. "I'll gut you like a fish!" He reached down to reclaim his knife, scooping it up off the ground with an evil chuckle—

—that turned to a loud groan, which then tapered off as the big man's eyes crossed. He wavered, still in the act of straightening up, and then swayed, eyes sliding shut right before he slumped on the ground, as limp as a bowl of day-old noodles.

Kagiri stared down at the unconscious man at his feet, and then back up—at the small, spindly, bent old woman behind the hulking intruder, a heavy iron-rimmed wooden tankard still clutched in her hands from when she'd brought it down hard upon Batsu's skull.

"Guess he won't be paying his tab any time soon," Taki commented, setting the tankard down onto a nearby table. She turned her narrow eyes toward Kagiri. "Okay?"

"Yes, ma'am," Kagiri replied, having done a quick mental inventory of himself and pleased to have discovered that, against all odds, he still possessed all his limbs and most if not all of his faculties. He was equally surprised that the tavern owner had expressed any concern for him, but that vanished a second later, when the tiny woman nodded.

"Good. Give me a hand with this," Taki insisted, squatting down and reaching for the door. Batsu had very conveniently puddled just shy of the downed portal, so between them Kagiri and Taki managed to lift the heavy door and lug it back over to its yawing entrance, propping the door up against the sturdy frame so that at least it once again covered most of the opening.

"We'll have to replace the hinges and the latch come morning," the tavern owner declared, scowling at the detached door. She turned and aimed a kick at Batsu's foot, which did not even stir the felled giant. "Probably can't even dock your wages for it, can I, you useless lout?" she raged. Then, suddenly, Taki glanced up and speared Kagiri with a sharp gaze. "Speaking of useless, where's that idiot brother of yours?" she demanded.

Kagiri gulped. "Uh—he ran for help," he managed after a second. "We figured both of us still wouldn't be a match for Batsu, but at least this way he could slip out and try to find a guard or something."

Their employer scowled at him, those little eyes glaring holes in Kagiri's flesh. Finally, however, she grunted. "Well, fat lot of good that did us, hey?" she griped at last. "Still, not a totally brainless idea." She yawned, covering her whisker-ringed mouth with the back of one wrinkled hand. "When he gets back, get him to help you tie that oaf up, hm? We can report him in the morning, when the guards come for their wake-up drink."

And with that, Taki turned and began making her way back toward the tavern's rear, and the stairs that which led up to her rooms up above, muttering and grunting with each laborious step.

Kagiri just stood there, frozen, watching his employer go, his mind racing. He would have to tie Batsu up himself, he guessed. Since he had no idea where his brother was, or how long he would be gone.

He was just lucky that Taki had believed him. And that the tavern owner hadn't thought to ask how even a brute like Batsu could have removed the door's security bar—which was safely on the inside.

No, that must have been the work of Kagiri's numbskull brother, no doubt sneaking out to perpetrate yet another of his idiotic schemes. And leaving the door vulnerable to attack on the very night that the vengeful laborer had decided to come and vent his ire upon them.

What the hell were you thinking, Noniki? Kagiri wondered as he headed for the bar, searching for any bits of rope or leather he could use to tie Batsu's wrists and ankles before the giant could awaken and attack again. And where are you?

And, he added, glancing up at the moon and sending up a quick prayer, are you all right?

Chapter Five

Noniki was frozen with fear. He lay there, peering out from behind his rotting human shield, as the two bannin strode into the crypt, spears at the ready. "Who's in here?" the one in front demanded, waving his weapon about so that the steel head clattered against the stone of the doorway. "Show yourself!"

Even Noniki knew better than to respond to that. But, as the guards began to stroll around the inside of the small stone structure, poking and prodding at the decaying bodies laid out on its shelves, he also knew that it was only a matter of time before he and his new acquaintance were discovered.

And when they were, well, there wasn't anywhere to go. And no way the two of them could fight off a pair of large, armed guards.

Which meant, if they were going to come up with a way to get out of here, it was going to have to be quick.

Craning his neck a little but moving slowly so as not to make any sound, Noniki glanced across the narrow aisle, to the body that was covering Seikoku. He thought he could a quick flash of her equally panicked gaze, but then it was gone. The corpse she was hiding behind didn't move, didn't even tremble. Noniki repressed a sigh. The bone thief wasn't going to be much help here, he gathered. He would have to come up with something on his own and hope she would at least follow his lead.

He frowned, peering up at the guards who were getting closer by the second. One of them nudged a body on the lowest level, literally laying tucked away inside an alcove on the floor, and then jumped back as the corpse's desiccated arm shifted, rag-covered bones changing position ever so slightly.

The other bannin chuckled. "What's wrong, Haru?" he teased his companion. "Afraid it's gonna bite?"

"Shut up," Haru growled, kicking that same body to show that he wasn't afraid. But he turned away hurriedly as soon as he had, and, watching all this, Noniki started to grin.

That was something he could work with.

He continued to lay still, waiting with bated breath, his eyes narrowed so any reflection from the lantern the bannin carried would not give him away. A little closer, he thought at them, waiting impatiently as the guards took their time inspecting each and every ledge. Just a little closer …

At last one of the guards—he thought it was the other one, Fumati, but was not entirely sure—reached Noniki's hiding place. Tentatively, showing at least as much trepidation as respect, the guard reached out with a gloved hand, his leather-shrouded fingers drawing closer and closer to Noniki's deceased covering. Just as the guard was about to brush the corpse's shoulder, Noniki made his move.

First he shifted beneath the corpse, causing it to move with him. The bannin practically flung himself backward as the dead body angled upward, from laying flat to a semi-reclined position.

"Bones!" The guard shouted, his cry almost deafening in the small space, both hands going to his spear even though he didn't really have the room to brandish that weapon effectively here.

Noniki wet his lips. Show time!

"Who ... disturbs ... my ... rest?" he demanded in his best creaky old-person voice, the one he'd gleaned from years of mocking Old Lady Cheshni back in the village. "Leave ... me ... be!"

And, gritting his teeth against the smell and the feel and everything else, and sending up a silent prayer asking forgiveness, he took hold of the corpse's wrists within the rotted but still mostly intact cuffs of what had no doubt once been a sumptuous burial robe—and shook the body's hands at the shocked guard.

"Atakai!" the big man all but shrieked, backing up until his shoulder collided with the ledge on the other side, making him stumble back forward again. "Atakai!"

The other guard had been jumpy from the start, and it didn't take much to set him off again. "What?" he demanded. "What? Where?"

The first guard waved a trembling hand at Noniki and his corpse-puppet. "There!" the man's voice was high and shrill from fear, and even in the dim light of the lantern Noniki could see that his face had gone pale, his eyes wide, his forehead beaded with sweat. "There!"

"Leave ... me ... be," Noniki repeated, waving the body's hands at the guards in what he hoped was a dismissive fashion. "This ... is no ... place for ... the living!"

At that, a body on the opposite ledge sat up and turned its head toward the guards. Noniki almost screamed himself at that, before realizing what was happening. Yes! Seikoku had caught on! As he watched, and the guards trembled, she manipulated her corpse-shield the same way he had, making its rotted head swivel toward the two bannin and its hands gesture in a shooing motion. "Begone!" she intoned, her voice not as ancient-sounding as his but more otherworldly, the syllables rising and falling like the wind whistling through the trees. "Leave here—or join us in death!"

Noniki quickly picked up on that. "Yes, join us!" he insisted, raising his corpse's arms so that it seemed ready to lunge for the two men. "Join us!"

That was the final straw. Shrieking like little girls, the two big men fled the crypt, their spears clattering to the ground behind them in their haste.

Seikoku wasted no time. "Quick!" she hissed, shoving the body aside and all but leaping out of the alcove. Noniki scrambled out after her, less gracefully but no less quickly, and sent up another quick prayer of apology to the corpse he had manhandled so disrespectfully. Then the slender bone thief was rushing from the crypt, and he was hurrying right after her.

"That won't keep them away for long," she warned once they were back out in the open air of the cemetery. "We need to get out of here before they come back with the rest of the bannin."

Noniki nodded, though he was also busy gulping at the cool, fresh air. He never wanted to be trapped in such a small, musty little space again!

"Do you have a way out?" she asked him after a second, and sighed when he shook his head. "How were you planning to get away from here, then?"

He shrugged, his face flaming. "I thought I'd just retrace my steps," he muttered finally. "While they were chasing after that firecracker."

His new companion snorted. "That was never going to fool all of them," she pointed out. "You'd have jumped back over the wall, and found yourself surrounded, spears aimed right at your throat."

"So you have a better idea?" he demanded, annoyed at her superior air.

"Of course," she answered smugly. "Follow me."

She led him deeper into the cemetery, which he thought was odd but her steps were swift and sure and she'd certainly been right so far, so he followed without a word and with as little sound as he could manage. Behind them he could hear the shouts of the guards, and knew that she'd been absolutely right about that as well—Haru and Fumati had clearly mastered their fear and returned to the crypt with their fellow bannin, hoping to cow the ancestral spirits into submission. Once they saw the bodies strewn about, they'd realize they'd been duped, and then the hunt would be on. He and Seikoku had to be out of her before then.

Just as he was about to ask her where they were heading, the bone thief stopped. "Up here," she instructed, patting a dark shape behind her, and Noniki realized that it was an ancient beech tree, its trunk gnarled and its bark rough as uncut stone. It towered over them, its top lost among the mist, but the young woman wasted no time in leaping up and grabbing a branch just above her head, pulling herself up onto it with all the ease of a trained acrobat. Noniki tried to follow, but although his arms and chest were powerful his legs were bowed, and each time his fingers scraped the branch but couldn't get high enough to gain purchase. Finally Seikoku lay down, both arms extended to either side of the bough, and caught his hands as he leaped. Then she sat up and leaned back, drawing Noniki up so that he could wrap a leg around the branch and then use his arms to pull himself onto its broad surface as well.

"Not a lot of trees where you're from, hey?" she asked softly, a gleam of amusement back in her eyes, and Noniki shook his head, too winded to speak. Their village had been on the water, so other than bamboo, lotus blossoms, lily pads, and a few scraggly bushes they'd had no large plant growth to speak of.

She only gave him a second to rest. Then she was nimbly rising to her feet, balancing perfectly on the broad branch. "Come on," she whispered, and Noniki heaved himself up as well. He was pleased to discover that the branch's rough bark provided ample traction, making walking along its length no more difficult than navigating a narrow path between two buildings, and a good deal easier than balancing along a water-slicked beam such as they used to use back home to provide makeshift bridges and docks. The branch proved to be long and winding, twisting its way through the mist, and Noniki was too busy concentrating on his feet to do more than keep Seikoku's trim back in sight, so he was surprised when she suddenly stopped—and then vanished from view.

"What?" he blurted out, managing at the last second to lower his voice so the sound did not carry too far. Her name was on his lips, but before he could utter it he heard a sharp hiss from somewhere below.

"Drop!" she ordered, and Noniki complied with only a second's hesitation. He wasn't sure the best way to go about something like this, and finally settled for dropping to his knees on the branch, the bark scraping him right through the thin cotton of his trousers, then wrapping both arms tight around the branch before leaning to the side and letting his legs slide over the edge. He dangled like that for a second, legs hanging below and arms still clinging, before slowly loosening his grip and allowing himself to fall. He landed in a heap on the solid ground, the impact knocking his breath out of him with a soft woof, and it was several seconds before he'd recovered enough to look up and see a pair of shapely legs right beside him.

"Took you long enough," she griped, reaching down and hauling him to his feet for the second time that night. "Come on." Then she was off again, all but invisible in the mist, her footsteps making not a sound on the hard-packed dirt of the road they were now standing upon. A road that ran behind the back of the cemetery, Noniki realized as he traipsed after her. That must have been how she got in as well. He'd circled the entire graveyard any number of times seeking a way in, of course, but the tree's branches had to be a good ten feet or more off the ground, and without a rope or a ladder he'd dismissed that as impossible to reach.

Obviously for the agile little bonethief, the height had not been a problem.

They moved at a fast walk, quick enough to put some distance between themselves and the graveyard but slow enough not to look too suspicious, for several more minutes. Then, finally,

Seikoku ducked behind a building of some sort—a warehouse, Noniki guessed from its broad beams, lack of windows, and the smell of flour and meal wafting up from within—and stopped.

"Far enough," she declared as she turned to face him. She'd removed both cowl and scarf, and was no nothing more than a pretty young woman out for an early morning walk. A very pretty young woman, Noniki amended, once again captivated by her dark eyes.

Eyes that flashed at him as she added, "Now go away." And turned away.

"What?" He rocked back on his own heels, stunned. "What do you mean?"

That made her round on him again, and he shrank back from the ferocity in her gaze. "Do you have any idea what you've done?" she demanded, lips drawn back from her teeth in a fierce scowl. "That place is always crazy dangerous, so I try not to go unless I absolutely have to. And just as I finally decide I need to, you appear out of nowhere and screw the whole thing up!"

"Me?" he protested. "We were fine until you laughed!"

But she brushed aside his claims. "All that risk for nothing!" she declared, stepping closer to glare him full in the face. "Not a single aishone to show for it! And they'll double the guard now! I'll never be able to get back in there!"

"I—I'm sorry," he stammered, surprised by her fury. And dismayed to realize that she was right, and for him as well. It had taken everything he had—not just money but also energy and effort—just to get in there this time. With more guards and new patterns and whatever other safeguards they added next, he'd never have a second chance.

The whole night had been for nothing.

"Sorry doesn't do me any good," Seikoku retorted, pushing him back with both hands, hard enough that he stumbled a step. "Just go away. I don't ever want to see you again."

And, with that, she turned and vanished into the mist.

Noniki stared after her, tears coming to his eyes and a sob threatening to rise in his throat. How had it come to this, he wondered. Everything had started off so well, and then he'd met her and it had been even better. And now here he was, broke and still boneless, this lovely girl hating him and blaming him for their shared failure, and nothing to do but return to the inn and admit what had happened to his brother.

He sighed, already imagining what Kagiri would say once he heard about all this. "Acting without thought, yet again," Noniki muttered, shaking his head. "Squandering everything on some crazy notion, and where did it get us? Worse off than we were before."

Which was, sadly, all too true. But there was nothing he could do about it now except trudge back to the Inn as the mist began to settle and the night started to give way to those first, early tendrils of the waking dawn. Go back, and accept the rebuke he so richly deserved.

CHAPTER SIX

"Your Imperial Majesty?"

Hibikitsu glanced up. He had been seated upon his throne—sprawled, really, slouched down with his upper back pressed against the carved latticework that fanned out behind him but nothing but air behind his lower back where it curved down toward the rich silk cushions upon which he sat, his legs kicked out in front of him, crossed at the ankles, elbows set upon the throne's ebony-inlaid arms, fingers laced together above his waist. Now, at the sight of the men and women gathered just before the dais, he sighed and straightened, untangling fingers and ankles as he pulled his legs in, setting his feet flat upon the floor, once again the ramrod-straight picture of Imperial dignity and might as he glared out upon his unexpected audience.

For a second, no one moved. Then one of the women bowed, the rest quickly following suit. "You sent for us, Imperial Majesty," the slender but unbent old woman reminded gently as she straightened, not the slightest hint of amusement or condescension on her ancient, lined face, her eyes still sharp beneath snow-white brows and an equally white and severely constrained bun, her narrow lips firm above a wrinkled chin. Her name was Amani Denbi, and she was the most senior of Hibikitsu's Rojiri, his Imperial councilors, seasoned nobles who had served his father before him and who could, with only a few exceptions, speak with the full authority of the Emperor himself behind them.

The question was, Hibikitsu mused silently, when they did speak thus, did they in fact have anything to say?

"Yes." The Echo of Victory frowned at the assemblage before him. "I have summoned you here to speak of our empire and her plight," he announced, forming his words clearly and precisely, projecting his voice so that each syllable rang from the pillars and columns and latticeworks and screens all around them. He saw a few of the old elderly nobles wince at his unexpected volume, and contained a secret smile. It pleased him to remind these doddards, occasionally, that while they held one of the highest offices in the land, he was still their Emperor. They still answered to him.

"Ah," Denbi replied, hands folded in front of her. She frowned, her lips all but vanishing amid the stern, thoughtful expression. Hibitkitsu wondered if the old woman had practiced making that particular face, and suspected she had. "Yes, the empire is indeed in dire straits," the councilor agreed, her tone mild and soothing as ever, like a patient teacher still trying to get through to a wayward student.

"I know that," the young emperor snapped, gritting his teeth. "I just said that!" He often felt that, just as he liked reminding them who was really in charge, his Rojiri delighted in treating him like a small child, reminding him of his youth, especially compared to their own age and experience and supposed wisdom. "Now, what can we do about it?" he pressed, leaning forward and resting his hands on his knees as he glared at his aged councilors, each one in turn.

"Hm." That was the only response he received at first, as Denbi turned away and began to pace before the dais, hands now behind her back, one cupped in the other, the very picture of wisdom. "Yes, that is a weighty problem," the councilor stated after several short circuits, and behind her the other Rojiri nodded and mumbled their agreement to this somber assessment.

Hibikitsu could feel his temper fraying, his patience pushed once again nearly to is breaking point by this little display from these men and women who did nothing all day but parrot back his own questions without a single genuine answer. "I am well aware of its weight," he grated out. "That is why I have put it before you, to receive the collected wisdom of your esteemed personages." He let his tone sharpen. "So, please, let that wisdom gush forth as a cooling torrent, to assuage our empire's wounds and act as a balm upon its turmoil." He was quite pleased with that particular turn of phrase, and even more so when he saw several of the councilors blink and glance at each other, surprised that their young, impetuous emperor could speak with such calm and courtly grace.

But Denbi was an old hand at such twisted diplomatic gestures, and she was not to be outdone by anyone, not even the Emperor himself. "We live to serve your Imperial Majesty," the elderly noble began, sweeping into a graceful bow that belied her advanced age, "and would happily share our thoughts on this matter, but surely it is a topic of such significance that we could be more useful if we were given time to prepare a proper presentation? With enough time, we could unpack the conundrum and present it in all its myriad elements, so that we could then examine each one in turn and provide more apt responses than a single, hurriedly prompted answer might provide?" The emperor thought he saw the old woman's lips twitch in a smirk for just a second, but an eye blink later and that was gone, if it had ever existed, leaving only the very image of dutiful attention.

Hibikitsu was not fooled, however. Nor was he willing to be put off yet again by flowery language and empty promises. "So what you are saying," he stated, speaking each word slowly, hands clenching into fists that began to bang his knees with each utterance, "is that, if I were to grant you, let's say, a week, you could prepare a clear and concise answer to the problem of our nation's decline? Is that it, Denbi?" As the Emperor, he did not need to use honorifics, since no one in the empire could match his own status, but when he was in a good mood he chose to generously award "sir"s and "master"s and "madam"s, "minister"s and other titles. He was glad to see that Denbi's brow furrowed the tiniest bit, aware that the emperor had just clearly signaled that he was not, in fact, in a good mood right now.

And yet the old woman still could not bring herself to speak any more plainly than to reply, "Indeed, Your Imperial Majesty, such time would be most beneficial in formulating a response closer to that which you desire." Which was, of course, not a promise that they could or would deliver anything even then, only that more time might help them get closer.

Hibikitsu rose to his feet, his hands moving to rest on his hips, still in fists, as he glowered down at these men and women who claimed to offer sage advice but in reality did little more than preen and peck and strut about, stuffed with their own importance. "And if I were to ask for some form of answer to my question right now, Denbi?" he asked, keeping his tone as soft as his gaze was hard. "What then? How would you answer your Emperor?"

"Why, Your Imperial Majesty," the chief Rojiri replied, "I could only say that the problem was too thorny a tangle, too weighty a matter, to treat with such hasty remarks."

"So you have no answer for me," the Echo of Victory restated plainly. "I have asked you what we can do to fix our empire, and you have only told me that you need more time to come up with anything even approaching a response. Is that an accurate depiction of your stance on the topic?"

Denbi began to open her mouth, but before she could frame a suitably elegant—and empty—reply, Hibikitsu took action. Flexing his legs, he leaped down from the dais, landing among the Rojiri like a fox suddenly bursting into a chicken coop. And, just like those farmyard birds, the councilors scattered, arms wheeling, embroidered sleeves flailing about, as they fell back, trying to maintain both balance and dignity and yet clear space for the emperor who had just alighted in their midst. A few actually fell, toppling onto their backsides, and if he had not been filled with fury right now Hibikitsu would have laughed at the sight. Where was their precious dignity now, he wondered, but he refused to let the sight distract him as he rounded on Denbi and the others.

"Useless," he declared, the word hissing from between his teeth like air escaping a fat man's backside. But his face twisted into a fearsome scowl, and he repeated the word, this time bellowing it with the force of a winter gale. "Useless!" His hand shot forward and tangled in the gilt and jewel-encrusted lapel of Denbi's robe, dragging the councilor forward, slippers skidding on the tile-inlaid floor as he hoisted the old woman up so that they were face to face, their eyes mere inches apart. "You are all nothing but fools playing at being wise," he snarled, flecks of his spit dotting her cheeks and making her flinch and then freeze even as she started reflexively reaching up to wipe them away. "You have no answers for me, no help for your Emperor or your empire. You are dead weight, and by all rights I should jettison the lot of you, cast you down into some dark hole where even your own egos will no longer be able to convince you of your supposed value, and find someone else, someone who can actually help me, someone who can do more than just posture all day!"

"You cannot do that!" Denbi protested, eyes wide, before remembering herself. "Your Imperial Majesty." Her face was pale, but she gathered her tattered composure and continued, "We are your Rojiri. As we were your father's. As our mothers and fathers were his father's. Our families have always provided council to the throne, back to the first generation."

Hibikitsu grimaced and thrust the old woman away as if he'd been burned. "Is that all you have to offer me?" he demanded, spinning to take in all of them at once. "Your only defense is that your families served me, so you must, too? Your only value, your only claim, your only credit, is that your families won this honor, and so it must still be accorded to you as well?" He shook his head, his topknot quivering with the gesture. "You live upon the empty reputation of your forebears," he proclaimed, "and do nothing to honor them or to advance those claims, merely feeding off them like parasites intent upon gorging and not caring that your very appetites are killing off that upon which you survive!"

"And are you any better, Imperial Majesty?" someone asked, and Hibikitsu's head snapped up, his eyes sweeping over the men.

"Who said that?" he demanded, but no one answered. Had he in fact heard it, he wondered for a second, but no, the words had been clear enough, the voice aged but still strong, the tone as cutting as the language. That none of them would now own up to the statement did not change the fact of its utterance—or the knowing looks he saw glimmering in many of the councilors' eyes.

A glimmer that changed to naked fear as he drew Kosshiki, the blade clearing its scabbard with a steely hiss that all but promised death and pain to all within hearing.

"I asked who said that," Hibikitsu repeated, the sword rising before him like a sliver of silvered light, the other men falling back to leave ample space between themselves and the deadly blade their clearly unhinged emperor wielded. "Come forward now," he ordered, and the ring of command crackled across the room.

For an instant, no one moved. Then someone cleared his throat. "I did, your Imperial Majesty," the man said, his peers shrinking away from him like he were plague-ridden. He was shorter than Denbi or Hibikitsu himself, wider but not fat, merely stout, his hair steely gray rather than white, his squared jaw clean of whiskers, his nose short and upturned. A fighter, had he been born to a different rank, but here his solid bulk was wasted, as was the rebellious streak visible in the clench of that jaw and the glare of those dark eyes.

"Ah." Hibikitsu nodded at the man. "Etsuya Kenshin." He extended Kosshiki to the full length of blade and arm, the Bone Spirit's tip holding rock-steady only inches from the councilor's right eye. "Explain yourself, sir."

If he'd thought to cow the old man, the Echo of Victory found himself sorely mistaken. Instead Kenshin's chin rose in defiance. "You say that we merely trade upon the honor and accomplishments of our ancestors, your Imperial Majesty," he stated plainly, not shouting but speaking loudly enough for all to hear. "Yet surely you do the same? As does everyone in Rimbaku, if we are being honest. We are a nation of ghosts, living on our family's past glories—and you, our esteemed Emperor, are no different from the rest of us." He bowed his head as if in respect, but his tone and his glare showed that there was little of that emotion present.

For a moment, Hibikitsu considered ending the man. A simple thrust forward, little more than a lean, and Kosshiki would spear through the man's eye and deep into his brain, the arrogant councilor's life dribbling out along the blade before he fell limp to the floor, one eye ruined and the other glazed over in death. The Emperor could all but see the scene, and it woke a certain savage glee within him, a desire to howl and tear and shatter and slaughter any who stood in his path.

But he mastered himself. He was the Emperor, the guiding light of his nation. He would not succumb to such base desires, even if he felt the punishment they would inflict on others was richly deserved.

Instead, he nodded in return. 'At least you have the courage to speak your mind," he told Kenshin, flicking his sword back and away and watching the relief flicker across the other man's face. "That is a start. Next time, instead of insulting me perhaps you can turn your forthrightness toward finding an answer to my question?"

Kenshin studied him for a heartbeart, as if unsure whether he was being somehow ridiculed, before bowing again. But this bow was deeper, more genuine. "I will try my best, Your Imperial Majesty," he murmured, and the others around him followed suit. Even Denbi, though her bow was more shallow, more perfunctory, than the rest.

"Good. Then perhaps we will be able to get somewhere." Hibikitsu resheathed his sword and turned his back on the men. "Now leave me." He did not move, not even a muscle, as he listened to the rustling of cloth and leather and silk against flesh and over tile. It was only once the room was quiet that he strode toward the dais, hopping back up onto it and settling back atop his throne to survey the now-empty room before him.

Pushing aside his lingering anger, he considered what the Rojiri had said. Was he right? Hibikitsu wondered. Was he as guilty of living off his ancestors' accomplishments as they were? Certainly he held the throne, not by some action of his own, but merely because he was the only child and heir of the late Hirokuni, his father. Who had been Emperor by virtue of blood as well, as had his father before him, and so on, all the way back to their original forebear, the great Taido Segei, the first Relicant Emperor.

But what had any of them done to deserve such an honor? How had any of them made good on Taido Segei's legacy?

How had he?

And what could he do now to redeem himself, and to save his land and its people?

CHAPTER SEVEN

Misataki Shizumi stood unmoving as a statue, her skin glistening with sweat, every muscle taut, feet planted well apart, nihono raised to head height, silk-braided handle even with her eyes and clasped securely but loosely in both hands, the long curve of the blade glittering in the early morning light. This high in Awaihinshi, the white marble of the City of Polished Light dazzled the sight, but Shizumi knew better than to let herself be distracted by something as minor as mere loveliness. Her intent gaze was instead locked upon the space before her, a space occupied only by the phantoms of his imagination. One such phantom rushed forward, crossing the invisible line Shizumi had painted there in her head, its own sword extended before it, and suddenly Shizumi exploded into motion.

"Hai!" Her shout shattered the pre-dawn calm, echoing from the marble-tiled roof surrounding the bare earthen yard even as she stamped her lead foot and then lunged, her coiled muscles releasing in a beautiful but deadly ballet. Her left hand released its grip upon the sword's handle even as her right rotated, bringing the blade up and over like a silver circlet carved out of the air, then around in a lethal arc, its edge slicing the air exactly where the phantom's throat would be. The illusory attacker fell, head toppling to one side even as his body crumpled to the other, but Shizumi had already forgotten that foe in order to concentrate on the next. And the next.

She stalked forward, each movement fluid and precise, her sword flashing as it spun and sliced. She blocked imaginary blows, careful to take the weight just above the sword's guard, where the blade was strongest, and to deflect it rather than attempt to absorb the full force of the attack. Far too many green recruits thought they could simply block with their sword, much as they had when they were youths and "fought" with sticks, only to have their blade shatter from the impact. "You do not fight with a club, or one of those graceless chokoto," her instructor had lectured her when training her for the Honjofu. "A nihono is an elegant weapon, sleek and swift and deadly, but it must be treated with great care and finesse, too." Now, after all those hours of training, Shizumi shifted her nihono into proper position without conscious thought, but in the back of her mind she was constantly checking over such minute details, making sure her angles were correct, that she was driving at each opponent's center line while stepping aside from their blows, watching her footing so that she was never off-balance or overextended. It was the little things that killed, the minor elements most people ignored, and Shizumi had trained herself to never overlook them. It was how she had stayed alive so long, how she had gone from a mere aiashe foot soldier to a gocho, how she had been recommended for application to the Honjofu, how she had earned a place in their elite ranks, and how she had risen there from warrior to gocho again and now even to gunso.

At last she reached the far side of the yard, all of her phantom foes dispatched, and paused, panting slightly for breath. Behind her and off to the side there came the sound of clapping, slow and condescending, and Shizumi stiffened, automatically raising her sword again before recognizing the tenor of that sound and lowering the blade. Instead she straightened as she pivoted, both hands going to the hilt again as she whipped the nihono down and back in a fast salute before sheathing it once again in the scabbard tucked into her sash.

"Hai, Taikoro," she called out, bowing in the same fashion as her sword had.

The man standing on the white marble walkway that ringed the yard nodded in reply, barely a dip of the head. "You show good form, a credit to your aishone as always," he replied, striving for the same crisp, ringing tone Shizumi had used but managing only a coarse bellow. "Truly yours must be a nearly endless supply, for you to be able to squander it upon such exercise, especially each and every day." His sneer would have been enough for her to recognize the dig even if she hadn't understood the meaning behind his words, suggesting that she was a poor judge and wasted valuable aishone merely to show off.

Shizumi had long since schooled herself not to react, however. Fujibuki Haro was the Lord Commander of the Honjofu, the Emperor's own Bone Warriors, and Shizumi's direct superior. The fact that he was at best an indifferent warrior, a middling strategist, and a poor leader did not change that fact, and Shizumi had learned long ago that her best course of action was in showing respect and obedience to her commanding officers, whether they deserved such behavior or not. Besides, when push came to shove Haro had access to extremely valuable aishone, and thus could transform himself into a proper warrior in the blink of an eye.

Which was why she merely said, "Thank you, sir," now, and waited. She doubted that Haro had come out here just to watch her morning practice or to needle her about her habits or even to ogle her as she stood in only hosode and ponmei, both of which clung to her slick skin.

Sure enough, after a minute her superior grunted. "Fyushu has made another incursion," he stated, stroking his well-oiled mustache. Haro was always impeccably groomed, more like a courtier than a field commander. "We must teach them the error of their ways." Fyushu lay to Rimbaku's north, and had become much bolder about pushing those borders of late. Thus Shizumi was unsurprised when Haro continued, "Gather a shotao and demonstrate to them the folly of encroaching upon our lands."

Shizumi bowed. "Hai," she replied, raising both hands to her chest, the right cupped over the fist of the left, and pressing them inward just above her breasts, right where her aishone pouch rested. "It shall be done." Only a gunso, a chuisu, or the taikoro himself could lead a shotao, and the Honjofu were a small enough unit that they only had at most one chuisu and two gunso at any given time. Their current chuisu, Ritsuro Okari, was currently incapacitated with the flux, and incapable of even rising from his bed, much less leading soldiers into battle. Which left Haro with the options of entering combat himself, recalling his other gunso, Norio Shinjuru, from Iwikaru where he was testing the latest batch of potential recruits, or handing the task to Shizumi. Evidently expediency was on her side.

Haro responded with another shallow nod, that of a man acknowledging the allegiance of a vassal, and then turned and walked away. At least he had not stared at her chest this time, she thought with relief. Shizumi did her best not to notice how the commander's turn was sloppy, how his feet splayed apart with each step, how he did not hold his balance, how his hand rested upon his sword hilt but not in a way that would allow him to draw the blade in a hurry. Some people retained a hint of whatever talents and skills their aishone had imparted to them, long after the influence of the bones had faded. Fujibuki Haro was not one of them. But she had grown adept at not noticing such things, or at least at not showing that she had.

Instead she turned her mind to the mission ahead. Her own gear was stowed and ready as always, and she could depart as soon as she had dressed, armored, gathered her bag, and saddled her horse. But she was taking a shotao with her, which meant she would need to select the score or so men and women accompanying her as part of that troop.

She was already drawing up a potential roster as she hopped up onto the walkway and made her own way toward one of the doors leading into the building, running through the list of Honjofu currently here in the Imperial barracks and who could be relied upon, who worked well together, who could command the bantao within her planned shotao.

Shizumi's blood still sang from her morning exercises, and her heart was racing as she hurried back to her pallet. But besides the simple reaction to her recent exertions, she was also excited for the prospect ahead. Off to the border! Enemy warriors to face! No mere phantoms this time, but actual flesh and blood! She could already feel the impact of blade against blade, and the lesser resistance of her sword cutting through armor and flesh.

She could hardly wait.

CHAPTER EIGHT

Awaihinshi was a tiered city, each of its six levels representing a level of the soul and each surrounded by marble walls of the corresponding color, growing lighter in shade as they ascended, until one finally reached the gleaming white purity of Aihiri, the Imperial compound at the city's peak. Outside the lowest and outermost wall, however, leaning up against that glossy water-pale surface as if for shelter from the horrors in the wilderness beyond, was what had grown to become a seventh tier, the huts and tents and stalls there forming a crude shanty town, a suranmui, in which dwelled many of the most unfortunate—and least reputable—of all Rimbaku's inhabitants. Many of the people who huddled there had not even a bronze to their names, and survived only by begging, and by random charity. Others worked, often taking whatever menial job was offered for whatever pay was tossed their way. Many toiled at tasks and activities which were not, strictly speaking, entirely legal, but then again, neither were the refugees and beggars and thieves who made Suranmui their home. It was a place of despair and hunger and terrible need, filled with the stench of hopelessness and the sour stink of deeply ingrained fear.

For some, however, the outer level presented an opportunity. Labor could be found for cheap there, and all manner of services. Goods could sometimes be acquired, for less than the going rate at market, and often those same goods were of the type that should not have been available to anyone save perhaps the soldiers or nobles. If you had an eye for talent and an ear for desperation and a nose for a bargain, and were not afraid to get your hands dirty, the town outside the city could be a veritable goldmine of opportunity. Particularly since the Emperor and his Dojo Kuge chose to pretend the slum did not exist, which meant that they could not demand taxes on items bold or sold or services rendered in that supposedly nonexistent place.

Oda Razan smiled as he strolled down the narrow alley that comprised the shanty's widest thoroughfare, whistling softly to himself. His robes were silk but largely unadorned, his jacket cut from rough brown muslin, his cap of the same cloth and plain style, his sash a marginally brighter coppery wash, his sandals simple hemp. The fan he carried in one hand, slapping it gently into the opposite palm, was carved wood rather than ivory or metal, with a single silk tassel dangling from the hinge. He bore no jewelry save a single brass hoop in his right ear, a tarnished silver ring on his left little finger, and a set of onyx beads looped around his right wrist. He was the very picture of a man who managed to survive and maintain himself but had no money to spare for others, nor anything worth stealing.

That look was a carefully crafted lie, of course. Razan was in reality a wealthy man with a handsome walled home on the fourth tier, Sakiriti, that of the cherry blossom walls. When he was at home he wore robes stitched with gold thread and decorated with seed pearls and jade discs, a cap of brilliant blue silk with silver and gold thread forming a dazzling pattern across its surface, and gems and jewels at his throat, his ears, and upon every finger. But he knew better than to walk Suranmui so attired. Here he dressed down, so as to escape notice—nice enough to not invite contempt from the other dwellers, mean enough to not draw their interest.

It was a guise he had learned to adopt several years before, when he had first realized what profits stood to be made off the less fortunate. Now he came down here at least once a week, sometimes more, to see to his various interests and search for other opportunities.

The soft, hitching sound of a girl sobbing drew him from his reverie of self-satisfaction. Glancing about, Razan soon spotted a figure crumpled against the rotting wood planks of a small lean-to. It had begun to rain, and the gentle patter of droplets everywhere nearly drowned out her sorrow, but the noise had filtered through to his ears nonetheless. And Razan was never one to pass up a potential for personal gain.

"Hello?" he called out, taking a step toward her. He glanced warily about, aware that many thieves used decoys to draw in their prey, but he saw no one else about. Plus he was hardly unarmed—tucked under his sash was a plain but sturdy knife, and his fan was good steel beneath its wood and canvas, capable of stopping a blade or slicing a throat with equal ease. That same fan sat comfortably in his grip now as he approached the girl. "Miss? Are you all right?"

Moving closer, he began to make out details in the dim light of night and fog. He had thought from the sound of her crying that she must be young, and what little he could see of her face confirmed that impression. Young, but no longer a child. And lovely, he saw as he drew nearer, with an oval face, a small, delicate nose, an equally graceful mouth, and large, long-lashed eyes that quivered as she turned her dark, liquid gaze up toward him. She wore no cap or cloak, only a threadbare scarf wrapped around the waterfall of her hair, and even in the near dark the strands gleamed a glossy black. Her beauty took his breath away.

Which only made him more cautious—Razan had not gotten where he was today by letting his guard down, or by being swayed by mere looks. Still, he felt his curiosity growing, and other parts of him were responding with great interest as well. Such a pretty little thing, he thought as he approached, and so distraught! Surely he could help her, take her under his wing, see her to shelter, perhaps, and a hot meal. And she would be grateful, he was sure, oh so grateful. And after, perhaps, other, more long-term arrangements could be made …

"Are you injured?" he asked, keeping his tone gentle and his movements slow and nonthreatening so as not to startle her further. "Might I assist you? My name is Razan, Oda Razan, and if you let me I—"

He had reached her by now and stretched out his free hand to help her to her feet. The girl blinked at him once, lower lip trembling, and then settled her delicate, pale-skinned hand in his.

And then, with a single sinuous surge, she had sprung upward, her hand tightening into an iron grip that crushed his fingers beneath it, her lips flattening into a tight line, her other hand darting up and across in a sweeping gesture that lit an answering streak of pain across Razan's throat. He staggered, groping at the sudden fire there with clumsy fingers, and reeled back as he encountered something wet and sticky spurting onto his hand. Blood. His blood. He had been cut. She had cut him!

He tried to pull away, but her grip held him like a steel band. He tried to scream, to cry for help, but the cut had torn something, and all he could manage was a wet, breathy sob. He tried to reach for his own knife, but his hand had lost its strength, the vitality draining from his body even as the blood gushed forth from his wound. Razan felt his legs grow rubbery, and sagged downward, no longer able to support himself. His vision began to cloud, darkening at the edges, and his breath hitched, becoming labored. He gasped for air but gurgled blood instead. Still the girl held his hand, tugging him upright and gazing down at him with lovely eyes turned cold as ice and hard as stone. She kept him there, unmoved by his plight, as his struggles and groans weakened, until, finally the darkness swooped in to claim him, and with a final rattle and a foul stench, his body surrendered and his soul fled from this world to the next.

Chimehara waited until she was sure the man had stopped twitching before she finally lowered him the rest of the way to the ground. Then she released his hand and crouched beside him. With deft fingers she searched his body, quickly locating the small pouch tied on a leather cord around his neck and the other, slightly larger pouch tied into his underrobe behind his sash. The former made a dry, rattling sound when she shook it, the latter a heavier clinking noise. Aishone and coin, then. Excellent.

She stripped the corpse of its other valuables as well: earring, ring, beads, fan. She even claimed Razan's knife for herself—it was better quality than her own, and its blade far sharper. That done, she rose to her feet, tucking everything away among her rags so that no one would be able to spot her sudden bounty. The body she left there for someone to discover or not, dispose of or not, as they saw fit. It mattered not to her.

As she stepped away from the scene and back into the shadows of Suranmui, Chimehara smiled to herself. Her first deliberate murder had gone quite well, she thought. And now she had better tools and better resources for the future.

She began to whistle as she departed, the same tune that had ushered from the hapless Razan's lips only moments before.

Truly, Awaihinshi was a place rife with opportunity!

CHAPTER NINE

"I still can't believe it," Kagiri muttered, thrusting an armload of empty cups at his brother. Mostly empty, as it turned out—a few still proved to have at least a few dregs in them, and bits of the thin, sour rice wine splashed out across Noniki's hands, arms, and chest as he accepted the load. He grunted but didn't dare complain, not when he was still smarting from his brother's displeasure. Which he'd fully deserved, he knew.

Kagiri had reacted exactly as he'd predicted, once Noniki eventually made his way back to the Foamy Cup. Of course, that was after his big brother had grabbed him in a bone-crushing embrace, then thrust him back to arm's length to make sure he was in fact healthy and unharmed. "Are you all right?" Kagiri had demanded, obviously fighting to keep his voice down, and

Noniki had smiled, touched by his brother's concern even as he puzzled over it.

"I'm fine," he'd replied, wriggling free of his brother's hands. "Why?" It was only then that he'd noticed how the tavern's front door was not just open but completely detached and leaning against the wall. "What happened here?" he'd been the one to demand then.

Kagiri had recounted the tale of Batsu and the door and the wok and all the rest. "I told Taki you'd gone to find help," he explained quietly, just as the wizened old tavern owner emerged from the stairs in back.

"Hmph, back at last," she'd muttered, shaking a narrow fist in Noniki's direction. "Don't think I'm paying you extra for running around like that, either," she'd declared. "Or you, for distracting the big oaf," she'd added for Kagiri's benefit. "As it is, I'm the one's got to pay for getting the door fixed. Now get to work!" And she'd stomped out through the empty doorway, no doubt to Genjiya's for steamed buns. Taki never ate her own food if she could help it.

No sooner had their employer vanished than Kagiri had turned back to Noniki, all humor absent from his lean face. "Now, where were you really?" he'd asked. And, after Noniki had explained, Kagiri had indeed shaken his head. "Oh, Niki," he'd said sadly. "What'm I going to do with you?"

The answer, as it turned out, was to nurse a grudge for the next several days, and to display that in tiny little acts like not bothering to empty the discarded cups onto the rush-strewn floor before passing them over for Noniki to take them back and rinse them out. But Noniki accepted the minor abuse silently. If this was the worst his brother did to punish him for acting so foolishly and squandering what little money they'd had, well, he could manage.

After washing the cups in the bucket in back, Noniki refilled several and began circulating among the tables, delivering them to any patron who held up a hand—and had the coin to pay for them. Taki didn't allow anyone to run up a tab at the Foamy Cup, so either you had coin or you went thirsty.

One of the men Noniki served was a familiar face, and Noniki smiled as he took the man's coin and passed him a mug in return. "How are you today, Jitu?" he asked.

"Fine, fine," the other man replied, accepting the mug almost reverently with both hands and bringing it immediately to his lips to slurp down the top layer of liquid there.

That wasn't just overeagerness on his part, either. When the brothers had started working here, Taki had made it very clear that they were only to fill the heavy mugs to a finger's width below the lip, where the shadows made it impossible to tell that the rice wine did not rise farther. But both Kagiri and Noniki felt that was simple pettiness, and staged their own tiny rebellion by instead filling each mug to the brim every time. Taki had reprimanded them, and threatened to dock their already meager wages, until Kagiri had pointed out that the tavern's custom had increased noticeably since they'd started that practice. "People get excited any time they think they're getting something extra," he'd pointed out in that dry, quiet voice of his. "It doesn't matter if they really are or not. You're making more than enough extra each night to cover the tiny cost of filling the cups all the way up." Taki had grumbled, and muttered about hired help knowing their place, but she couldn't argue with the results and so she'd allowed the new system to stand. Which meant that, as each patron received his mug, he drank down the top quickly to keep it from spilling. Even with rice wine as cheap and mean as Taki's, no one wanted to let so much as a single drop go to waste!

"Good," Noniki said, turning away to serve another customer. "Let me know if you need anything else, okay?"

Jitu wrinkled his broad forehead, heavy brows lowered in thought. After a second, he shook his head, the thick bun at top wiggling with the motion. "No, just rice wine and maybe some stew," he replied.

Noniki tried not to laugh. Jitu Kanai was one of the first people he'd formed any kind of connection with here in Ginsai.

The man was a potter, and a decent one but not great—his pots were solid, clean, and well-made, but there wasn't anything fancy or clever about them. The same could be said for their creator, and while the brothers appreciated his honesty and his direct nature, they sometimes had to struggle not to roll their eyes at how he took everything so literally, or how he had to stop and consider any statement carefully. This was especially hard for Noniki, whose mind had already jumped to a different topic and who was already three customers away.

"There has to be something we can do," he muttered as he swapped with Kagiri a few minutes later, passing his brother the empties he'd collected—and shaken out to make sure they were truly empty—and taking a handful of refills back in return. "Otherwise we'll be stuck here serving Taki's cheap swill forever."

"Sure," Kagiri replied, his tone laced in acid. "If only we had some money—oh, wait, we did, before my idiot brother threw it all away on some idiotic notion. Now we're broke, and it'll take us months or even years just to save up enough coin to strike out for another village. Not that we'd have any easier time finding work there either."

"So we save up and buy some aishone instead," Noniki argued for what had to be at least the hundredth time. "Once we have that, with my Suponichi and your Chosinichi, we'll be unstoppable!"

"Of course," his brother retorted, his words even sharper than before. "I'm sure the fraction of a copper we can save each week will be enough to purchase us some top-notch aishone in no time at all." He shook his head and turned away, leaving Noniki with no real argument but an armload of mugs and a bunch of thirsty patrons clamoring for service.

Sighing, Noniki went back to work. His brother was right, of course. Kagiri usually was. Taki was a shrewd operator and paid them just enough to give them hope but not enough for them to actually be able to put anything away. As long as she did that and provided food and shelter at the same time, she knew the brothers couldn't afford to leave.

"But there has to be more than this!" Noniki groused, slamming a mug down on one of the tables so hard the wine within sloshed upward, a fine spray escaping the mug's heavy wooden lip.

"There is!" the man he'd nearly drenched declared, laughing. "There's the next cup, too!" And, thrusting a copper into Noniki's hands, he clutched a second mug, dragging it free to join its mate there on the table. The man's companions all roared with laughter, and Noniki mustered a weak smile himself before turning away. Was this really his future, he wondered as he circled the rest of the taproom, distributing more mugs. To serve other people drinks, and not even for himself but for someone else? Was that all he was good for?

He was going back to the kitchen for the next round when one of the patrons at the farthest table gestured at him. "Over here," the man called, and Noniki nodded, raising a hand in reply.

"Be right there!" he shouted to be heard over the general clamor of the crowd, and quickly grabbed the next batch of mugs from Kagiri, who had just emerged with them. "Yes, sirs and madams!" Noniki announced as cheerfully as he could once he'd reached the table. "Drinks for everyone?" He didn't recognize the men and women there, which meant they weren't regulars, but they wore fine clothes and no doubt had money to pay for their wine, and might even be inclined to leave a tip for good service, so he did his best to appear amiable and attentive.

"Sure, sure," the man who'd summoned him, a broad-shouldered fellow with an equally wide face, replied. "They're, what, a copper each?" He pressed a single coin into Noniki's palm and smiled, though there was something about the expression that reminded him of the face a fox made when it spied a stray hare. "Keep the rest."

Noniki had just set the last mug down on the table, and now he stole a quick peek at his palm. The disc there glinted in the tavern's low light, shining with the cool gleam of silver rather than the dull glimmer of copper. "Yes, sir!" The man had four others with him, and a silver was worth ten copper, so he'd just given Noniki twice as much as the drinks had cost. That was five copper for Noniki himself, as much as they'd had when they first left their village! "When you're ready for more, just wave at me and I'll bring them straightaway," he promised, and the group chuckled at his obvious enthusiasm.

"We will, thanks," the first man assured him. "What's your name, anyway?"

"Noniki," he answered. "And that's my brother, Kagiri." He flicked his chin toward where Giri was delivering mugs to the other side of the room.

"Ah, brothers," the man said. "That's nice, to have family with you. I'm Kishin Narai."

"Sir, it's a pleasure." Noniki inclined his head. He could tell from the cut of his clothes and the high quality of the cloth, plus the way his hair and beard were so well styled and trimmed and slicked back, that Narai was a man of money. His companions all looked equally prosperous.

"Are you from here, Noniki?" Narai was asking, and Noniki quickly pulled his attention back to the conversation.

"No, sir," he replied. "We came from a village some ten days' walk away. We've only been here in Ginzai a few months."

He must have grimaced, because the man and his companions all chuckled. "And I gather this is not all you had hoped for," one of the women said, waving a well-manicured hand at the crowded tavern.

"No, sir," Noniki admitted. "As soon as my brother and I can gather some money together, we mean to strike out on our own," he confided, leaning in a little. "We just need to purchase some proper aishone first."

"Hm, yes, of course," the woman agreed, nodding and stroking a narrow chin. "A good plan—if you are willing to wait a few years." She smiled, reminding Noniki of yet another hungry fox. "But perhaps a better opportunity will arise."

"I hope so," Noniki said. "If it does, I'll grab it with both hands!" His fists clenched as if to do just that, provoking more laughter from the assemblage, but approving nods as well. Then he sighed. "But I'd best get back to work now. Let me know when you want refills."

He turned away and hurried to collect the mugs that had piled up during that conversation, but even as he worked Noniki could not tear his thoughts from those men and what they'd said. Had the one woman meant to imply that he and his companions might know of such an opportunity? It had certainly sounded that way! And they clearly had money—maybe they needed someone to run errands for them or something? Noniki would happily do that, or whatever else was required if it meant him and Giri getting out of here!

The night slid by in its usual blur of wine and cups, shouts and song, fights and spills. The group at the far table nursed their cups and only asked for refills once, again paying Noniki a whole silver for the privilege. He'd hoped they would drink more, but could hardly complain when he now had twice as much money in his pocket as he and Kagiri had ever had before! Taka came out several times to supervise, always eyeing the brothers closely as if he expected them to steal from him, though they never had. Noniki didn't even take the insult personally anymore—it was just the suspicious old tavern owner's way.

Finally Taki stepped up beside the bar and, raising an empty mug, slammed it against the pitted brass gong hanging there. "Last call!" she shouted as the gong rang out, her shrill voice and the gong's resonant clang cutting through the usual clamor. "Last call!"

Noniki was kept busy for the next few minutes, delivering one last cup to most of the patrons who were still here and still alert enough to request another drink. A flicker of motion off to the side caught his eye, and he glanced over to see Kishin Narai waving him over again. Noniki quickly grabbed up the last few mugs, eliciting squawks from a few patrons who'd been about to reach for the drinks, and hurried over to the far table.

"Here you go, sirs and madams!" he said as he set the mugs down carefully in front of each man. "Last one of the night!"

"Thank you, Noniki." Narai's voice was grave, and impressively free of drunkenness, as he handed over a third silver. "Do you have a moment, then? We'd like to talk with you, if you do." And he gestured at the space on the bench beside him.

Noniki glanced around. Kagiri seemed to have the rest of the taproom covered, and Taki was deep in conversation with one of the other regulars over by the bar. "I can sit for a second," he agreed finally, plopping down onto the bench with a sigh. As always, by the end of the night his back and feet felt like they had been laced with fire, and his arms and legs were more like wet noodles than functional appendages. He'd also have bruises all up and down his arms and chest from where he'd been slammed with mugs.

"Good, good." Narai studied the room a second as well before leaning in and lowering his voice a little. "I'll be truthful with you, Noniki," the man began. "My friends and I, we are not from here. We hail from Awaihinshi, in fact."

Noniki gasped at that. These men and women were from the nation's capital itself, the fabled City of Light? No wonder they looked so fine and had such money to throw around! But "What're you doing here?" he blurted out without thinking, only to curse himself for his usual lack of tact.

The group didn't seem to mind, though. "We're actually just passing through," Narai explained. "We are on our way to a sacred place called Tawasiri. Do you know of it?" Noniki shook his head—he'd never heard that name before. "It is called the Tower of Ghosts," the man continued, "and it is said that aishone litter the ground there, free for the taking by any who possess the courage and the fortitude to reach it." He smiled. "We have decided to undertake that quest. But, in all honesty, we knew that it might benefit us not at all, even if we did reach it. Because you see," and here he lowered his voice still further, forcing Noniki to lean in and strain in order to hear, "we are all either Tokimichi or Sokuichi. The greatest aishone in the world would not help us for long."

Noniki nodded, his mind awhirl. "I could help!" he announced, then lowered his voice. "I could help. My brother, too. He's Chosinichi. And I'm Suponichi." Of course, he was a bit of a Tokimichi himself, and Giri was also Sokuichi, but Noniki chose not to mention that just now. Besides, he figured their gifts canceled out their flaws.

"Are you now?" Narai rubbed at his chin. "That is a stroke of luck. Yes, you and your brother might be just what we need, then." He turned to his companions. "What do you say, my friends? Should we bring these two young men with us and entrust them to absorb these fabled aishone on our behalf? I'm sure we could then trust them to use their newfound gifts to our benefit."

"Oh, absolutely," Noniki agreed. "We'd be happy to."

The group all seemed to consider this carefully. Then, one after the other, they each nodded. "Excellent, we're agreed then!" Narai stated, clapping Noniki on the back. "We'll hire you both on for, let's say, a dozen silver a week, plus new clothes and whatever else you need. In return, you will come with us to Tawasiri, claim and absorb the aishone we find there, and then use those bone relics in our employ afterward."

Noniki sat back, stunned. "A dozen silver?" he repeated softly, glancing from face to face, he frowned, trying to even imagine that much money.

The merchants seemed to mistake his expression, or at least the reason for it. "A dozen—each," Narai corrected, and the group visibly relaxed when Noniki stared.

"Done!" Noniki practically shouted. He was grinning ear to ear, he knew, and when Narai offered his hand he pumped it vigorously. "When do we leave?"

The men and women were all rising from the table, which was perfect timing since any minute now Taki would bang the gong again and order everyone out. "We will collect you and your brother here at first light," Narai instructed. He offered another of his tight-lipped, slightly predatory smiles. "We'll bring proper traveling clothes for both of you." He clapped Noniki on the back again, and then turned and followed his friends out the door.

Noniki watched the group go, aware that he was gaping but not really caring. This was exactly what they'd needed! Silver in their pocket, new clothes, a better job, and best of all, aishone waiting at the end of it! He couldn't wait to tell Kagiri.

He also couldn't wait to tell Taki that they were done with slaving for her. Noniki pictured the face the old tavern owner would make when she found out that she was losing her hired help and would have to handle the entire evening crowd herself, and laughed aloud.

It was shaping up to be a beautiful night!

CHAPTER TEN

"Have you completely and utterly lost your mind?" Kagiri demanded, careful to keep his voice down. The last thing he wanted was for Taki to come clomping back downstairs, all bristly because they'd cut short her sleep or her counting money or whatever she did up there after hours. "You told these people you'd go with them?"

"No," his brother argued, also speaking softly. "I told them we would go with them!" Even in the dimness of the empty and unlit taproom, his brother's eyes shone. "Think about it, Giri," he insisted. "They have money! And they're going to get these aishone, but they can't use them! So they want us to use the aishone for them! It's perfect!"

"Yes, it is," Kagiri agreed with a sigh. "A little too perfect, if you ask me." He drummed his fingers on the tabletop—they were sitting down for now, because Noniki had said he'd had something to tell him. "These men and women just happen to show up here, just happen to tell you they need someone to help them, when we're looking for a way out of this place? How does that work?"

"It must be the First Emperor," his brother replied in all seriousness, his broad face completely earnest. "He heard our prayers, and sent us this opportunity! We'd be fools to turn away, Giri!"

"We'd be fools to just blunder into it, too," Kagiri shot back. He scrubbed at his face with one hand. "What if they're bandits, looking for servants? Or worse?"

But, as usual, his brother could not be dissuaded—once he had an idea in his head, Noniki was like a mountain, unfazed by even the strongest gusts. "Why would bandits bother to hire anyone?" he argued now. "They'd just grab people out on the road, or on the plains, or something. Narai offered us a dozen silver a week! Each!"

"That's a lot of money," Kagiri agreed. "Which is what worries me. Why pay that much for a pair of brothers who only say they've got good aitachi?" And didn't mention their flaws, he added silently, but decided not to get into that for the moment. "Still," he admitted after a second, "for people like that it might be barely a pittance. Especially if they're truly from Awaihinshi."

"Exactly!" His brother beamed. "So they think they're getting a bargain, and we know we're getting a fortune! Everybody's happy!"

Kagiri sighed again. "You're going with them, aren't you?" he asked, but he already knew the answer to that.

"Absolutely," Noniki replied. "No question."

Kagiri shook his head, but there was only one thing left to do. "Then I guess I'm going with you," he stated, and managed a smile when his brother crowed and lunged forward to enfold him in a tight hug. Of course there was no way he was leaving Noniki to face this—or anything else—alone. They were brothers, and the only family they each had left. So, even though he thought this was crazy and foolish and possibly dangerous, if Noniki was going, he would go too.

At least that way, he thought, he might be able to balance out Niki's tendency to dive headlong into trouble without even considering it first.

"Good morning!" Noniki called out, clearly projecting as much cheer into his voice as he could despite the early hour. The sun was still not visible yet, though it had begun to send tendrils of light questing out from the horizon, slowly writhing their way into the dark night sky and shedding a pale radiance that only served to throw the world's shadows into sharper relief, but even in such faint illumination the brothers had been able to spot the group riding toward them.

Riding! Kagiri resisted the urge to rub his eyes and blink and look again in case he might be dreaming. He had seen horses here in town, of course, but not that many of them, and most were hitched to wagons or carts. These beasts were sleeker than those draft animals had been, with slimmer lines and narrower heads and longer legs, and each bore a finely worked leather saddle Kagiri was sure cost more than his entire birth village would have been worth, probably several times over.

And the last two horses, ambling along behind the rest, carried empty saddles, their reins draped across their long, curving necks.

Did that mean what he thought it might?

"Good morning," the man in front agreed. He was the one Kagiri had seen speaking with his brother at the end of the night, and now Kagiri took the opportunity to study the man properly. He was not terribly tall but not short either, or at least so he appeared from horseback, but he had broad shoulders and a broad face that looked as if it might have been meant for humor until every grin and gape were driven out of it. Instead the man wore what might have been intended as a mask of geniality but instead came off more as a dismissive smirk. His clothes were well-made and looked expensive but also dusty, and he bore a sword at his side which Kagiri noted was not a nihono but instead something a little shorter with a straight blade and a thick metal ring at the handle's end. Not a noble, then, since it was punishable by death to wield a nihono if you were not of noble blood. Interesting.

"You must be Kagiri," the man continued, and Kagiri bowed. "I am Kishin Narai, it's a pleasure to meet you. I'm very glad you and your brother agreed to assist us in this quest."

"You honor us," Kagiri replied, setting his misgivings aside for the moment. "Thank you for this great opportunity. We will strive to prove worthy of it."

"Of course, of course." Narai waved, and another man appeared, this one on foot. The newcomer was clad in full armor, the iron and leather scales of his breastplate jangling softly against each other, as did the panels of his armored skirt. His menatu hung loose from one side of his helmet, revealing a young and unshaven face with a long nose and wide lips, and his sword, of the same straight style as Narai's, slapped against his leg as he approached them. Laid atop his gauntleted hands was a pile of clothing, which he thrust toward Noniki, who was closer to him.

Niki accepted the bundle and nodded his thanks to the man, who merely grunted and turned away.

"Ignore Joshi's bad mood," Narai instructed with a chuckle Kagiri thought sounded forced. "He dislikes early mornings and dislikes delivering packages even more." The man gestured at the clothes Noniki held. "Traveling clothes, as promised. Your horses already have all the rest of your gear, so as soon as you've changed and mounted up we can be off."

Kagiri blinked, even as he reflexively accepted half the pile from his brother. So those two horses were for them! Astounding! He wanted to protest, or at least ask for an explanation—the man Joshi was standing near Narai's horse and seemed like he would be traveling on foot, so why couldn't they?—but the man didn't seem like the kind to tolerate delays. So instead he hurried back into the inn long enough to strip off his old, ragged clothes and pull on the new garments instead, then returned to where the men waited.

"Much better," one woman approved, and despite his doubts about this whole venture Kagiri had to agree. He and Niki had grown up on the water, rarely wearing much more than loincloths or smallbreeches with the occasional smock-like shirt tossed on over it. Taki had insisted they wear pants when in the tavern, and of course they'd had to pay for those themselves, so Kagiri and Noniki had bought the thinnest, cheapest pants they could find, and had patched those several times from tears where the flimsy fabric had caught on benches and tables and whatever else. These new clothes consisted of sturdy cotton trousers, loose and comfortable and tied at the waist by a simple drawstring, with a plain silk hosode over that and then a short, dark brown jacket of stiffer material, probably hemp. There were new hemp sandals as well, and Kagiri slipped his feet into them with a sigh. Though he had always gone barefoot growing up, crossing the desert to get here and then walking about Ginzai's hard-packed dirt streets during the day, and the inn's equally hard floor all evening and night, had taught him to appreciate the value of footwear.

Noniki emerged right behind him, and Kagiri studied his brother with a critical eye, then nodded. The strangers had done a good job of sizing them up, he saw, providing longer, slimmer garments for him and wider, shorter ones for his brother. Now they looked like proper people, even people of substance, though not compared to the men and women on horseback in their elegant kitoros and jewelry. Still, he had to wonder if perhaps he had been mistaken after all. Could Noniki have gotten it right for once?

"Have either of you ever ridden before?" One of the other men asked, and Kagiri shook his head quickly, even as Noniki opened his mouth to no doubt make up some story.

"No, sir," he replied to cut off his brother, "and perhaps it would be safest for us to simply accompany you on foot, as noble Joshi clearly does." He bowed in the guard's direction, but only got another grunt in reply.

"Nonsense!" A third, this one a sharp-featured woman with a tidy bun, argued. "Tawasiri is near the bottom edge of Nariyari, many miles from here, and we will need you both in top form when we reach it. Come, we will have you riding like you were born to the saddle in no time!"

An hour later, the party finally set out from Ginzai, Narai and his four companions on their horses, Joshi and a handful of other guards marching along before and behind—and Kagiri and Noniki walking with them.

"I almost had it," Noniki protested, then grimaced as Kagiri prodded him in the side. "Stop it! I did!"

"Oh, yes," Kagiri agreed with a smirk. "That last time you fell off was much closer to staying on than the first six."

"You fell off too!" his brother pointed out, and he sounded so personally insulted Kagiri had to laugh.

"True," he acknowledged. "But only twice." Then he'd given up, using those two falls as proof that they were better off walking, at least for now.

Naturally Noniki had been far less willing to accept the inevitable.

"Do you think we'll ever see this place again?" Noniki asked, changing the subject as they trudged through Ginzai's main square, over the wide wooden bridge that spanned its bisecting river, and toward the town's eastern edge. They had just passed the cemetery, and Kogiri noted but did not comment on the fact that his brother had shuddered and looked away from those high walls and the crypts beyond. No point bringing that failure up yet again.

"I hope not," Kagiri replied instead. "But I'll tell you what, if we do let's make a point of not drinking at Happoa Kappua, eh?" They both laughed at that. Taki had been first shocked and then furious when the brothers had woken her to tell her they were leaving, and not just at some indefinite future point as they'd always claimed but this very instant. The little tavern owner's screams and curses had followed them a good four buildings or more, carrying through the sounds of the town waking to life with the start of the day.

"Agreed," Noniki said, his usual good cheer returning quickly. "But look, Giri! We're really leaving! In good clothes, with silver in our pockets, and a whole party of men and guards all around us! We're really doing this!"

"We really are," Kagiri confirmed. I only hope it's everything you hope it will be, he added silently. More than anything, he wanted for his brother's boundless enthusiasm and hope to actually be rewarded—and not squashed flat, as it had been so many times before.

Over the course of the next few weeks, Kagiri and his brother did in fact learn how to ride, albeit stiffly and with a great deal of pain at the end of the day. They also got to know the rest of the merchants they were accompanying, from Shizu Yokori (she of the pointed chin and equally pointed wit) to Jiro Masute (cadaverously thin but with long beautiful hair and eyes like a hunting bird) to Eien Kawatai (long-nosed, close-eyed, a bit dim but Kagiri kept thinking the man was laughing at him behind his back) to Fujiko Oritano (short, stout, loved numbers and facts of all sorts), plus crude, grouchy Joshi and the rest of his men and women. The brothers quickly found that they were in a strange no-man's land within the extended party, not learned enough or wealthy enough to be considered equals by the merchants but too sheltered and protected to be accepted by the guards. "It feels," Kagiri said to Noniki one night as they sat by the campfire and picked at the meal one of the guards had prepared, which was arguably still better than Taka's stew, "like we're pampered children. Or pets."

"I'm okay with being a pet for a little while," Noniki shot back, sucking on a duck's leg bone. "At least we get fed well, we're learning to ride horses, and the longer this trip takes, the more silver we'll have in our pockets as a result."

Which was at least true. Narai had already paid them their first week's "wages," handing each of them a dozen silver like the handful of coins couldn't matter less to him. Which might be the case, considering how rich his clothes and jewels were. But it was a lot to the brothers, and they had carefully squirreled the shiny coins away in the belt pouches they'd found tucked into their horses' saddlebags along with the blankets and other useful items.

Kagiri was about to reply when a sound emerged from the darkness beyond their fire's ring of light. Instantly, Joshi was on his feet, his sword—it was called a chokoto, he'd grudgingly revealed to the boys just the other day—suddenly in his hand, its long, straight blade casting reflections of firelight all around them.

"Who's there?" the guard demanded, advancing to the edge of the ring while, behind him, the other guards did the same on other sides. "Show yourself!"

The night beyond was quiet. Then, silent as the grave, two figures wafted out of the darkness.

At first Kagiri thought they might be akatai, they moved so quietly and were so pale, their skin white as ivory. But their hair was inky black in the night, and their eyes were dark as well, and when one opened his mouth, regular human sounds emerged.

"Please, sir," the boy said, for he was only a boy, Kagiri saw, a few years younger than Noniki. Shorter as well, and slight as Masute, though on the merchant it looked more like he was naturally that thin despite his impressive appetite, whereas this boy was clearly half-starved, his cheeks all but caved in, his eyes pools within deep pits, his every bone visible beneath his skin every time he so much as shifted. "We mean no harm," the lad continued. "My brother and I were only hoping you might spare a bite to eat."

Brother? Kagiri exchanged a glance with Noniki. The two boys did look clearly related, it was true. "What's your name?" he asked the first one, who seemed to be the elder of the two.

"Ibaru, sir," the boy replied, turning to face him fully. "And this is Iraku." Both boys bowed, and Kagiri nodded back, not used to anyone showing him such respect.

Noniki was already on his feet, of course. Grabbing up a loaf of bread and two chunks of duck meat from tonight's meal, he advanced toward the two boys. "Here," he offered, holding out the food.

Before they could reach for it, though, a sword blade intercepted the offering, blocking its passage. "Why are you so hungry?" Joshi demanded gruffly. "Why don't you just work for it instead?"

Kagiri started to protest—he and his brother knew firsthand how difficult it could be to find work!—but the boy slumped, staring down at his feet. "No one will hire us," he admitted finally.

That clearly piqued Noniki's interest. "Why not?" he asked, food still in hand. "You're skinny, sure, but nothing a couple decent meals wouldn't fix."

The boys didn't answer, not until Joshi's sword shifted and swung toward them instead. "Answer him," the guard insisted.

Ibaru huddled, seeming almost to fold into himself. "We're Mukanichi," he admitted finally, his words so soft the crackling fire nearly swallowed them up.

But Kagiri managed to hear him. And so did Noniki, who reeled back like he'd been stung. "What?" his brother yelped. "You're Untouched?"

The boys nodded miserably. Now their pitiful state made sense. As Mukanichi, they had no aitachi at all. They could not use aishone, not even a little bit—for them the relic bones were merely bones, nothing more. Which, in the eyes of Rimbaku, made them all but useless themselves. Mukanichi were shunned, often beaten, and most survived only by begging and the occasional task no one else was willing to do. Few survived very long.

Noniki was still backing away, his face twisted with distaste and disgust and even a little fear. Joshi looked like he was debating whether he should just run the boys through here and now and save them years of grief. But even as he pondered, Kagiri rose to his feet.

"Give me that," he demanded, striding over to his brother and holding out his hands. Noniki frowned but did as requested, passing over the food.

Then Kagiri turned and walked right past Joshi, straight over to the boys. "Here," he told them, offering them the bread and the meat. "Go ahead, take it." Behind him he heard Noniki gasp, but he ignored that.

The older boy—Ibaru—stared at him for a minute before reaching out and snatching the food. "Thank you," he mumbled. Then he and his brother turned and fled, disappearing back into the inky black that swallowed the world beyond the group's cozy little encampment.

"Waste of good food, you ask me," Joshi muttered, sheathing his sword and returning to the spot where he'd been lounging on his blanket before the intrusion. Kagiri didn't bother to respond to that.

"I wish you hadn't done that, Giri," Noniki said quietly as Kagiri rejoined him. "What if you touched them? What if it's spreading somehow?"

"They're not sick, Niki," Giri replied, rubbing at his face. "They're just hungry."

"Yeah, but not just that," his brother countered.

"What, you mean being Mukanichi?" Kagiri frowned. "So what? Don't you see? If we'd been born without aitachi, we'd be just like them! So how are we any different, any better, just because we have the Touch?"

"That's why we're better!" Noniki burst out. "We're better because we can do things they can't, that they never will! That's how we know we're better!"

"But we didn't earn that!" Kagiri shot back. "We didn't work for it, or study for it, or practice for it! We were just born with it—and they weren't. It's not right, Niki—don't you get that? It isn't right that we have all this"—he gestured around them at the camp, the horses, their saddlebags and blankets— "and they've got nothing, just because they're Untouched. There has to be more to it than that—or there should be, anyway." He shook his head. "I'm tired." And with that he stretched out, tugging his saddlebag over so he could rest his head against it, and closed his eyes.

He was out within seconds, but even as he faded from consciousness Kagiri wrestled with the problem he'd been forced to live through today. Two sets of brothers. Two wildly different lifepaths. And, as far as he knew, the only distinction between them was that he and Noniki had the Touch. Why was that more important than anything else, he wondered as he lay there, staring up at the stars but not really seeing them. Why did no one care what else people could do as long as they could cannibalize their ancestors properly? What did that say about the world they lived in? And about them, and everyone else who accepted such a ludicrous situation and thus allowed it to continue? What did it say about him?

Sleep snuck up and claimed Kagiri before he had a chance to figure out the answer—assuming that there was one.

CHAPTER ELEVEN

Hibikitsu was glancing over the latest treasury report when someone knocked on the outer door to his study. Both relieved at a reason to set aside the depressing scroll and annoyed at being interrupted, he barked out, "What?"

The lacquered door slid open just enough for a servant to glance in. "Apologies, Imperial Majesty," the old man intoned, unfazed by his emperor's glare, "but Dogenriku Sunao and Taikoro Fujibuki are here and say that they must speak with you right away."

"Oh, they must, must they?" Hibikitsu snapped back, but then schooled himself. The servant in question, Seisen, had been in service to his father and grandfather before him and had always been faithful. "My apologies, Seisen," he said now. "Please send them in."

The old man nodded, acknowledging both the order and the apology with only the faintest flicker of a smile, then disappeared from view. A second later the door swung wide and Sunao Tadazi and Fujibuki Haro strode into the room.

Hibikitsu set the scroll atop his desk, concealing a sigh. Many of his nobles were difficult to deal with, and the men now intruding upon his private study were among the worst, both of them preening popinjays who thought themselves warriors but were little more than trumped-up courtiers granted a high rank thanks to their family names and nothing more.

"Your Imperial Majesty," Haro declared, clicking his heels together and executing a deep bow. Both motions were clearly meant to occur with military precision, yet even to Hibikitsu's eye the man's form was sloppy. And Tadazi's was no better. Still the emperor acknowledged the obeisance with a nod.

"What can be so urgent, gentlemen, that it requires you to disturb me here?" he asked the nobles before him. The throne room was where Hibikitsu received most visitors and dealt with most of the public business of the empire. This study was his private refuge, the place where he retreated to study accounts, pen notes, and contemplate in peace. Now his Lord General and Lord Commander were standing here amid his books and scrolls and paintings, invading a sanctuary of bonsai and mediation pools with their silk and armor and steel.

"My apologies, Your Imperial Majesty," Haro replied, bowing again. "We felt this matter was one which could not wait for a formal audience, as every second could be critical to our success."

"Oh?" Hibikitsu lounged back in his chair—a comfortable construction of willow reeds woven into a standing basket and lined with cushions, far different from the heavy, carved throne in the room beyond. "And what might require our attention in such a hasty fashion?" He emphasized the word "our" and watched Haro flush as the man realized he had overstepped his bounds. But Tadazi picked up where his companion had left off, continuing as if he had not noticed the pointed rebuke.

"Bandits, Your Imperial Majesty," the man stated instead. "Bandits have taken control of Nariyari."

"What?" Hibikitsu rose from his chair and stalked around the low desk to confront his general, not stopping until his face was inches from the other man's. Tadazi gulped and leaned back ever so slightly, but knew better than to retreat unless given permission to do so. "Explain," Hibikitsu demanded, glaring at the noble, his green eyes spearing into the other man's dull brown.

"They call themselves Kindichi," Tadazi said quickly, the words spilling out beneath his perfectly groomed mustache. "They're rebels, thieves and killers. They've been plaguing the province for months, but now they've declared it belongs to them completely."

"Well, send a bantao to discipline these 'kings,'" Hibikitsu ordered, but his eyes narrowed when the other man shook his head.

"We did," the ashen-faced general insisted. "The Kindichi sent back their heads. Then we sent a shotao—with the same result." He gulped again, and his eyes shifted, clearly desperate to escape his emperor's stare but unable to do so. "We believe they may have as many as fifty men, possibly even more."

Hibikitsu frowned, his own gaze narrowing. "So?" he demanded. "Fifty country bandits against forty trained warriors, and you are telling me that these rebels, these self-styled 'bosses,' were the victors?" He pressed in, his forehead nearly brushing Tadazi's, his eyelashes all but beating against the other man's brow. "How is this possible?" he demanded. "How could my Aiashe lose to such rabble?"

"I–I do not know, Your Imperial Majesty," his general stammered out, "but I promise you, I will find out." He took a deep breath before continuing, sweat already prickling his brow and threatening to muss his neatly oiled back hair. "That is why I asked Taikoro Fujibuki to accompany me here. I believe this matter has become more than my Aiashe can handle, and humbly request assistance from the Honjofu." And he executed a quick bow in the other noble's direction.

The emperor fought hard not to roll his eyes at the political drama unfolding before him. Tadazi was in charge of the army but Haro commanded the Honjofu, which were an elite force and not part of Tadazi's domain. To ask him for help was to acknowledge that the army was outmatched, and normally Haro could have used that as leverage to demand some kind of concession or favor from Tadazi in return—Tadazi was not just a military leader he was also one of the Rojiri, and that meant he had a lot more influence than Haro ever could. Which was why the Lord General had brought the matter here, into Hibikitsu's presence—this way the Honjofu commander could not refuse, nor could he try to bargain for anything in return.

Sure enough, Haro bowed, the motion doing nothing to hide his flushed cheeks or pursed lips. "I am happy to lend any and all necessary aid to my fellow commander," he declared, his eyes glinting as the apparent demotion of his rival sank home. "Unfortunately, my chuisu is indisposed, one of my gunso is otherwise engaged, and I have already dispatched Misataki Shizumi to the north, where Fyushu is testing our border again. But as soon as she returns, I will—"

"No," Hibikitsu cut him off, pivoting away on his heel and beginning to pace the room, hands clasped behind his back. "There is no time to wait for your gunso, however talented she may be. Tadazi is right—this is a matter for the Honjofu to handle now, and without delay. You will assemble a chotao and go yourself. We will teach these bandits to respect our rule, or we will crush them beneath our feet and decorate the walls with their heads to dissuade any others who think they can flout our authority."

Behind him, Haro made a noise like a bleating sheep. "Me?" the man blurted out, his face blanching. "You want me to go myself?" Tadazi uttered what might have been a laugh, but smothered it when the emperor swiveled back around, glaring them both to silence.

Ignoring the general, Hibikitsu focused on Haro. "Yes, you," he snarled, invading the other man's personal space. "You are

Taikoro of my Honjofu, are you not? Lord Commander of my Bone Warriors, leader of my most elite force?"

Haro could do nothing but nod. "Yes, but—" he started, only Hibikitsu did not let him finish.

"Then you will do your duty," he instructed sharply. "You will gather your warriors, and you will ride out for Nariyari with all due haste. You will teach these Kindichi that they have no right to lay claim to my lands or to ignore my orders or my duly appointed representatives." He glared at his commander. "Is that perfectly clear, Fujibuki Haro?"

The man stiffened at the use of his full name and the pointed reminder of his ancestral house, and performed another bow, this one marginally tighter than the first. "Hai, Your Imperial Majesty," he managed to grate out through clenched teeth. "It will be done."

"Good." With a nod, Hibikitsu dismissed him, and watched as Haro turned and stormed from the room, all but slamming the richly painted door behind him. He heard shouts in the hall and guessed that the Lord Commander was assuaging his bruised ego by yelling at Seisen and any other servants who might be passing.

Tadazi had remained behind, and now he bowed as well. "Wisely done, Your Imperial Majesty," the wily old general stated.

"Do not think I am pleased with you either, Lord General," the emperor warned, wiping the smirk from the nobleman's face. "You will find out exactly why your soldiers could not handle this matter themselves, and you will see to it that their training is increased. If the men cannot handle a simple band of thieves and brigands, they do not deserve to be Aiashe any longer."

Face flaming, Tadazi bowed again. "It will be as you say, Your Imperial Majesty," he agreed briskly, his words taut with an anger he could not openly express toward his ruler, and when he departed a second later it was with just as much rage as his rival had only a moment before. At least his departure was not followed by any shouting, though that only suggested that the servants had been smart enough to hide this time.

Hibikitsu settled back into his chair with a sigh. Why, he wondered, did he have to put up with such fools and ingrates? Haro was no military genius, and judging by his form he was barely even a competent warrior, yet he had control of the Honjofu and was second only to the emperor and the Lord Commander and Lord Admiral in military rank. True, the Fujibuki had always commanded the empire's elite troops—their ultimate forebear, Fujibuki Sato, had been a brilliant tactician and a phenomenal warrior, and had risen from the ranks to control the small force of expert fighters that helped Taido Segei gain control of the lands and found the Relicant Empire Hibikitsu himself had ultimately inherited. But while that might certainly entitle the Fujibuki to noble status, why did it mean they should automatically command the finest warriors in the land? Why should Tadazi, who was not any better, command the armies, or Watane Yatahei the navies. Should not that honor, that responsibility, go to one with more ability?

He sighed and reached for the intricately enameled teacup sitting upon its carved jade saucer near the desk's edge. The jasmine tea inside had cooled, but still its delicate floral aroma soothed him as he sipped, letting the lukewarm liquid slide down his throat. Haro was just another example of the same problem as the Rojiri, he mused. People living off the accolades and accomplishments of their ancestors and in no way contributing or even living up to that legacy. Much like the men and women who utilized their ancestors' skills and knowledge but never added anything new to that store, instead merely depleting it little by little. The entire Relicant Empire was built upon the talents of the old, and devoured those same gifts year after year without giving anything back. It was a cannibalistic graveyard, rapidly depleting its only resource.

But was there any way to change that pattern before it killed them all, he wondered, draining the last of the tea and setting the cup back down. Was he doomed to appoint another equally inept Fujibuki as Taikoro when Haro eventually fell or retired or died, and Tadazi's heir Dogenriku? Was he bound to make

Amani Denbi's eldest a Rojiri when the old woman eventually passed away? Was it impossible to flout centuries of tradition and appoint for ability instead of heritage?

And would it make any difference if whomever he chose instead merely had better aitachi and aishone? Wouldn't he still be trading off the merits of the dead rather than those of the living?

Hibikitsu sat there as the day began to lengthen, the sun's light shifting through the carved screens of the window, and stared off into the distance, hoping desperately to spy there an answer to his ongoing dilemma. But instead he saw only fading light and lengthening shadow.

Chapter Twelve

"Come in, child. Show me what you've brought me." The voice was rich and warm as sun-touched honey, but Chimehara hesitated, the heavy drape of the tent's front flap clutched in her hand. Still, standing outside would do her little good, so she marshaled her courage and stepped through, letting the flap fall shut again behind her.

"Good day, Senkousa Medeiko," she intoned, bowing deeply to the small, squat woman perched on a thick pile of cushions at the tent's far end. "I hope I do not intrude upon you at such a late hour." For it was nigh on twilight, and most regular merchants had already closed their curtains and packed up their stalls and bundled off toward home, their wares and their profits clutched tight to their chests. Yet the senkousa's lantern had remained lit on its pole outside, indicating that she was still open for business.

"Not at all, child," the older woman replied. "I often stay late, since many wish to see me after their own day's business had been concluded. Come closer, closer. I will not bite." She gestured to a more modest stack of cushions a few feet from her, and Chimehara complied, settling herself carefully. She hated that her back was to the tent flap, and the skin along her neck prickled, but she forced herself to seem as relaxed and nonchalant as she could manage.

"Ah, you are a pretty thing, aren't you?" the Bone Reader cooed. "And so young!"

"Thank you, Senkousa," Chimehara said, smiling as she felt at least some of her unease dissipate. Her beauty was her greatest weapon and had disarmed many she'd encountered, so knowing the old woman was falling under her spell gave her back some of her usual confidence.

"Now, show me what you've brought me," the older woman added, patting a small, ivory-inlaid table resting between them. "I can smell it from here." "Of course." Chimehara pulled out the pouch she'd taken from that fool of a merchant and emptied its contents carefully onto the table. They were a modest grouping, to be sure, a half dozen fragments and slivers, none larger than a finger bone, but still they represented the most wealth Chimehara had ever held, and a part of her was loathe to part with them, even for a moment. But they did her no good as they were, unknown and unused. That was why she'd finally forced herself to come here.

"Hm," Medeiko half-hummed, sucking at her lower lip as she reached out for the aishone. She stopped when her palm was only inches from the bones, however, and closed her eyes, breathing in deeply. "Ah, yes." She blinked and studied the girl in front of her. "You are a merchant?" she asked, her eyes sharp despite the wrinkles surrounding them.

"My father was," Chimehara answered, having already prepared her story. She mustered her most sorrowful expression. "He passed only a week ago. Most of his aishone went to my eldest brother, his heir, but these he left to me."

"I see." The older woman's tone was more guarded than it had been before, her gaze more wary, and Chimehara tensed. She crossed her arms over her chest, her hands sliding into the opposite sleeves as if she were cold, but her right hand gripped the handle of the knife sheathed on her left forearm. She hoped not to have to use the blade, but if the old woman cried out or called for a guard, she would. She could not afford to get caught.

Medeiko was still studying her. "It is rare for a father to gift aishone to his younger children, especially a daughter," she pointed out, her gray bun bobbing with her words. "Typically that is for the mother to do, as her gifts would prove more useful."

Chimehara nodded. "My mother has indeed promised me her aishone when she eventually passes," she admitted, doing her best to look stricken at the mere thought of it. "But I was my father's favorite. That is no doubt why he left these for me."

Her hostess sniffed. "Yes, no doubt," she agreed, her tone making it clear that she was not entirely convinced. Still, she finally returned her attention to the bones themselves. "These are a fine collection, if a modest one," she stated, using her the gilded nail of her little finger to prod each sliver loose from the pile. "This one is from an accountant, very good for keeping books. This one is from a trader, talented at haggling and at appraising goods. This one ..."

As the old woman talked, Chimehara let her mind wander, though outwardly she remained attentive. In truth, she did not much care what each aishone was for, only that it would fetch a good price. That was, after all, why she was here. Bone Readers had such strong aitachi they could actually sense what memories, knowledge, and skills each aishone possessed. Because of that, they basically set the value for such gifts, and people often brought aishone to a senkousa to evaluate and possibly buy whatever bones they possessed. The women—for all senkousa were female—were like relicant banks, and were expected to be just as honorbound. For a senkousa to lie about an aishone's contents or value was punishable by death. Of course, that also meant that they were very careful who they dealt with, which was why Chimehara had taken so long before coming to this one. Even here in Mazihini, the outermost level of Awaihinshi, she had to be careful. If Medeiko suspected the aishone had been stolen, she could have Chimehara arrested—or worse. Her only hope was that it had been long enough that no one would be able to connect these bones with the merchant she'd killed, and that the old senkousa would be so glad to see such comparatively valuable bones that she would not raise a fuss about where they had come from.

"I can see why a merchant would want these, especially all together," Medeiko was saying, and Chimehara brought her mind back to the present, and the tent, and the old woman across from her. "I can only assume that the aishone your brother received were of a similar kind and quality, but perhaps a larger size."

"Yes," Chimehara agreed. "Father left him a pouch three times this one in size."

"Oh, very nice," the senkousa murmured. "Well, if he ever wishes to sell any, or to trade them for others, please send him my way."

"I certainly will," Chimehara agreed, inclining her head. She hesitated a second, playing the role of reluctant petitioner to the hilt. "I—I loved my father, Senkousa, and cherish his gift to me, but I cannot help thinking—"

A sly smile crossed the older woman's plump face. "That you might be better served with some silver to add to your dowry?" she asked, and chuckled when Chimehara nodded, blushing and looking down at her own hands. "Oh, don't fret, child," the senkousa exclaimed cheerfully. "There is no harm in thinking ahead! And your father would have wanted to know you put his gift to its best possible use."

"I hope so, Senkousa," Chimehara agreed. "So, if I were to …"

"Oh, yes!" Her hostess clapped her hands together, the flesh wobbling along her arms. "I could give you, let's see, hm, two gold for the lot. I think that's quite fair."

Two gold! Chimehara almost frowned—she was sure they were worth more than that! But then she saw the way Medeiko's eyes narrowed ever so slightly, and schooled her own expression back to bland hopefulness. Inside, however, her heart was racing. The old woman knew! She knew the aishone were illegally got, and she was deliberately offering a cut rate! But of course there was nothing Chimehara could do about it, and the senkousa knew that as well. After all, if she protested too much the old woman would start asking more questions—like the name of this dead father and where he lived—and then the jig would be up. Or she'd simply summon a guard and have Chimehara arrested, keeping the aishone for herself.

No, all Chimehara could do was play along. So, gritting her teeth on the inside, she fluttered her eyes and pressed a hand to her chest, the very picture of gratitude. "Oh, really?" she managed to utter. "So much? Thank you, Senkousa!"

"My pleasure, my dear," the older woman replied, her eyes laughing even as her tone stayed serious. "Here you are, then." She reached into her robe and extracted a small silk pouch, from which her thick fingers plucked two discs of gleaming gold. These she proffered to Chimehara, who accepted them with only partially feigned eagerness.

"Thank you again, Senkousa," she said, rising gracefully to her feet. She set the pouch from the aishone down on the table as she stood, and kept the coins clutched tight in her hands as she bowed and retreated for the tent flap. "Thank you, thank you."

"Of course, child." The Bone Reader watched her go, a self-satisfied smirk on her round face. She still had not moved by the time the flap fell shut again, banishing any sight of her from Chimehara's suddenly furious gaze.

"Oh, that old witch!" she fumed as she stomped away. "Cheating me! I should—" But of course she wouldn't. Going back would be far too risky. It was one thing to knife a merchant slumming it in Suranmui, but she was inside the walls now, and senkousa were well-regarded and well-protected. So instead Chimehara kept walking, not stopping until she was several blocks away. Then she paused long enough to open her palm and quickly regard the twinned coins trapped there before sliding them into a hidden pouch sewn into her sash. While not as much as she'd hoped, two gold was still a great deal, and far more than she had ever had before. For a start, it would do nicely.

Especially since that was not the only thing she had left with. Chimehara unclenched her other hand, and smiled down at the bone fragment nestled there. She had palmed it when she'd risen to leave, and it wasn't like the old senkousa could send guards after her, not without revealing the entire sordid exchange. Chimehara had in fact listened when the other woman had rattled off the use of each bone, and this one had belonged to the trader. Her smiled widened as she added that to her concealed pouch.

Between the bone and the coins, now she had a plan.

Still smiling, she continued on her way, looking for some place with a room to let. Because she was inside the city walls now, and she intended to never set foot beyond them ever again.

CHAPTER THIRTEEN

Noniki glanced around with great interest as they disembarked the barge. This side of the river was evidently Nariyari, or so Mistress Oritano had informed him as they'd shepherded their horses onto the crude, flat-bottomed boat. They had now left Bezenkai behind for the first in his life, and he was curious what this new province would be like by comparison.

Thus far, he was unimpressed. The terrain had become rougher and rockier as they'd traveled east, leaving the wide open plains behind, clumps of trees replacing the fields of rice and grain he had grown accustomed to and which were much more like the rice paddies and bamboo groves along the coast near their village, but on this side of the river that seemed to continue. He had hoped that, here, the ground would suddenly become rich and fertile again, sprouting bean stalks and lotus blossoms and other exciting produce, or simply providing a welcoming carpet of green grass dotted with bright flowers, yet all he saw was still dirt and rock and the occasional scrub brush. "How do we even know we are in Narayari?" he asked, kicking at the ground and raising a cloud of dust that made him cough and caused his eyes to water. "Perhaps this is still Bezenkai, and that bargeman lied in order to charge us more for crossing a fake border."

"What did you expect?" Mistress Yokori called back from where she had already mounted her horse. "That the whole world would turn, transform and tilt and colors would invert themselves just to prove we had traveled to another province? That people here would wear their clothing backwards and their hats upside down and their boots inside out?" She laughed in that sharp, slightly insulting way of hers. "It is another province, young Noniki, but it is still Rimbaku."

"Leave him alone," Master Narai instructed, and his second grimaced but nodded and turned away. "Yokori is right, though," the leader of their little group added more softly, pulling his own horse up alongside Noniki. "You will see more and more differences, both in terrain and in people, the farther you get from home, but here we are merely in another province, and a neighboring one at that. We are still within Miniri, after all, and you cannot expect such a drastic change within a single region." He smiled indulgently and patted Noniki on the shoulder before spurring his horse and following Yokori and the others who had already started down the road that led from the docks.

"Well, how was I supposed to know?" Noniki muttered, scowling as he planted a foot in the stirrup and hauled himself up into the saddle. Kagiri was already mounted, and together they managed to get their horses pointed the right way and ambling after the rest of the group, Joshi and another guard lingering with them to bring up the rear.

Two days later, however, Noniki learned about a significant difference between this province and the one of his birth. The sun was just reaching its zenith, its radiance beating down on them harshly enough that his clothes clung to his skin and his hair was plastered to his head with sweat as he half-draped over his horse's back, letting the poor beast carry him even though it had to be suffering just as much. Master Masute, who had the sharpest eyes of any of them, suddenly sat up straight in his saddle and let out a piercing whistle that drew all their attention.

"There's a town up ahead," he reported, brushing his long, silky hair back from his face. "Most likely they have a well."

A collective sigh rose from the gathering. Though they had filled their skins at the river before leaving it behind, that had been days ago and what water they had left was now both warm and stale. The prospect of cool, fresh water revived them all, and without discussion they all picked up the pace, the horses picking up on their riders' mood and neighing with shared excitement.

But as the town slowly appeared on the horizon, and then grew in everyone's sight from a mere speck to a dark blot to a cluster of small squares to actual buildings, Noniki saw Master Masute frown. "There are people there," the rail-thin merchant announced. "Waiting for us, I'd wager."

Master Narai tugged on his horse's reins, slowing from a canter to a trot, and the others followed suit. That gave Joshi and the rest of the guard a chance to catch up and jog out in front. "Weapons ready," Narai ordered, "but do not move to attack. Let us see what they want, first."

As they drew closer, Noniki could make out the dark shapes spread out between the buildings huddled to either side of the road. They did not seem to be on horseback, which was a good sign, but there were several of them. At least a half dozen, he estimated. But perhaps closer to eight or nine, he amended as he began to make out more details. They had only eight guards, including Joshi himself, but there were fifteen of them total, so he relaxed a little, confident that if these strangers were hostile they would at least be outnumbered by Noniki and his friends.

"They don't look much like honest villagers," Kagiri whispered from right beside Noniki. Noniki frowned, squinting to study the strangers, then nodded. He could now see the men and women well enough to make out that they were dressed in a variety of clothes, much far flashier than he would have expected for a small village in the middle of nowhere and none of it coordinated—one man had on a full kitoro, for example, but it was of some lilac-shaded silk, patterned with blossoms and leaves, and looked more suited to a woman than a man, especially one wearing a fur vest and glossy black pants beneath it. All of them had wild hair pulled back in buns but otherwise unrestrained and unkempt, and most of the men had scraggly beards and mustaches as well.

And all of them were armed, he noted. Much like the bannin back in Ginzai, they seemed to mostly favor clubs and spears, though the one in the kitoro had a nihono shoved through a gold sash. Still, they were clearly not farmers, and possibly not regular craftsmen and laborers, either, not with that attire and those weapons.

Just to be safe, Noniki turned to the merchant closest to him, which unfortunately was Master Kawatai. "Do you have any aishone we can use in case we're attacked?" he asked, keeping his voice low.

The long-nosed merchant frowned. "Aishone?" he repeated, his voice loud enough to carry to the entire group. "Why would you need that?"

Noniki sighed, but it was Kagiri who saved him by answering first. "If those men prove to be hostile," his brother pointed out, "we could help fend them off. Provided we had the right aishone within us."

"You want us to just hand over some aishone, just in case?" Mistress Yokori asked with a snort. "Perhaps you'd like our coin purses as well?"

But Narai silenced the other merchant with a raised hand. "The idea has merit," he agreed. "You will not use them unless you must, of course?" His words were soft but his eyes glittered as sharp as the jagged rocks that often lurked just offshore to snare the unwary.

"Of course," Noniki agreed quickly, and Kagiri nodded beside him. The master merchant glanced around at his fellows, and first Kawatai and then Oritano and Masute and finally even Yokori nodded.

"Very well." Narai gestured at Oritano, and the stout, cheerful merchant deftly slowed her horse, sliding it behind the others, and then sped up again to glide between Noniki and his brother.

"Here you are," Mistress Oritano announced, drawing a small pouch from somewhere within her kitoro and handing it to Kagiri. "The bones of a true warrior, a great Honjofu of years past. Use them sparingly and well." That task done, she reversed her earlier maneuver and reclaimed her usual place in the procession, just to the right of Masute and to the left of Kawatai.

Kagiri wasted no time opening the pouch and inspecting its contents. "It should be enough," he whispered, extracting a pinch of bone and passing that over. Noniki accepted it without comment, keeping his hand clenched tight to keep the aishone from escaping. They both knew that he needed only a little to absorb a skill, whereas Kagiri would require a great deal more—but then Giri would retain that skill a lot longer than he would, in return.

Noniki started to say something, but was startled by a sudden prodding on his other side. The intrusion, and his reflexive flinch, nearly made him toppled from his horse, and he flailed about momentarily, clutching at the reins even as his legs tightened around the horse's flanks. When he had finally regained some semblance of balance, he glanced up, prepared to glare at and curse whoever had poked him—and was startled to find himself looking down the length of a sword.

"I can never seem to get the hang of this cursed thing," Master Kawatai declared, proffering the scabbarded weapon. "But perhaps you can."

"Thank you," Noniki managed, accepting the sword. The merchant nodded and turned away, giggling a little at something only he could see or hear, and Noniki shared a glance with his brother. More than once on this trip they had wondered if Master Kawatai was really as dim as he seemed.

One of the guards offered Kagiri a sword as well, and the brothers straightened in their saddles and grinned at each other. Noniki knew Giri must feel as relieved as he was to have some sort of defense on hand, and as excited at the prospect of holding a fancy metal blade instead of a mere club or staff.

They had reached the front edge of the village now, and the men and women spaced out across the road, blocking their path. Narai slowed to a halt, and the others did the same beside him. "Greetings," he called out, his voice as mildly pleasant as ever. "We are travelers, hoping to purchase a sip of fresh water from your well and perhaps some other supplies as well."

"You can have some water, all you can bear," the man in the kitoro replied, sauntering forward with a rough swagger. "But it will cost you your horses, your weapons, your wealth, and your clothes." The others laughed, and he grinned, revealing uneven teeth.

"Ah, that seems a bit too steep a price," Narai stated. He nudged his horse, and it shifted back a step. "We will simply go around, then, and hope for better luck at the next village."

The stranger frowned. "You misunderstand me, friend," he declared, stroking his thick beard. "It wasn't an option. You will dismount, disrobe, and surrender your gear and your goods."

"Or what?" Joshi retorted, moving in front of Narai, gauntleted hand resting on his sword's hilt. "There are more of us than there are of you."

That made the stranger laugh. "Are there?" he replied. He inserted two thick fingers between his lips and let forth a loud, crude whistle, and four more men emerged from the nearest buildings and trotted over to join his little band. There were twelve of them now, but still fifteen merchants and guards and brothers, Noniki thought. The odds were still in their favor.

He was surprised, then, when Narai leaned forward and tapped Joshi on the shoulder. "Stand down," the lead merchant ordered. "We will do as they say."

"What?" Noniki burst out. He couldn't help it. He looked around at the rest of their party, at the guards who looked annoyed but resigned, at Joshi who was as belligerent as always but already nodding in obedience, and at the merchants who were already beginning to dismount. "The bones we will!"

The stranger's eyes narrowed as he paced to the side to stop right in front of Noniki. "Ah, we have a fighter here, do we?" he asked, still grinning. He stroked the nihono at his side. "Do you think you can take me, child?" he taunted. "You and your friend there against me and all my people, while your companions stand around gaping and do nothing?"

"If that's what it takes," Noniki shot back. He was no stranger to bullies—growing up there had always been older children and even adults who had picked on him and Kagiri, until they'd gotten big enough and strong enough to defend themselves. Then those same bullies had gone after younger, weaker children instead—until he and Giri made them stop that as well. He'd seen a few in Ginzai, too, but none who'd tried to mess with him more than once. And he wasn't about to back down from one now. Because that's all this man was, he could see. A bully who threatened and swaggered and browbeat others into giving in, even when they could have stood against him.

Well, Noniki wasn't having any of that.

Raising his clenched hand, he quickly dumped the pinch of aishone into his mouth, swishing it around with what little saliva he could muster and then swallowing the still-dry powdered bone. At once Noniki felt a surge of power race through him, confidence and skill shooting through every nerve and vein, and he straightened in his saddle, automatically adjusting his seat so that he was balanced properly and could guide the horse with only his knees, while his hands went to the chokoto in his lap. An inferior weapon, he couldn't help but think, no match for the other man's nihono when it came to speed, grace, or cutting power, but good for thrusting and blocking. It would suffice.

"Noniki," Narai was urging from where he stood several paces away, holding his own horse by its reins. "Do not do this. It is not worth dying over."

"I will not die," Noniki shot back, his new expertise filling him with reckless courage. "But they will, if they try to stand against us."

Beside him he heard a dry-sounding gulp, and glanced over to see Kagiri swallowing convulsively. Then his brother's posture also changed, from a novice rider and nonfighter to a trained warrior. Giri nodded at him, and in a perfectly matched motion they both unsheathed their swords.

"Joshi!" Noniki called out, the guard stiffening at his name. "Prepare your men to charge!" The guard scowled but couldn't help nodding at the tone of command, and with a hand he beckoned the other guards to join him. They drew their swords as well, and now the strangers faced eight armed men and women, two of them on horseback. Judging by the way they held their clubs and spears Noniki doubted if any of these bandits—for that was what he judged they were—had ever received proper combat training, and he felt confident that they could defeat this rabble with ease.

Apparently he was not the only one to think so, either. Because suddenly the man in the kitoro held up his hands. "Enough!" he shouted, making all his men pause from where they'd started to step forward, weapons raised. "I am feeling magnanimous today," the stranger continued. "I admire bravery, and would hate to see you boys throw your lives away just because you had found your courage. Instead I, Daro Barindo, chief of the Kibichi, grant you safe passage." He bowed sweepingly and somewhat mockingly, then made a big show of stepping aside and gesturing them toward the town beyond—and the well at its center. "You may pass through, take water, and continue on your way."

Noniki glared down at the bandit chief, sure that this was some sort of trick. But Narai, who had somehow remounted already, slid his horse forward between the brothers and the bandits. "Your generosity does you great honor, noble Barindo," the merchant declared. "And we are grateful to accept it. May you know all the prosperity such richness of character deserves."

"Indeed, indeed!" Barindo replied, guffawing. He slapped the nearest of his men, who smiled as well even though it was clear he was not sure what was going on or exactly what the merchant had said, but the bandit moved aside all the same. So did the rest, and Narai led the way as they walked their horses into town to the well.

"That was well done," Master Narai murmured to Noniki as they quickly set about watering their horses and refilling their skins. "Your show of force was enough to make him think twice."

"Thank you." Noniki bowed, pleased at the compliment. He just hoped that the bandit chief would keep his word. Already he could feel those skills leeching back out of him, all knowledge of swordsmanship and mounted combat and tactics vanishing like a fog scattering before the morning sun, leaving him once again awkward and leaden within his own body. He envied the way Kagiri still sat his horse so well, still moved with military precision, but there was nothing for it, and the short burst of martial talent had done what they'd needed.

Still, Noniki couldn't help but wonder as they mounted up again and rode through the rest of the town and then away. They had outnumbered the bandits from the start, yet Narai had surrendered at the first hint of threat. Why do that, when you had the numbers and the weapons and the horses? Even with half them not being soldiers, they still would have been able to take those bandits, he judged. But perhaps the merchant knew something he didn't.

Or perhaps, he thought as they left the town behind them, dwindling away like water down a drain, the merchants were too fond of their own skins to ever consider risk them, even when the risk was small. Whereas he and Kagiri were young and had less to lose, and so had been more willing to take a chance.

It was the first time he had realized that he and his brother really might have something to offer their wealthy employers after all, and the idea warmed him well into the chilly night.

CHAPTER FOURTEEN

"They've dug in pretty well," Isano reported. He'd just returned from scouting, and now stood beside Shizumi as she studied the terrain ahead. They were near the very northern tip of Korito, which was the northernmost province in Rimbaku and the one that, along with neighboring province Tabichi, butted up against Fyushu's land. But mountains protected Tabichi and the western edge of Korito, whereas here those same peaks gentled into tall, sharp-edged hills, still steep but more manageable. Especially if your soldiers were on foot. It was here that Fyushu had yet again sent warriors to cross the border, and they had already frightened off or killed several shepherds and farmers and a handful of border guards. There wasn't enough room for a full army, and the terrain was tricky, so you needed troops better able to maneuver and think on their feet and deal with strange situations.

Which was why the Emperor had instructed Fujibuki Haro to handle the matter.

And Haro had sent her.

The problem was that, exactly as Shizumi had suspected and Isano had just confirmed, the Fyushan troops had chosen their incursion point with great care. The hills here were tightly spaced, with only a narrow gap between them, and it was in that gap that the warriors had settled themselves. That gave them the hills in front and behind for cover, and only a thin, winding path by which they could be attacked.

Of course, it also meant that they couldn't muster a full charge either. Nor could they beat an easy retreat, if it came to that.

Which gave Shizumi an idea. "Could you see them at all?" she asked Isano now, frowning impatiently as he considered his reply. He was one of her best, sharp-eyed and strong, a devil with the bow, and always dependable, but the same patience that made him so valuable as a sniper could also make him maddening when he was called upon to answer quickly. Like now.

Finally, having thought the matter through thoroughly, he shook his head. "No," he replied. "Not clearly enough to get off a shot, at least. Just brief glimpses of the tops of heads."

Shizumi nodded. "But could you get off a shot that landed in their midst?" was her next question, and her scout grinned as he realized what she had in mind.

"Easily," he confirmed, this time quickly. "The way they've situated themselves, I almost can't miss."

"Good." Shizumi was putting the pieces together in her head even as she gestured to a few of the other Honjofu clustered nearby. "Akino, Geniji, Dairumu," she called. "Here." The three quickly hurried over, and she outlined her plan. "Get everyone ready," she ordered when she was done, and they all saluted and spread out among the rest of the Bone Warriors, calling out orders. Meanwhile, Shizumi had turned back to Isano and, with an impatient wave of her hand, sent him off as well. He was still grinning as he saluted and hastened off to do her bidding. Left alone for the moment, Shizumi flexed her hands in their gauntlets, idly testing the flexibility of the armored fingers, then ran through a quick weapons and armor check, making sure everything was secure and in its proper place. Finally she grabbed her naritaba, her hands closing comfortably around the polearm's long wooden shaft, and settled in to wait.

It didn't take long—less than an hour had passed and the sun was still low in the sky, having not yet fallen fully, when she was roused from her thoughts by the call of a spotted owl. Only it was still too early for the nocturnal predator to be swooping about, even up in these hills. That was why she'd chosen the signal, because it would not seem too out of place to anyone who was only half paying attention but she and her soldiers wouldn't mistake it for an actual bird as long as there was still even a little daylight. Which meant Isano was in place and ready.

"Ready for the attack," she called softly, and Akino, who was nearest, nodded. He turned and conveyed the order down the line, and Shizumi heard the faint, reassuring creak of leather and rattan and iron tightening and settling as the last straps were adjusted and as swords were loosened in scabbards. There was also the soft whisper of silk and the faint gulp of people swallowing, even as she tugged her own pouch free from under her breastplate and loosened the ties before tilting it into her waiting palm. She waited until a small mound of coarse yellowish-white powder had collected there, then tossed that into her mouth, swishing the contents around before swallowing and then returning the re-tied pouch to its normal resting place. Shizumi closed her eyes, letting the expected calm wash over her, feeling her body relax and adjust. She knew that, all up and down the line, her warriors would be doing the same, their posture and stance and weapons handling improving as the aishone were absorbed into their blood, granting them the martial prowess of their ancestors. Everyone here had long experience at taking aishone right before an attack, of course, so she knew that in only a few seconds her entire troop would be ready. When her second finally nodded back, Shizumi lifted her face toward the sky and gave the call of the owl in return.

She did not hear the arrows fall, of course, though she imagined she heard the faint twang of Isano's bowstring as he loosed each one. Nor could she hear the soft thump of the arrows striking home, or the sizzle of the burning cotton and twine wrapped around their heads and shafts. Many of those would fizzle out, of course, or strike nothing but dirt and burn out a few seconds later. But if the enemy had planned ahead as well as she suspected, they had set up tents in their little redoubt, and those would be made of waxed canvas to keep out the rain.

Which meant the Fyushans were essentially sitting under large, flat sheets of wax, like enormous candles without a wick.

Shizumi thought she made out screams and cries rising up into the night from among the hills. Then those sounds increased, and she knew she had heard them for certain. "Now!" she ordered, raising her naritaba high and charging forward. Her warriors were right there with her, Geniji deliberately upping her own pace so that she was just a little ahead and to the left of Shizumi in order to protect her better, Akino right behind and to her right, Dairamu just past him. They covered the distance from their own base to the foot of the first hill in a matter of minutes—

—and reached it just as the first Fyushans began pouring out from that narrow gap, stumbling and coughing, eyes watering and throats raw from the smoke of the burning wax that had been all around them, faces and heads and arms pocked with burns from the molten drips that had rained down upon them.

They were barely able to draw and raise their own weapons before the Honjofu were upon them.

"Lay down your arms!" Shizumi commanded, and Geniji echoed her, the big warrior's powerful voice amplifying her cry. "Surrender, and you will be unharmed!"

Several of the invaders did just that, dropping their swords and spears and bows at once from hands that had barely been able to close about the weapons in the first place, much less have any hope of wielding them effectively. A few of the Fyushans actually dropped to their knees, still gasping for air.

But not every one of them was so shaken, or so ready to give up. Some had converted their surprise and discomfort to anger, and had correctly deduced that they owed the nasty surprise of a few seconds ago to this Rimbakan troop, and in particular to the young woman calling out orders. One of the latter type spotted Shizumi, snarled, and charged her, his chokoto held high. Before he could reach her, however, Geniji had sidestepped into his path, the blade of her naritaba flashing out and down, slamming against the soldier's chokoto with such force that the sword was knocked clear out of his hand. Then Geniji hipchecked the man, the power of her broad frame sending him flying into one of his fellows so hard they both went tumbling to the ground, groaning from the impact. He cursed and gasped for air where he'd hit, but apparently thought better of getting up again.

"Good strike," Shizumi congratulated Geniji. "But I had him."

"I know," the other woman agreed with a broad grin. She had long ago appointed herself Shizumi's bodyguard, and no protestations to the contrary had deterred the big soldier from this self-selected duty. Nor did Shizumi mind most of the time. But right now she really hoped one of the Fyushans was foolish enough to cross her path where Geniji couldn't get to him, so that she would have a chance to whet her own blade!

She got that chance a moment later, when three Fyushan warriors appeared from the gap. These three were in full armor and stood straight and tall, so either they had been far enough from the wax to not be effected or they had simply taken the time to stop and recover before pressing the attack. Now they had, and after a quick glance about they made a beeline for Shizumi.

Geniji saw them and moved to intercept, but while two of the men slowed to engage her the third kept going, his eyes locked on Shizumi. Geniji saw this, but was in no position to go after him.

Which was fine with Shizumi.

"You are the one in charge here," the stranger declared as he closed the distance between them, his green-and-gold enameled menatu in place so that all she could make out were a pair of sharp blue eyes. "You set our tents ablaze."

"I am, and I did," Shizumi acknowledged, flexing her legs and settling into an easy half-crouch, naritaba partially extended before her, both hands firm on its haft.

"Clever," her new opponent acknowledged. He inclined his head, a mark of respect for an equal. "Aioi Kazuko, at your service."

Shizumi dipped her own head in return. "Misataki Shizumi," she replied, and saw his eyes crease in a smile.

"Ah, I am fortunate, then, to meet Rimbaku's greatest warrior," he announced. He drew his nihono and extended the blade, then dipped it in salute. "This is truly an honor."

"As it is for me," she said, saluting with her naritaba, her own nihono still snug in its scabbard at her side. "I hope we can settle this honorably and without unnecessary bloodshed."

She could tell by the way he stiffened that he took the suggestion as an insult, and cursed in her head though she only gritted her teeth outwardly. Damn that male pride! Sure enough, he answered, "A true warrior does not surrender, but fights until he cannot continue. I must do the same."

"So be it," she countered, biting back the accompanying sigh. Then she charged him.

Her naritaba gave her the edge as far as reach and she used that, closing the distance between them and stabbing in toward his chest. As she'd expected, he blocked that with his sword, the blade ringing off hers just above the guard. She quickly rotated her blade, dipping the entire weapon into a tight circle, but he was wise to the trick and disengaged before she could trap his weapon.

This time he struck, his nihono snapping forward in a sweeping arc aimed straight for her neck. Shizumi tugged the naritaba in close, lifting it straight up and down so that its blade caught the nihono again, stopping the swing several inches from her face. Then she lashed out once more but this time with the polearm's butt, the metal ball there rising swiftly and connecting solidly with her opponent's nether regions. She winced in sympathy at his agonized groan as he doubled over, his sword falling from his hands only seconds before he himself wound up on the ground, curling into a ball around his injured groin.

"My apologies for such an ignominious defeat," she told him, stabbing the polearm's blade down to knock his sword farther away. "Feel free to change the story of how it happened when you tell the tale to your children and eventually grandchildren."

Aioi Kazuko just stared up at her with wide, pained eyes. He did not attempt to rise again, however, and after a second he nodded tightly, acknowledging his defeat.

That defeat had coincided with the last few pockets of resistance being handily quashed, and now as Shizumi stared out over the makeshift battlefield she was pleased to see not one Fyushan left standing and armed. The entire battle had last perhaps four minutes, possibly less.

"That was awesome!" Geniji shouted, emerging from the chaos to slap Shizumi on the back. "Half of 'em still don't know what's going on!"

"It was well played," Akino agreed, sheathing his blade as he joined them. "Took them totally by surprise, and we were right here waiting to mop things up." He offered Shizumi a short, crisp bow. "Brilliantly done, Gunso."

"Thank you," she replied, acknowledging both the salute and the compliment. "You too." She frowned, already thinking past this engagement. "Let's round them up," she ordered, indicating the downed Fyushans. "I doubt any of them are sufficiently important to ransom, or have actionable intelligence about other attacks, so once we check to make sure we'll just send them back home. No reason to kill them or to drag them all the way back to Awaihinshi." Many officers would disagree, feeling that a show of force required death to truly sink in, but Shizumi knew that wounded pride could cement a lesson more than mere bloodshed and she was loathe to waste lives, even those of people who had just attacked her and her troops moments before, unless absolutely necessary. Killing was sometimes a necessity but should never be a pleasure. She was also careful to select Honjofu who shared her views—demonstrating a lust for death and violence was a sure way to ensure that you never wound up in one of her commands.

Her warriors saluted and moved to obey, dispersing to make sure the Fyushans were all dead or bound. Shizumi watched them go, the battle elation fading now, to be replaced by fatigue, guilt, and sorrow as usual.

It had been a good plan, she had to admit. It had worked beautifully, forcing the Fyushans to abandon their well-chosen defensive position and instead stumble right into her arms.

And she probably would never get much more credit for it than she had already. And none of that would ever reach Fujibuki Haro's ears, much less the emperor's.

She scowled, her fingers tightening around the naritaba until the wooden haft creaked in protest. She had little right to be upset, she knew. Here she was, a gunso in the Honjofu, the favored sergeant of the Lord Commander himself. That was a tremendous honor, especially for one so young. And for a woman, who could draw strategy and tactics and memorized maneuvers from aishone but not muscle memory and reflexes and actual swordsmanship, to advance so far in a martial field was nothing short of incredible.

Yet here she was. And here she would stay, because the next step up from gunso was chuisu, and there was no way Haro would ever appoint a non-noble to that rank. That a commoner had become even a junior officer had to rankle him, she knew, even if he did his best to hide it. He would never promote Shizumi to anything higher.

And of course if he knew her secret, he wouldn't just demote her, he'd probably have her arrested at once. Or executed. Or both.

She was still mulling this over when Akino found her. "Message from Awaihinshi," he reported, holding up a carrier pigeon in one hand and a tiny message tube in the other. He passed the tube over to Shizumi, who carefully extracted the tiny scrap of rolled parchment within. This she unfurled and read, then read again.

"It is from Fujibuki Haro," she explained once she had fully absorbed the information. "I am being recalled, and ordered to meet him in Nariyari as quickly as possible." She looked up at her scout and frowned. "Apparently they have been experiencing a problem with some bandits, and our taikoro has requested my presence." She made a point of sighing. "Ah, the drawbacks of being so well known and so admired!"

Her scout laughed, as did she, but inside Shizumi was still smarting a bit. Because the truth was, Haro could trot her out like a showpiece any time he pleased, and there was nothing she could do about it. That was simply part of the price she had to pay for rising so far and so fast.

And, she reminded herself forcibly as she turned away from what was left of the battle's cleanup, this was why she had managed to rise as high as she had. Because she'd been willing to do what was necessary, and to put the needs of the Empire first.

Considering her commanding officer had just reached out to her and ordered her to travel almost the entire length of the country to assist him, she could only assume that it was working. Shizumi was a Honjofu, and first among them.

That was worth everything she had given up to get here, and possibly even a great deal more.

CHAPTER FIFTEEN

Seikoku smiled as she scaled the tree. This was almost too easy! Why was it, she wondered as she scampered across the bough, the toughened soles of her bare feet gripping the bark and providing her with steady purchase, that people could be so cautious about locking their doors and barring their lower windows but then never consider that the trees they'd placed around their property for fruit and shade and bouquet could also provide such ready access to their upper floors? Not that she was complaining, since it certainly made her task considerably easier, but she never understood that mentality of not looking up.

The thought made her instinctively glance around herself, surveying Ginzai as it stretched out silent and still in the pale moonlight, and her eye caught on the tip of a pale marble mausoleum in the cemetery, which was only a few blocks away.

Seikoku scowled. She had wandered past the graveyard several times since that ill-fated night, and had been unsurprised to learn that her guess had been completely correct. The number of bannin stationed there had doubled, and their patrol pattern had added an additional layer of complexity, with multiple guards interweaving their paths so that not a single inch of the wall was left out of view for even a second. But what was far worse was that someone had either figured out her entry point or simply chosen to take precautions—the grand old tree she had used to gain access that night had been savagely mutilated, its handsome branches hacked free with great, vicious blows that had left wide swaths of pale wood jutting out in tufted shards.

It was yet another thing that boy had to answer for.

She gritted her teeth, remembering him. Noniki. She would never forget his name, or his face. Or his broad shoulders. Or the way his dark eyes had crinkled when he'd smiled. Or—

Seikoku shook herself, forcibly dispelling such images. She was angry with him, she reminded herself. It was his fault she'd botched that attempt, his fault she might never be able to go back. His fault she was forced to return to smaller, pettier thefts like the one she was in the middle of assaying tonight.

That made her turn her concentration back to the task at hand. She had continued across the branch without having to think about it, but now the branch was narrowing, splitting into an array of smaller, more delicate limbs, each one decorated with fragrant white blossoms and small, dark green leaves that bore serrated edges sharp enough to cut any exposed flesh. She would have to be more careful from this point on.

Crouching lower and angling her torso forward, Seikoku crawled the last body-length along her chosen path, putting her a long reach from one of the house's back windows. The shutters were drawn against night and mist, of course, but she stretched out and managed to brush her fingers along the seam, then tried again and hooked the toughened tip of her gloved forefinger into that narrow gap. A quick tug and the shutter swung open, the two sides sliding apart without a sound. She was fortunate—

the trader who lived here took great care to maintain his home, which include oiling every hinge. She'd have to thank him for that later.

Now the window was wide open, the expanse beyond it dark and inviting. Seikoku had studied this house as best she could without being obvious, and was all but certain the room she faced was a bedroom reserved for visitors. The trader did not have any guests at this time, so the room should be completely empty.

She hoped. Because this part did not allow for subtlety.

Coiling in on herself, Seikoku tensed, eyeing the opening before her. Her feet curled, gripping the branch as best she could, and her gloved hands did the same. She took a deep breath, let it out, took another.

And then she sprang.

Like a cat she lunged, pushing off with hands and feet at the same time, launching herself forward with all her strength. Silent as an owl gliding down on its prey, she vaulted through the air, clearing the branch's flowering edges and the windowsill with ease and diving headlong into the room beyond. She ducked as she passed the shutters, arms tucking in across her chest, head bowing down, neck curving, and hit the floor with her shoulders, rolling forward and tucking her knees in tight before pushing out again and bouncing to her feet. The entire maneuver had taken only a second and had made only the faintest thump on the polished teak of the floor.

Nonetheless, Seikoku froze, ears straining for any hint of movement.

None came, and after a moment she relaxed slightly, freeing herself to straighten from the half-crouch she'd automatically assumed. Then she turned and pulled the shutters closed, though she left them ever so slightly ajar. This way, anyone who happened to pass by and glance up would not wonder at why one window was open while all the rest were shut, but she also still had a way to exit in a hurry if that became necessary.

That complete, Seikoku turned and surveyed the room she was in.

It was exactly as she'd guessed, an unused guest room. The furnishings were clean and simple but looked sturdy and well-made: a bed with a handsome rattan headboard, a small table, a low-slung chair, a writing desk, and a small wardrobe. Crossing the room, her bare feet sliding across the smooth wood, she examined the desk drawers and then the wardrobe, but the former contained only paper and ink and pens and the latter only bedding. A lamp and a water pitcher and bowl sat on the bedside table, but were not worth the effort of lugging away.

Besides, she was not here to steal household items.

Instead she slid the door open, the paneled wood and parchment whispering along its track, and stepped out into the hall. The trader had a wife and two small children, but they had gone away to visit relatives, she knew from lingering near the woman in the market a few days earlier. It was why she had chosen tonight to strike—the trader had been on his own for the past few nights already, which meant he had gotten over the discomfort of being alone in the house and had begun to sleep more soundly. At least, so she surmised from watching him leave in the mornings, weary-looking the first few times but more rested as the days passed and he settled into his new, solitary routine.

She hoped that he was sleeping well tonight.

Creeping down the hall, Seikoku ignored the side doors, which she was sure would lead to the children's quarters, and made for the door at the far end instead. This was the master bedroom, where her prize waited—and where the trader himself would be, as well. Reaching the door, Seikoku paused a second, making sure her breathing was low and calm, unhurried, and that her gloved hands were cool and dry and steady.

Then, gently, she slid open the door.

The room was not that dissimilar from the guest room she'd entered, she saw at once, only a little larger and with two bedside tables, two chairs, and two large wardrobes.

And with a figure huddled in the middle of the large bed, the thin blankets there rising and falling with his breath.

Taking extra care in case any of the floorboards squeaked, Seikoku crossed the room. The trader slept peacefully, his fleshy face relaxed in slumber, his eyes twitching a little as he dreamed. After watching him for a second to make sure he wouldn't suddenly startle, Seikoku glanced over at the small table beside him—and smiled, careful not to let a relieved sigh escape her lips.

Because there, beside a water pitcher and a small basin, nestled in front of a small wine bottle and cup, was a pouch of dark silk on a long, sturdy cord.

Most people liked to keep their aishone within arm's reach, but very few were so paranoid as to sleep with them on, if only because it would be all too possible to roll over in your sleep and wind up strangling yourself with the pouch's cord. Instead, people routinely shed their pouches at night, setting the little bags of relic bones somewhere close by. Many thrust the treasures beneath their pillows, especially when they were traveling, but here in his own home she had hoped the trader would feel comfortable merely having the pouch on the table beside him instead.

Which he had.

Now came the tricky part. Seikoku stepped forward until she was right beside the little table, her shins all but brushing against its smooth, polished ebony edges. Reaching out, she placed her hands on either side of the pouch but did not touch it yet. Instead she waited, steadying herself.

Then, as the trader breathed out, his sheets shifting around him, she closed her hands on the prize, her fingers clamping down on the smooth silk.

Another breath, another faint rustling, and she lifted the pouch clear, holding it tightly so that its contents could not rattle about.

Next she retreated from the room, out into the hall and then back to the guest room.

Once she was there she went to the writing desk and, crouching beside it, used that surface to carefully nudge free the pouch's contents. The bag was twice the size of her own, and comfortably full, with many pieces as big as a thumbnail while others were more like the sliver of a nail above the finger.

Seikoku did not bother to empty the bag completely. Instead she selected two medium-sized fragments and carefully wrapped them in a bit of silk she pulled from her pocket. The small bundle then returned to her pocket, while the rest of the aishone went back into their pouch. After that it was simply a matter of retracing her steps and restoring the pouch to its normal resting place, which she did without causing the trader to stir even once.

Finally, after what felt like hours of tense silence and steady, stealthy motion, Seikoku was back in the guest room, easing its door closed behind her before striding toward the shuttered window that awaited. Easing the shutters open, she studied the street below and the houses to either side, listening as well as looking. All was quiet, with no sign that anyone but her was still up and awake at this hour. She nodded once, pleased, then gripped the windowsill, her hands well apart. A quick hop and she was perched on the sill, bare feet between gloved hands, knees up against her chest. She pulled two thin threads from where they'd been tucked into her sleeve, and tucked the knotted end of one in between slats on one of the shutters before tying the rest of the thread around her ankle. The process was repeated on the other side, so that she was now tethered, albeit loosely, to those open partitions.

This was one of the hardest parts—and one of the most exciting. After several deep, steady breaths, Seikoku flung herself out of the window. She stretched to her full length as her feet pushed off, arms at full extension, hands wide—and as soon as those hands came down on the tree branch she pushed off again, whipping her legs forward over her head so that she wound up flipping over entirely, her whole body catapulting farther down the branch before landing, feet down, body low, hands spread for balance, close enough to the trunk that the branch was easily wide enough and sturdy enough to support her without even the slightest tremor to indicate her presence.

That done, she became immobile once more, waiting to make sure no one had noticed her rapid exit from the house. The threads had done their work well, tugging the shutters closed before being pulled free by her momentum, so that the window was once again shut, with no evidence that it had ever been opened. Nor were there any outcries from below, so Seikoku was confident that her escape had not been noticed.

After that it was a simple matter for her to scamper from that branch to another, putting herself just a little farther from the trader's home before swinging down and dropping to the ground.

The night was quiet, the city asleep as Seikoku straightened and walked away, moving quickly but calmly, just a woman out for a late night stroll before the pressures of the day. The pair of aishone were nestled deep in her pocket, a reassuring presence she sensed but could not feel. Hopefully the trader would not notice their absence, or if he did he would simply think that he had misremembered how many he'd had left. That was why she had only taken two, and not gone for the larger fragments, which he would be more likely to recall.

Still, even if he did realize he'd been robbed, he would have no way of knowing how anyone had pulled that off, much less who had done it. And tomorrow morning Seikoku would visit Madam Akari, who she had done business with several times before. Akari was a Senkousa, but she had started out as an orphan and still remembered what it was like to have nothing and no one and to do whatever it took to get by. She would buy the aishone off Seikoku, no questions asked, and then find a way to sell them without attracting any suspicion.

Seikoku smiled again as she made her way back home. Although tonight's little escapade in no way made up for the massive windfall she would have experienced if the cemetery heist had gone off as planned, it had still been a good night's work. Plus she loved being out and about when the rest of the city was asleep, leaping from branch to branch, prowling through other people's homes, making off with their valuables without them ever realizing she was there. That sense of freedom was half of why she did what she did.

The other half, though, was the part that put food on the table. And she wasn't about to forget it.

CHAPTER SIXTEEN

Noniki leaned back, unconsciously reining in his horse, as he stared at the rocky cliff before them—and the strange, spiky tower that glittered atop it, its jagged spires rearing up so high it seemed as if they might carve bloody furrows in the sun itself. "Whoa," he whispered.

"Whoa is right," his brother agreed from beside him. Belatedly Noniki realized that Kagiri had also halted his steed. In fact, all of the party had paused, strung out in a nearly perfect line across the wide path that had led them here, almost as if the strange tower had erected an invisible boundary they could not see but were nonetheless loathe to cross.

"We made it," Master Kawatai muttered, and for once he sounded entirely lucid. "I was not completely sure we ever would."

"Of course we made it," Mistress Yokori snapped, shaking her head at her companion's pessimism. "I never had the slightest doubt." She lashed her horse with the ends of her reins, forcing it to reluctantly step out ahead of the rest, then glanced back over her shoulder. "Well? Aren't you coming?"

Master Narai shrugged at the others, as if to say, "what would you have me do?" Then he was following after her. One by one the other merchants joined him, and then Joshi was standing beside Noniki's horse. The guards had actually reached the tower first, going ahead to scout it last night and returning this morning to report that "all was clear and quiet," at which point Narai had ordered everyone to saddle up and ride out.

"Better get a move on," the gruff soldier warned now, and Noniki swallowed. The others were getting farther and farther ahead, though, and he couldn't see any reason to refuse—this was why they had come, after all—so finally he kicked his horse gently and nudged it forward. Kagiri was right behind him.

"What is this place?" Kagiri whispered as they rode, quickly closing the gap to the others and then settling into a steady canter. "I mean, I get that it's got to be this Tawasiri they talked about, but what does that even mean?"

"It means 'Tower of Ghosts,'" Mistress Oritano called back over her shoulder. Evidently her hearing was excellent! "It's said that it's haunted by the ghosts of those who once lived here, though who those people were and what they were doing constructing such a strange edifice in so distant and forbidding a place, no one can say." She pursed her lips. "But no one ever goes in. Most people won't even get as close as we are now."

Noniki could understand why. Already, as they slowly threaded their way along the narrow path cut into the side of the cliff, he felt an enormous sense of dread weighing down on him, dampening his spirits and threatening to smother him with its cold, clingy despair. And the closer they got, the stronger that feeling became.

"Giri—" he started, and his older brother, riding right behind him, nodded.

"I feel it too," Kagiri confirmed. He shivered audibly. "There's something really wrong with this place."

That much was evident just by looking at it. Noniki had grown up with the mud-and-wattle and woven reed and occasionally wooden huts of his village. In Ginzai he'd seen houses of stone and wood and plaster. During their travels, he'd seen more of each of those types, to varying degrees of plainness and complexity and elegance.

This place, the Tawasiri, was something altogether different.

For one thing, there was its composition. All of the buildings Noniki had seen thus far were one to two stories, nothing more, and typically had sturdy wooden beams at the corners and clean walls between, broken only by doors and windows. This tower looked to be solid stone, but not the standard pale or milky varieties he was used to—this edifice had evidently been carved from something gleaming and black as the night sky, and as glossy as still water on a lake. That was a little difficult to tell, however, because not a single inch of it appeared to be flat and empty. Instead the entire tower was covered tip to base with carvings, all of which ran in bands about it. Much of the carving looked to be geometric in nature, with sharp edges and crisp angles, and for most of the upper half each level ended in tiny spires that mimicked the final peak, so that it was as if a thousand baby birds clustered around their mother and threw back their heads to shriek for food.

For another, there was its placement. The space immediately before the tower widened into a small plateau, but the only way to reach it was by the narrow path they were currently traversing. To their left, the waves crashed against rocks every bit as brutally sharp as the tower they protected. To their right stood a thick cluster of scraggly, twisted bushes whose roots emerged from the cliffs around them, forming a solitary patch of green and brown against the grey rocks. Shadows behind those bushes suggested that they actually extended farther back than Noniki could see, possibly settling into a more traditional wooded area once the sea was lost from view. But that initial row of scrub brush formed a barrier none but the bravest—or most foolhardy—would ever even consider breaching. The tower was effectively cut off save by the one road they had already taken, a road that was treacherous enough all on its own. But clearly that had been the builders' intent, to make this site as inaccessible and secure as possible.

In that they had succeeded admirably.

"Just how old is this place?" Noniki asked. The others had all stopped and dismounted a dozen paces from the tower, and now he and Kagiri did as well. It felt like he was swaddled in layer upon layer of cloth, he thought as he took a step, then another. Every motion was an ordeal, like trying to battle his way uphill while carrying a sack of rocks on his back and more draped from his arms and legs and even his neck.

It was, again, Mistress Oritano who answered. "No one knows for certain," she replied as casually as if she were discussing what to have for tea, but her eyes were bright and her smile looked too fixed to her broad face. "Some say it dates to before the Schism, though."

"Before the Schism?" Noniki stared up at the strange, overly ornamented structure with mingled awe and terror. "Is that even possible?" He and Kagiri had heard of the Schism, of course—though their village had been too small to require formal schooling, the elders had passed down stories and tales to their children and grandchildren, sharing what little store of knowledge they had gleaned from their own ancestors. Many of those stories were of the golden times long ago, before the land was broken and its magic all but lost. No one knew how or why that had happened, the elders had always claimed, but they did have a name for the terrible time when it occurred: The Schism.

And now the merchants were saying that this strange place predated that? Certainly if it had been carved by magic that would explain its strange architecture and materials, Noniki judged. But it still didn't explain why it was here, or why he could barely stand to look at it.

Master Kawatai had wandered over, and now he draped one arm over each of the boys' shoulders. "They say it was the home of wizards," he confided, tugging them close. "And that entering it is enough to drive a man mad." Then he grinned at them. "I suppose we'll soon find out, eh?"

That reminder was enough to awaken a jolt of fear so powerful it shivered Noniki's legs to jelly, and he might have crumbled if the long-nosed merchant's surprisingly powerful grip had not kept him upright. "Soon?" he managed to squeak out, his voice wavering and thin. "Like, how soon?"

At that, Mistress Yokori, who had just stepped in close, grinned. "Well, no time like the present, is there?" she pointed out, her smile as sharp-edged as ever, and her eyes equally hard.

"Uh, wait," Kagiri protested, though his voice sounded as weak as Noniki's. "We need some time to think about this. To figure out a plan."

"Plan?" Master Masute scoffed. "What plan? You go in, you gather whatever aishone you find, you come out. That's it." All around them, the other merchants nodded.

"This is what you were hired for," Master Narai reminded them, his tone quiet but stern. "We have paid you good silver to come all this way with us, so that you might obtain and absorb the aishone said to wait within."

"Well, yeah, okay, sure," Noniki stammered out, trying to think, to come up with something, anything, to slow the horrible fate he could already see rushing toward him and Kagiri. "But you wouldn't want us to screw it up, right? What if we just stumble in and miss the really important stuff? That'd be a wasted trip. We should stop and walk around a little, get a sense of the place first."

The merchants frowned, but after a moment Narai nodded. "That is not unreasonable," he acceded, and stepped back, waving for Kawatai to release the brothers. "By all means, take a look around," he suggested, a hint of mockery in his tone.

Still, Noniki was happy for whatever respite he could obtain. Grabbing Kagiri's arm, he dragged his brother forward, away from the merchants—and their armed men, who he now realized had cut off their way back to the horses and the path behind.

They were trapped.

"What're we going to do?" he whispered to his brother as they started slowly approaching the tower.

"I don't know," Kagiri replied, and Noniki took it as a mark of just how serious the situation was that his brother didn't point out that this was, really, all his fault. Again.

"Maybe there isn't even a way in," Noniki offered, but almost as soon as he'd said that his spirits fell a bit, because there, right in plain sight, was a doorway. Its carved frame stood out from the rest of the tower, though it had clearly been carved out of the same stone and in the same style, complete with a jagged, peaked top made up of many small spires clustered close together. The door itself was of the same stone but instead of bands it had been carved with a series of circles set one atop the other, each one bearing a strange, unfamiliar pattern that made Noniki's skin crawl just to look at it. He shivered.

"Maybe it won't be so bad," Kagiri said, though his voice lacked conviction. "Maybe the floors within really are littered with aishone, and we just have to duck in, scoop some up, and run."

Neither of them bothered to claim they believed that.

"Stop stalling," Master Masute called out. "Just get it over with."

"We, ah, we're still thinking about the best way to do this," Noniki hedged, but the merchants all scoffed.

"There's only one way," Mistress Yokori argued. "And it's going to happen, whether you like it or not." There was no mistaking the threat in her tone, or in her glare. "Now get to it!"

"We could run," Noniki suggested softly. "Charge them, duck past, get to the horses, mount up and wheel about and ride away while they're still trying to figure out what's going on." Even to his own ears that idea sounded ridiculous, so he was nearly struck senseless when his brother nodded.

"We might be able to run," he agreed. "I doubt we can get to the horses, though, not with Joshi and the others guarding them." Obviously going off the cliff would be suicide—if the jagged rocks below didn't kill them, the raging waters beyond that would. Instead his gaze swept to the side, toward the brush there. "But if we can make it across to that, we can duck under and hide in the woods beyond."

"You think so?" Noniki was a bit thrown—normally it was him coming up with insane plans and Kagiri acting as the voice of reason.

But this time his brother was the one with the plan. "It's worth a try," he argued now. "I don't think we're going to come up with anything better." He shuddered a little. "And I don't know about you, but I really don't want to go in there."

"Right." Noniki nodded, putting on his best front. "Let's do it, then." He considered where they stood, and where the merchants were. "We'll wait until we're closer to it, then both jump."

"All right." Kagiri smiled. "It'll be fine, Niki. You'll see."

Noniki tried to act confident too, but knew he wasn't fooling anyone. Including himself. Still, he had faith in his brother.

Together they continued toward the tower but also around it, heading inland toward that scrub brush. When they were parallel with the ragged foliage, Kagiri rested a hand on Noniki's shoulder. "Now!" he suddenly shouted, shoving Noniki forward and leaping as well—

—but in the wrong direction.

"Giri!" Noniki screamed, stunned into immobility as he watched his older brother charge straight at the gathered merchants. Kagiri's headlong rush took them by surprise and he barreled several of them over, flailing about him with his arms as he did.

"Run, Niki!" Kagiri yelled back, and Noniki was torn. He understood, all at once, that this had been his brother's plan from the moment he agreed to the idea. He was distracting the merchants, holding them off, so Noniki could escape.

He was sacrificing himself for his little brother. Protecting him like he always had, one last time.

"No!" Noniki shouted, spurred to motion again finally as he turned to help his brother. But then his eyes met Kagiri's and the despair there—but also the resolution, strong as the stone upon which they stood.

"Go, Niki," Kagiri urged softly. "Please. For me." Then he had turned and started laying about him again, forcing the merchants and their guards to keep back.

And Noniki, tears streaming down his face, finally did what his brother asked. He turned away and, with a heart as heavy as iron, fled, racing across the plateau and diving headfirst into the thick bramble that bordered it. Sharp thorns tore at his arms and hands and face but he didn't care. He thrashed about, forcing his way through the thicket by sheer force, until suddenly he tumbled clear, onto rough, loose dirt on the far side.

He'd done it!

"Kagiri!" he shouted, springing to his feet and facing the tower again. "Come on!"

But the words died in his throat.

Because, through the thicket, he could see the tower and its clearing as if through a carved screen—and, even as he watched, Joshi slid up behind the wildly gyrating Kagiri and, with a single judiciously placed blow from the ringed butt of his sword to the back of the boy's head, sent Noniki's brother tumbling to the ground, senseless and splayed upon the bare rock.

"NO!" Noniki screamed, his voice tearing from his throat, but if his former employers heard, they gave no sign. Instead he was forced to watch, powerless to intervene, as two of the guards lifted Kagiri by the arms and legs and carried him over to the tower, where another two had just pried upon the heavy stone door.

And then, with a single coordinated heave, they flung Noniki's brother inside and slammed the door shut behind him.

CHAPTER SEVENTEEN

"Uhhh."

Kagiri came awake to a blinding headache, narrowing his vision to a mere tunnel, a patch of shadow that barely seemed empty but felt more like a hazy prison, wrapped around him in a cocoon that threatened to suffocate him with each labored breath. He gasped for air—and choked, doubling over from where he had just levered himself into a sitting position, retching and trying to suck in fresh air at the same time. Tears streamed down his cheeks, clinging to dirt there before trickling between his lips, adding to the bile and mucus already swirling in his mouth. He swallowed convulsively, and the bitter, acidic mixture nearly made him hurl it back out again but he fought the urge, pounding a fist against his chest, and finally forced the foul liquid sludge down, where it roiled about his stomach but at least left his throat empty. Sneezing vigorously made his head throb and his vision strobe but cleared his nose so that he was able to at least draw a weak, shuddering breath and hold it.

The air was thick around him, and he realized now that this was no illusion, no strange notion of his addled mind, but a reality. Whatever he had swallowed, it was all around him, dust or dirt or something else but it seemed to coat everything and to float freely in whatever space this was, as well. His hands were gritty with it where he'd pushed off from the floor, and when he finally managed to drag himself to his feet more of the substance flaked away from his clothing.

Where was he, exactly? He wracked his brain, seeking answers, but only caused another burst of pain, fierce enough that he pressed both palms to his temples, trying in vain to keep his skull from cracking open—or perhaps hoping to split it apart like a nut and release the hurt so that it could no longer torment him, he wasn't quite sure. What had happened to him? Last he remembered—ah!

It came back to him, then—the Tawasiri, that strange, terrifying, clearly ancient tower. The merchants and guards he and Noniki had fooled themselves into thinking were friends or at least considerate companions turning on them, ignoring their fears and threatening to force them into the old ruin against their will if necessary. Him realizing that there was no way both he and his brother could escape this fate—but one of them might. Tricking Noniki—that was something he knew Niki might never forgive him for, but it had to be done. Attacking Joshi and the others to keep them away while Niki fled, and then almost having the whole "noble sacrifice" thing be for naught as his stupid, courageous, bull-headed brother threatened to turn back for him instead. Watching as Niki disappeared into the bramble, hearing him cry out, then something hard striking him from behind—

And now here he was.

Inside the Tawasiri. It was the only answer that made any sense. The merchants had made good on their threat. They had shoved him in here, and, what? Left him to die?

No. That didn't fit. They wanted the aishone from the place too badly to just walk away.

Which meant Narai and the others must still be here. Outside. Waiting.

Peering about, Kagiri managed to make out a faint difference in the overall shadows of this place. There were lighter patches and darker ones, he discovered. But his first thought, that the brighter areas were open space, was rudely disproven when he reached for the nearest and yelped in pain as his hand collided with something stiff and unforgiving. Stone. The lighter patches were stone, something rougher and far paler than the glossy black of the exterior. And the darker patches were the open space in between.

Well, at least that gave him something to work with. Kagiri stopped thrashing about and forced himself to stand stock-still, even though his skin still crawled and his lungs still burned and his eyes ached and he kept feeling as if he were being watched. He closed his eyes, counted to ten, and then opened them again. Now he could make out the walls a little better as his eyes adjusted. The space he was in was long and narrow, with only the faintest light trickling down from somewhere up above. A hallway, he surmised. And assuming that Joshi and his soldiers had been too scared to step foot in here themselves—not that he would blame them for that!—Kagiri guessed that the closer end of that hall was the door through which he had been thrown.

Turning in that direction, he took a careful step forward, then another, one hand outstretched. He had not even finished the second step before his fingers brushed against stone once more. Aha! Running both hands up and down the obstruction, Kagiri confirmed that it was indeed a door—he could feel the depression around it, a narrow but deep groove that ran all the way up one side, across the top, and then down the other. That was where the door sat in its frame. He also found what had to be a handle, roughly the same height as his stomach, the only element that jutted out more than a finger's width, which then widened into a cold, uneven loop. A metal ring, he assumed, pitted from centuries but still solid.

But when he tried tugging, nothing happened. And when he set his shoulder to the door and pushed instead it groaned but did not budge.

His actions did garner one result, however: a shout that went up from outside.

"Hello!" Kagiri yelled, his throat throbbing from such abuse when it was already raw. "Let me out!"

He did not get an answering shout, but a moment later he did receive a reply.

"Hello, Kagiri," Master Narai called out, his voice muffled by the thick stone but clear enough to hear. Kagiri had to guess that the merchant stood right by the door, possibly with his lips mere inches from where it met the frame. "I am glad to know that you are still alive and well—Joshi assured me that he did not hit you too hard, and we all saw that you were still breathing, but still we were concerned."

Kagiri had to laugh at that, though his chuckles quickly changed to rasping coughs that shook his entire body. "Concerned?" he echoed, not bothering to raise his voice since he doubted they would hear him, or care if they did. "For your own interests, maybe. Not for me."

The fact that Narai had continued speaking only confirmed his guess. "Now, I am sorry the matter had to be handled the way it did," the merchant claimed, his tone as mild and reasonable as ever. "But we did engage you and your brother for a task, and we still expect you to make good on that. We will not pursue Noniki, or seek any sort of retribution against him, provided you do as promised. Gather the aishone there and we will release you. Then we can discuss how our association can proceed."

"Our association?" Kagiri muttered, trying not to laugh again even though he could feel the hysteria building within him. "You mean when I stagger back out of here you'll decide whether to keep me alive and enslaved or just kill me and be done with it." He no longer had any illusions about the merchants' concern for his well-being. It was all too clear now that all they cared about was their treasure.

"When you are ready, bang three times on the door," Narai was instructing. "We will unbar it and open it. Be warned, however— if you do this without having the aishone in your possession, we will simply toss you back inside. Nor will you receive any food or water until you have completed your task." He paused for a moment before adding, "I suggest you make haste."

"Damn you!" Kagiri raged, banging impotently on the door. His fists barely made a sound as they connected, and he knew that the thick stone would completely muffle that impact from the men and women waiting outside. How did they expect him to let them know he was ready to be released, then? They would stand there impatiently, straining to hear his signal, while he wasted away inside. Perhaps they would grow curious enough to open the door before he died from hunger and thirst and suffocation—but he knew he could not count on that.

But perhaps the very treasures they had sent him here for could be what saved him.

With that thought in mind, Kagiri turned his back on the door and the people beyond it and, even though a part of himself screamed at the very notion, he staggered away from it, lurching and stumbling his way deeper into the dark tower he had been trapped within. He knew that every step he took made it less likely Narai and the others would even find him when they eventually searched, but waiting by the door would avail him nothing. If there was any salvation to be found, any chance of escape, it would be through the aishone, which would be placed in a spot of veneration near the tower's heart.

At least, so he hoped.

The stairs nearly killed him.

Kagiri had managed to clear his head enough that he could at least think clearly again, and his vision had adapted well enough now that he could make out the pale stone to either side, so he no longer needed to keep his hands up and feel his way along step by step. That, and the fact that he saw only darkness ahead, convinced him to pick up his speed a little, so that soon he was actually walking at a more normal pace down the hallway.

The problem, as he realized only after his right foot had collided painfully with something hard and pitched him forward, and he'd flung his arms out only barely in time to keep from smashing his forehead against something else hard and cold and rigid, was that his vision only extended a few feet ahead of him. And, it turned out, only a few feet down as well. So the first step had been hidden in the shadows that coiled about this place, completely invisible to him, as had the rest of the staircase until it was literally inches from his face.

Then he was able to make it out very clearly. Or at least as clearly as he could distinguish anything in this cramped, dark, oppressive place.

"Lovely," he muttered as he pushed himself back upright, wincing at the sharp pains radiating through his arms from where they'd struck. "Guess I'm going up, then." Which made sense, really, seeing as how the tower had loomed high overhead. He should have expected stairs at some point.

Just not quite so quickly, or suddenly.

Now that he knew they were there, proceeding to ascend the steps was simple enough. They were still solid, apparently untouched by the years, and although there was no railing the walls were close enough that Kagiri could run his fingers along each side as he went, for reassurance and just in case he needed to suddenly grab hold and stop himself from falling. He counted three dozen steps before his foot, nudging forward for the next one, dipped down several inches instead before finally planting itself level with his trailing limb. He was back on level ground, albeit considerably higher than the entranceway he'd started in.

Moving carefully, Kagiri felt his way around this new space. It was a room, he soon surmised, perhaps twenty feet wide and the same length, and the stairs continued up on the far side. His foot brushed against something on the floor in the room's center, but when he knelt to investigate his fingers found only dust. Whatever had been here had succumbed to old age long ago.

With a heavy sigh, careful not to inhale too much and start coughing again, Kagiri rose to his feet and made for the second set of stairs. "Onward and upward," he muttered.

At least, if he died somewhere along this path, he'd end up someplace high and dry, where his bones could rest for centuries before the next idiot blundered in.

Again the stairs numbered three dozen before ending in another chamber, and again it was empty, save for some dust and a continuation of the staircase. What was the purpose to these rooms? Kagiri wondered as he continued on after a brief pause for breath. Were they meant as way stations? Guard posts? Or just some kind of pause so people could catch their breath, exactly as he just had? He had no idea. Certainly neither of the two he'd found so far had offered any sort of window, which meant he was still relying upon the stifling and stagnant air and limited illumination that had pervaded the tower thus far. Still, he had not run out of air yet, so that was something.

The third chamber he found was significantly larger than the previous two, and, by the First Emperor, it did have windows! Kagiri nearly wept for joy when he saw the slivers of light outlining those squares, and he did sob after running to the nearest one and shoving against it, because the ancient stones slid apart with a shrill, piercing shriek and suddenly he was blind from the light that poured in around him, and deliriously near-drunk from the fresh, cool, salty air that engulfed him! He had not even realized just how accustomed to the darkness and the dust he had become until he was able to see again and able to breathe cleanly.

When his vision cleared and he'd stopped gulping, Kagiri took the time to look around.

This was the first chance he'd had to see any part of the tower's interior properly, and he felt something within him soar as he studied the room he was in. It was dizzyingly high, the ceiling invisible overhead but a series of tall, graceful arches crisscrossing the space just within the edges of the sunlight, their shadows creating a series of overlapping rings across the floor. The floor itself was not stone but tile, he saw now, each piece cunningly place to create an intricate pattern he could not comprehend but was still staggered by its beauty and complexity. The window frames were the glossy black stone from the exterior but delicately fluted, and the walls had bands of carvings around them, the details worn smooth from age but still somehow hauntingly lovely.

And this room was not completely bare.

Against one wall, the one between the stairs he had just exited and the window, was some sort of display, taller than him but only a foot or so deep, with crossbeams at varying heights. On the wall opposite that one was another display, this one divided into panels and each bearing several hooks and short bars. The wall on the other side of the lower stairs and the one facing it both had handsome wooden benches set before them, and the final wall, directly across from the window, had a broad table running its entire length, the surface still covered with dishes, bowls, and pitchers.

Food and drink!

Seeing that, Kagiri's heart leapt. He dashed over to the table, grabbing desperately for the first pitcher he saw, the hunger and thirst that he had pushed to the back of his mind now dominating all thought, his throat suddenly dry as bone and his stomach cavernously empty. He didn't even want to think about how long these things had sat here, or what state they might be in, as long as he could still quaff and chew them.

But the second his hand touched the pitcher, the graceful ceramic crumbled, its structure dissolving like a mud castle beneath a hard rain.

"No!" The cry burst from his throat, as painful physically as it was emotionally, as Kagiri grasped desperately, as if he could somehow preserve some of the pitcher's shape within his hands.

But in an instant there was nothing left but the ever-present dust sifting through his fingers, motes of it rising to tickle his eyes, nose, and throat anew.

Despondent, he slumped forward, his hands dropping to splay across the tabletop—

—which promptly collapsed as well, spilling him onto the floor amid a cloud that swirled about him and threatened to choke him once and for all.

That was the last straw, and Kagiri collapsed onto his back, laying there staring up at the ceiling and the light dancing beneath it, tears running down his face. Of course anything still here would be centuries old, and only preserved because it had been undisturbed. It had been foolish to think otherwise. But having let that thought, that hope, flit across his mind, however irrationally, it gutted him now to have the harsh truth thrown in his face once more.

There was no food here. No drink. And he was now three levels away from the tower entrance. Even if there were aishone, even if they had somehow survived when all else had fallen to ruin, the odds of him being able to find them and carry them back before he collapsed were frightfully small, and diminishing with every second.

He would probably die here.

Acknowledging the likelihood of that fate, Kagiri felt a part of him finally relax. There was an ease in accepting the inevitable, in no longer struggling against it. A sad sigh escaped him, and, closing his eyes, he slipped into a deep sleep.

CHAPTER EIGHTEEN

Two days.

It had been two days since Noniki had watched his brother disappear into that cursed tower.

Two days since Kagiri had essentially ceased to exist.

Noniki had spent most of that time sitting right here, perched in one of the trees he'd found behind the scrub-brush barrier he'd forced his way through. The trees were not terribly tall, and they were twisted like a thicket of reeds after a monsoon, bent every which way, but they were sturdy, their rough bark easy to climb and their leaves thin and soft enough that their edges did little more than tickle. On top of which, the trees produced a small fruit Noniki had never seen before but that reminded him of a satsuma, small and hard and filled with plump red flesh and tart juice once you got past the thin, sticky peel. He had consumed several to quench his hunger and thirst, and had filled his pockets with more, all the while keeping his eyes trained on the tower that had swallowed his brother whole.

The first day, nothing had happened. The merchants, whose names Noniki cursed with every other breath in a never-ending litany, sat around a small fire, sipping tea and nibbling fruit and cheese and otherwise acting exactly as they had the whole way here, as if they were enjoying a casual picnic rather than embarked on some crazed quest. Only the glances each of them kept stealing toward the tower door indicated their actual unease. The guards had been more active but only insofar as they kept pacing about the clearing, reminding him all too forcibly of the bannin in Ginzai as they swapped positions, weapons at their sides, their gazes alert.

Meanwhile, two stood in place to either side of the door itself, arms crossed, facing outward as if daring anyone to do anything stupid.

No—as if daring him to do something stupid.

Because, of course, that was exactly what Noniki wanted to do.

He wanted to charge back through the bramble he still bore angry, weeping scratches from, waving the sword he still carried, the one Master Kawatai had given him, and rush the tower, sweep the guards aside, knock loose the iron bar he'd watched them wedge against the door, wrest it open, and leap inside to find and rescue his brother.

But even someone as hotheaded as him knew that would never work. There were too many of them, and they were too well-armed, too well prepared. Too ready for him or anyone else who might happen by. If he even tried, he'd be dead before he could get halfway across the clearing—bones, he'd probably be dead before he even escaped the brambles! Either that or he'd find himself tossed into the tower as well. And while that would at least reunite him with Kagiri, it wouldn't help either of them escape the Tawasiri alive. Much less get away from the men and women Noniki now realized meant only to use him and his brother and then discard them when their value had ended.

Much as Kagiri had tried to warn him.

But of course he'd refused to listen. As usual.

Noniki gritted his teeth, his fingers digging into the bark of the branch he sat upon. This was all his fault. Why hadn't he listened? Why hadn't he looked for something else, something less impressive but also less risky? Giri had pointed out that this offer was too good to be true, but of course he'd leaped in anyway, like always. And dragged Kagiri right along with him.

And now his brother was trapped in that tower, and there was nothing he could do about it.

Noniki knew his brother was still alive. At least, he had been yesterday, or so he'd surmised. Because he'd been startled out of a half-doze by Joshi shouting from the door and all the merchants rushing over. Then he'd watched as Narai had switched places with the lead guard, practically pressing his face against the door's edge. Watching the merchant's jaw work, Noniki was fairly sure the man had been talking, projecting his voice into the tower as best he could.

And the only reason to do that was if he had been talking to someone inside.

Meaning Kagiri.

But that had been yesterday. They had not opened the door, and nothing else had happened since.

Noniki knew that they hadn't tossed any supplies in there with his brother. And he couldn't imagine that a place like this, which had been shunned for so many years, would have any food or drink secreted somewhere within. Which meant it had now been two days since Kagiri had had anything to eat or drink.

Food was one thing—you could go hungry but survive.

Water was another.

How long could a person live without water? Noniki didn't know for certain, but he was sure it would be measured in days or even hours, not more.

And it had been two days.

With each passing hour, he had to acknowledge that there was less and less chance Kagiri was still alive in there. Yet the merchants and their soldiers seemed unconcerned. They certainly hadn't bothered to go check, or to lob a waterskin inside, just in case.

Which told Noniki that, while they might hope his brother made it out alive with their aishone, they were perfectly willing to accept the notion that he might not. His death meant nothing to them except a little bit of lost time, nothing more.

But to him it meant everything.

Noniki scowled and kicked at the tree's trunk, chipping away a chunk of bark that flew upward, nearly catching him in the face. He ducked automatically, then grimaced, annoyed at himself all over again. What did it matter if it hit him? So what if it scratched him? If it left a long, ugly scar straight across his face, even took out an eye, well, it would be no more than he deserved, and a whole lot less if he were being honest.

Yet he had still moved to protect himself without thinking. Just like when he had run off and left Kagiri there to die.

"If only I'd had some aishone," he started to mutter, but then stopped himself, clenching his fists. No, that was the last thing he needed right now.

In fact, he realized with a sudden burst of bitter clarity, it was the last thing he needed ever again.

True, Narai and his friends were the ones who had brought them here, but really it had been their desire for aishone that had done the brothers in. It had been their own aitachi that had made them such ideal stooges for the merchants—and now, thinking back, something else occurred to him. That night in the tavern, he and Kagiri had been talking about their lack of prospects, and he had said something about how, between the two of them's aitachi, they should be able to do amazing things.

And he hadn't bothered to be quiet about it.

They heard me, Noniki realized now. Narai and the others. No wonder they waved me over, tipped me so well, showed so much interest in my plans and prospects. They already knew about my aitachi, and Kagiri's. The whole thing, them mentioning this trip and then admitting their own limits and acting so surprised when I told them what we could do, that was all fake. They planned all of it to lure us here. For this.

And he had fallen for it, the ultimate fool.

He had taken the bait—but Kagiri was the one they'd thrown to his death.

If we hadn't had such good aitachi, none of this would have happened, Noniki thought bitterly. If we were like those two boys we met on the way here, the Untouched, Narai wouldn't have been interested in us. We'd still be in Ginzai, still slaving away for Taki, still hoping for some way out—but Kagiri would still be with me.

He'd still be alive.

Barely able to breathe through his own self-loathing, Noniki glared at the tower once more, than hopped down off the branch. This was hopeless. Kagiri was gone, and he wasn't coming back. Staying here only meant the merchants might get tired of waiting and decide to come in here after him in order to double their chances.

Well, Noniki wasn't about to let that happen. His brother had died so that he might live. He was at least going to honor that sacrifice by making sure he didn't share Kagiri's fate.

Grabbing a few more nearby fruits, Noniki took one last look at the towering edifice that had sealed his brother's demise. I won't forget you, Giri, he promised silently, swiping an angry hand across his face to mop up the tears trickling down. I won't. And I won't ever let my aitachi lead me astray again. I'm done with that—for good.

I'm sorry.

With that, Noniki ducked his head and turned away. Then, before he could talk himself out of it, he stomped off, wending his way through the trees and deeper into the wilderness, the foliage quickly shielding him from having to see the reminder of his worst mistake, the one that had cost him the only family he'd had left. He left all of that behind, and all of his hopes and dreams and plans with it.

Wherever he went from here, he would do it alone. No Kagiri, no aitachi, no aishone, nothing.

Just him.

For whatever that was worth.

CHAPTER NINETEEN

Hibikitsu stroked his chin idly, lost in thought and shadow. He was in his private study again, brooding once more over the state of the empire, and still he had found no solutions. The Rojiri had not come back to him with any answers or sage advice, not that he had really expected any from them. Fujibuki Haro had also been absent, and was presumably still on his way to Nariyari to deal with the problem there—Hibikitsu could only assume that the general would send word if he managed to defeat the bandits, and an entreaty for rescue if he failed. At least the latest attempt by Fyushu had been put down, thanks to Haro's able-bodied second, Misataki Shizumi. That was something, but it was a single bright spot against an entire backdrop of gloom and despair.

A knock at the door roused him, and he glanced up, startled. "Enter," he called out, and the carved door slid open, revealing a short, heavyset man bearing a tray laden with tea pot, cup, fruit, and pastries.

"Your breakfast, Imperial Majesty," the servant intoned, bowing so low his nose nearly brushed the teapot's spout.

"Yes, thank you, bring it here," Hibikitsu ordered. A peek back over his shoulder showed that the sun was indeed already poking up above the distant mountains to the east, its rays starting to spread across Awaihinshi like water spilling across a shallow pool, puddling here and there in sparkles of brilliance while the rest created a soft sheen that glimmered more gently atop the lingering shadows. How had it grown so late already, he wondered, his hand reaching automatically for the pouch around his neck and smoothly enacting the ritual of opening, tilting, extracting, and swallowing that he had followed every day since he had reached adulthood. He had risen early, as he often did, bathing and dressing long before his body servants were even awake, and had slipped in here to sit and think during that lonely, peaceful solitude that could only be found late into the night and very early in the morning. Evidently he had lost several hours in such contemplation, and to what end?

The servant was sliding the tray onto the edge of the desk, and Hibikitsu shifted back to allow the man more room to maneuver. "Where is Seisen?" he asked, watching the man lift the teapot and pour a steady stream of gleaming-bright, steam-wrapped liquid into the cup. "Don't tell me he overslept!" In all the years that Seisen had served him and his family, the old servant had never once been tardy to a task.

"No, of course not," the servant agreed quickly, his hand shifting and nearly splashing tea onto the tray before he got himself back under control. "He was not feeling well, so I offered to bring the tray instead."

Hibikitsu frowned. "What is your name?" he asked, studying this man he now realized was a stranger to him. Was he truly so blind that he did not even recognize his own household servants?

But why would the man be so nervous about Seisen's illness, then, since that in no way reflected upon him?

"Yoshio," the servant answered, averting his gaze as he carefully set the teapot back down. He was nearing middle age, Hibikitsu noted, and was recently clean-shaven if the redness around his cheeks and throat were any indication, but wisps of unruly dark hair escaped from beneath his cap, and his jacket was ill-fitted, too tight across the shoulders and straining across his chest and belly. And his pants were too long, the hems nearly covering his sandals and no doubt threatening to trip him with every step. Never had Hibikitsu seen one of his servants so ill attired—his housekeeper, Takeji, would have the man flogged in an instant if she saw him displaying such a slovenly appearance, especially before Hibikitsu himself.

The young emperor's eyes narrowed. Something was clearly amiss here.

As if sensing the scrutiny, and the suspicions behind them, Yoshio flushed. "Will there be anything else, Your Imperial Majesty?" he asked, bowing again, both hands sliding into the cuffs of the opposing sleeves.

"No," Hibikitsu started to reply, but before he had even finished uttering that syllable the other man had straightened again, his hands reappearing—and a long, glittering blade emerging from each one. Then the supposed servant was leaping at him, knives outstretched.

An assassin! Hibikitsu knew at once that he was too close to effectively block either blow, and his sword was resting in its stand behind him, just out of reach. He had nothing with which to stop those hungry blades from piercing his flesh!

Nothing—except his wits, and reflexes that had been honed through years of training. Kicking out against the desk, he propelled himself and his entire chair backward, the carved feet scraping across the tiled floor with an anguished screech. The daggers plunged downward, but Hibikitsu was now several feet past them, and the blades met nothing but empty air.

At the same time, the emperor's hand had snagged the edge of the tea tray and, with a quick flip, upended that so that its contents all flew toward his assailant. The man cried out in surprise and instinctively raised both hands to protect his face—which gave Hibikitsu all the opening he needed. Leaping to his feet, he spun about, one hand on the chair's back as he pivoted, his other stretching out—and closing firmly around Kosshiki's handle. With a tug he pulled his sword toward him, his other hand rising to grab the scabbard as he slid the legendary nihono free in a single, smooth motion, its blade catching the early morning light and turning to a graceful arc of pure, blinding radiance. Then, weapon properly in hand, Hibikitsu turned to face his attacker.

The other man had recovered from his earlier misstep and was now charging his intended victim. But now, instead of a defenseless man trapped in a chair, he found himself facing a stern warrior armed with a naked blade. Yoshio faltered for a second, his dismay plain to read on his broad face, but then he set his jaw and continued forward, his choice made.

It was a fatal one.

Hibikitsu brought Kosshiki around in a fast, tight sweep, the Bone Spirit singing as it cut through the air. His would-be assassin tried desperately to block the attack, but the emperor's nihono dashed his knives aside as if they were mere blades of grass bent double before a stiff wind. Then the sword's edge found Yoshio's neck, slicing clean through in a single stroke, and a spray of blood erupted across the space between them.

The assassin's face registered surprise, shock, and pain even as his head toppled from his shoulders, his eyes going wide and then dull just before it struck the floor.

Hibikitsu shifted, hands automatically bringing the sword back to his side and settling one above the other on the grip, blade raised and ready, body poised in case a second attack came. But the assassin's body was already tumbling to floor beside its head, its knives dropping from fingers that had suddenly gone limp.

The threat was over.

Still, Hibikitsu hesitated a second before straightening. Then he slid Kosshiki between his fingers, wiping the blade clean before resheathing it. That done, he sank back into his chair, and discovered that he was breathing heavily, his whole body trembling slightly, his forehead damp with sweat.

That had been … amazing!

His mind replaying the events that had just transpired, the young emperor exulted in every second. He could not remember the last time he had felt so alive! Of course he had been beset by assassins before, both before and since he had assumed the throne. But none had ever come so close before—the man had been here in his private study, only inches away!

A sudden thought sobered him momentarily. Seisen was most likely dead, Hibikitsu realized. It would have been the only way to be sure the old servant was out of the way so Yoshio could take his place. The young emperor felt a pang of grief at losing the faithful old man, but his excitement quickly pushed all other emotions aside. He had dispatched an assassin! Not his guards, him personally! He had been in peril, his very life at risk, and he had defeated his assailant with nothing more than his sword and his skill!

But then his eyes fell upon the dead man, and the silk pouch that had fallen out of his stolen garb, sliding free now that there was no longer a head to keep its cord in place. The man's aishone—

—in a bag not all that dissimilar from Hibikitsu's own.

The same pouch he had dipped his fingers into as Yoshio had approached, just a moment ago.

It was not me who defeated him, Hibikitsu realized with a stab of both jealousy and sorrow. It was my father. And his father before him. And his before him. All the way down the line, right back to Taido Seigei himself.

It was the relic bones that had saved his life, by granting him the skills and talents of his ancestors.

He himself had done little more than serve as a conduit for those ancient abilities.

The study's two doors both burst open, and Honteno came pouring into the room, weapons drawn. "Your Imperial Majesty!" the one in front shouted as she approached, nihono high. "Are you injured?" It was Maniko Kohori, the head of Hibikitsu's household guard. Though no longer young, she still moved with poise and grace, and was considered deadly with the blade—an even greater feat since, as a woman, the actual handling of the blade came from her alone.

"No," Hibikitsu replied, waving a hand toward the headless body at his feet. "He tried, but I dispatched him. I suspect he killed Seisen."

"He did," Kohori confirmed. "We discovered his body only a moment ago, and came straight here. I am relieved to see you unharmed." She straightened, sheathed her sword, and bowed.

"Thank you." Hibikitsu dipped his head in acknowledgment. "Please dispose of this for me," he ordered, gesturing at the assassin's remains.

"At once, sir." The guard commander began calling out orders, and in seconds a pair of other warriors had grasped poor, dead Yoshio by the arms and legs and hauled his body away, while a third got the unenviable task of removing the head itself. "Will there be anything else, sir?" Kohori asked once the grisly remains had been carted off.

"No, thank you." The young emperor waved her away, and with another bow she turned on her heel and departed, taking the rest of the guards with her. No doubt they would be stationed outside the doors, Hibikitsu surmised, alert and ready in case Yoshio had allies who planned to make a second attempt. He was not worried, however. His guards were chosen from the best of the already elite Honteno and would use every ounce of skill to defend him to the death.

But whose skills? he thought bitterly. Not theirs, just as his had not truly been his. He had trained, yes, but it had been a forebear's expertise that had so readily dispatched Yoshio. If he had not taken a pinch of aishone right then, the outcome could have wound up being very different.

Which forced Hibikitsu to ask himself, who was he, really, when all of his talents came from someone else?

Was anything he did, anything he had, truly his own?

CHAPTER TWENTY

"What the bones do you want?" a voice called out, floating across to them over the otherwise empty path.

"Yeah," a second voice added. "There ain't nothing for you here."

"Crawl on back to whatever hole you call home," a third chimed in. "We don't need your kind filthying up our town."

Ibaru refused to look back or to respond. He simply hunched his shoulders and continued on the way they had been going. But beside him, Iraku had already stopped. "Don't," he whispered, reaching out, but it was too late. His brother had whirled back around to face those taunting them.

"You don't need us filthying up your town?" Iraku demanded, glaring at the three young men facing him. None were much older than they were, and only one was taller, though all three at least looked healthy and well fed. Ignoring that for the moment, he made a point of looking around, studying the rough dirt path that approximated a road, the crude mud-coated huts scattered along its length on both sides, and the empty expanses past them, long stretches of bare dirt where nothing grew. "Yeah, looks like you don't need any help with filth, you're right," he agreed at last, a grin splitting his narrow face and showing teeth yellowed from constant hunger.

Their three tormentors just stared blankly at him, mouths gaping, and for a fleeting, hope-filled second Ibaru, who had finally turned to stand by his brother, hoped that the insult might simply pass over their heads and vanish with the wind, leaving them free to be on their way. Then one of the boys, the shortest and thinnest of them but the one standing slightly in front of his companions, scowled. "Hey!" he started, glowering at the brothers. "You saying our town's filthy?"

Ibaru sighed. He knew when they had passed the point of no return, and that had been it. So, since the outcome was now inevitable, he was determined to get in a few licks of his own before they came to that. "Actually," he explained now, speaking slowly as if to a small child, "he never said that. You did." He gave the trio a second for that to sink in before continuing, "you said you didn't need us filthying up your town. That suggests that you can handle making it filthy all on your own. My brother was merely agreeing with you. He was backing you up."

He waited patiently and resignedly as the lead boy puzzled that one out. Finally the boy shook his head. "You're just trying to mess with our heads!" he shouted, shaking a scrawny fist at them.

"More than trying," Iraku shot back. "We're succeeding." He winked at Ibaru. "Always was good with rocks, and your head's just full of 'em."

As usual, Ibaru could tell when the light had finally dawned, and he watched as the lead boy's jaw clenched, a vein beginning to throb dangerously along his right temple. "That's it," he growled, his voice gone low and dangerous. "Get 'em!"

His two companions sprang forward, one going for Ibaru and the other for his brother. One on one, he thought as he tensed, arms out, feet well apart, body curled inward to present a smaller target. Maybe we can get out of this okay, especially if he just stands back and watches.

Except that the youth coming for him had several inches on him and half again his weight, and didn't bother slowing to consider tactics but simply barreled directly into him, bowling Ibaru over like a badly balanced rock perched on shifting soil. They both hit the hard, packed dirt of the path, but Ibaru was on the bottom and bore the brunt of the impact, which drove the air from his lungs only half a second before his foe's shoulder doubled him over, gasping.

"How's that for filthy?" his attacker snarled in his ear, leaping to his feet and yanking Ibaru upright with one massive hand, only to hammer the other into his gut hard enough to make him see stars.

As he was struggling to breathe and to clear his head, Ibaru saw that, off to the side, Iraku had received similar treatment. His adversary was not as large or as solid, but then neither was Iraku. Both of them dangled like dead fish in their tormentor's hands, gasping and writhing and helpless.

And then the lead boy closed the gap in order to thrust his face within an inch of Ibaru's, his words sending spittle forth to spray across Ibaru's face and drip slowly down his cheeks and chin and nose.

"No one wants you here, Mukanichi," the boy declared, his voice dark and filled with venom, as was his gaze. "In fact, no one wants you, period. So do us all a favor—end your miserable life now. Before somebody else does it for you." He pulled back then and nodded at his two henchmen, who delivered matching parting blows to the brothers' stomachs before dumping them both in heaps on the ground and, after a few desultory kicks, leaving them there to their misery.

"That … could've gone better," Ibaru managed to spit out, along with some blood and grit. It had taken a little time, but eventually he and his brother had managed to collect themselves enough to stagger to their feet and then stumble out of town and away, leaving the pathetic little cluster of ramshackle homes as far behind as their throbbing heads, aching backs, and sore, stabbing guts would allow.

Beside him, his brother grunted. "You think so?" he demanded, their recent beating clearly having done nothing to tamp down his constant fire. In fact, if anything the violence had served to fan those flames into a raging inferno. "How, exactly?" Iraku demanded now, turning so he could get in Ibaru's face. "How could it have gone better? When has it ever gone better, really?" He shook his head, inky-blank tendrils scattering around his face. "Honestly, Baru, when is it ever going to get any better?"

"I don't know, Raku," his older brother answered truthfully. "I wish I did, but I don't." He sighed, even though the motion made his stomach and back ache all over again. "Truth is, that little buttsore was right about one thing. We're Mukanichi—nobody wants us around." This hadn't been the first time they'd heard that, of course. Every village they set foot in, every town, the people had all been the same. Some had shown pity at first, but most had heaped only scorn upon them, mingled with hatred and fear. Sometimes they'd managed to flee before the violence could erupt, before the town could turn against them. Other times, like here, they hadn't been so lucky.

And there was absolutely no reason to think it would ever get any better. They would always be Mukanichi, after all. Which meant that, everywhere they went, people would consider them useless. And as far as the Relicant Code was concerned, those people would be right, too.

In a world where everyone survived by consuming the relic bones of their ancestors, being unable to tap those inherited gifts meant being incapable of participating in the most basic tenet of their culture.

It meant never fitting in, never having a place, never being seen as more than just some sort of horrific, monstrous mistake.

It meant today's beating, which had been only the latest in a long string, was as good as he could ever hope for life to get.

"Damn them all!" Ibaru burst out, pounding his own bony fists against his sides. "I hate them!"

"Yeah, me too," his brother agreed, the calmer of them for once. "So, now what? Next town?"

Ibaru stared at him a moment, then nodded heavily. "Next town," he agreed, hands going to his aching sides as he turned his back on this little smear of a village.

But deep down inside, Ibaru couldn't turn away so easily. In there, in the pit of his soul, he carefully filed away the town's location, its appearance, its citizens, everything about it. He held that knowledge tight, just as he had every other town they'd been chased out of, every face that had sneered at them, every hand that had struck them. Each detail was etched into his memory forever, so that he would never forget.

So that, some day, he could find a way to return the favor of each and every curse and shout and sneer and blow.

And he knew, from the dark glower he'd seen in Iraku's eyes, that his brother felt the same way.

Some day, they would make all of them pay.

CHAPTER TWENTY-ONE

"… at the state of this place …" someone was saying, a man with a deep voice and a strange, clipped accent that rendered his words nearly incomprehensible and the rhythm of his speech grating upon the ear. "… a disgrace to the Matekai …" The words cut in and out, fading and swelling like the tide, their sounds crashing in but then sliding away again, their meaning slipping free with only the faintest echo remaining.

Kagiri stirred, shifted, groaned. Where was he? Who was speaking to him, and why?

"… too serious, as always …" someone else was replying. Another man, his voice softer, milder, more pleasant, though with similar rhythms. "… hardly anyone's fault …"

"I'd disagree." This was a woman, her voice low and mellow, if somewhat dour. "There's always someone at fault."

"You would say that!" Another woman, her words followed by gentle chuckling. More laughter followed, from multiple voices, seeming to surround him.

Kagiri groaned. Whoever they were, why couldn't these people just leave him alone?

With a tremendous effort he managed to peel one eye open, blinking against the light that instantly stabbed in through the aching orb and speared deep into his brain. Ahh!

"... to wake up ..." someone pointed out, a new voice, male and so soft as to be nearly a whisper. "... should give him some space ..."

"Nonsense!" That was from the second man. "He'll need to meet us soon regardless, might as well make it now!"

Kagiri blinked, forcing the glare to settle slightly and the blurs beyond it to resolve into proper shapes. "Who ... ?" he managed to croak out, but the rest of his question was lost to his gasp as his other eye opened convulsively and he stared.

Because, save for him, the room he found himself in was completely empty.

Or not completely—the racks still stood against two of the walls, the benches against two of the others, and the dust that was all that remained of the table still mounded the floor around him.

He was still in the tower, the Tawasiri. Still in the room with the window. Still right where he had collapsed. Still utterly alone.

But at the same time, he wasn't.

He blinked, and the room changed. Now the racks were clean and polished, covered in weapons that gleamed with care. The other rack held armor, similar to that of an Aiashe or a Honjofu but not exactly the same, each set styled a little differently but all with the same basic style and all well maintained as well. The benches looked practically new, and held silk cushions to soften their sturdy surfaces. And the table! The table had been restored, shining with fresh polish, The decanters and pitchers and bowls and platters upon it filled with water and wine and fruit and cheese and bread. Even the tile floor had changed, its muted colors now rainbow-bright, each tile polished and perfect.

It was like the room was new again, and filled with light and life.

Just like its inhabitants.

Because now Kagiri could see them standing all around him—three men and two women, all of them in fine kitoros and ponmei, simple woven sandals upon their feet. All of them leaning in close to study him closely, expressions of varying degrees of concern, interest, and amusement etched onto their faces.

Then he blinked again, and they were gone. The room was dim and dusty, the racks and their contents corroded, the table collapsed.

Blink, and they were back.

Blink, gone.

Blink, back.

"Ahhhh!" Kagiri screamed, lunging up into a sitting position and slamming both hands down over his eyes. "Have I gone mad?"

"No, I wouldn't think so," one of the figures replied. "Or at least, not completely."

"Oh, I'd say you had, yes," a different one responded. "Utterly mad."

"Leave the poor lad alone," another warned, though playfully. "He can decide for himself, hm?"

"I am mad," Kagiri declared, gulping for air and promptly coughing as he inhaled yet more of the tower's ever-present dust. "Mad, and choking, and most likely dying."

"Well, yes, no doubt," the dour-sounding woman agreed. "That's what happens when you don't eat or drink for days, you know." The part of Kagiri's mind that was not panicking noted that the voices had stopped wavering in and out. All of them now sounded clear and strong, as if they were really right here in the room with him.

Except that of course they weren't. They were just figments of his imagination, a product of his fevered mind spiraling out of control even as he sank toward death.

"Hm, that's a bit harsh, isn't it?" the second woman, the one with the lighter tone, argued. "That we're some sort of death image? Not very welcoming."

Kagiri started to reply, then stopped.

Because he hadn't said that last bit aloud.

"That proves that you're all in my head," he pointed out, a sense of triumph warring with a wave of despair. "You know what I'm thinking because you're not real, you're just strange thoughts I've conjured up to keep my company in my final moments."

"That's awfully pessimistic for one so young," the deep-voiced man stated. "Perhaps we're just good at guessing what you're thinking."

"Or maybe we are inside your head, but we're still real," the second man suggested. "What about that?"

Kagiri gritted his teeth and pulled his hands down into his lap, then forced himself to look around again. He was still alone. "There, see?" he practically shouted, his words echoing off the walls. "You aren't here because you're not real!"

Except that, even as he said that, he blinked and the quintet flickered back into existence around him.

"Are we real now?" One of them, the second man, asked, eyebrows quirked mischievously over a strong-jawed, handsome face. He reached out and snagged a fruit off the table, then took a big, wet bite, the juice spilling down over his neat beard. "How's that for real?"

Kagiri's mouth watered at the sight of the food, which resembled a nafti with its spherical shape and dusky, mottled gold and green skin and even had the same crisp, sharp sound as the man bit into it again. He reached out, and the stranger smiled, one eyebrow arching up, then offered the half-eaten fruit. Kagiri grasped for it—

—and his fingers slid right through it.

"Bones!" he cursed, snatching his hand back as the man laughed. "See? Not real."

"Maybe not to you," the man agreed, tossing the fruit and catching it easily before consuming the rest of it in three quick bites, core and all. "But that isn't any sort of proof. Who's to say you're real, either?"

Kagiri shook his head. He didn't have the energy or the patience for some deep philosophical debate with the merry apparition. "Go away," he begged instead. "At least leave me to die in peace."

"You need to stop all this talk about dying," the soft-spoken man suggested, his whisper full of stern remonstrance. He was slight of build, with a lean, narrow face and sharp eyes. "Don't give up so easily. Show some backbone!"

"Yes, on your feet, you!" the more cheerful of the two women agreed. She had a broad, open face, not beautiful but appealing in its apparent honesty. "Stop lying about here, or you really will be dead, and what good would that do anyone?"

"It would do me good if it would make all of you stop yapping at me," Kagiri grumbled, crossing his arms over his chest. He knew that he was being ridiculous, sitting here sulking like a small child denied a treat, but he was tired and his head hurt and it was hard to breathe and he just wanted to lay down and go to sleep and not have to think about it anymore.

Besides, it wasn't like the merchants would be willing to let him out anyway.

"Of course they will," the deep-voiced man insisted. He was the biggest of them, built like a mountain with a rough, craggy face. "You were sent to obtain these … aishone, correct?" The word emerged strangely from between his thick lips, but Kagiri understood it well enough to nod. "Well, then!" the man slapped his knee with one huge hand. "Task complete!"

"What?" Kagiri stared at him. "What are you talking about?" he looked around, searching the room wildly, then sighed. "There's nothing here but me and some ancient, rotting furniture and some old, rusty gear, and a whole lot of dust!"

"And us," the other woman added. She was lovely, with delicate features and large, quick eyes that seemed to pierce him to his very soul. She smiled, and the beauty of her warmed his soul, but somehow there was something lacking to it, as if her own heart was not behind the expression. "We are here with you."

Kagiri frowned, for he did not think she was playing with him, phantom though she might be. "What do you mean?" he demanded suspiciously, studying her and her companions again. "I know I see you and hear you, at least part of the time, but that's not real. That bit with the nafti just now proved that."

"Maybe that part wasn't real anymore," the slender man whispered. "But we still are. We are here with you right now. All around you." He waved a hand, and the motion stirred dust motes in the air, sending them glittering about in a spinning aerial ballet. Kagiri stared, transfixed by the display, especially since, even when he blinked and his strange companions vanished, the dust remained.

The dust!

Suddenly it all made sense to him, and he nearly gagged at the realization. "The dust—is you," he managed to blurt out, his head throbbing and his throat aching and his belly threatening to rebel at the thought. It was one thing to deliberately swallow an aishone, but this! All this time he had been staggering about this place, searching for bones, when the whole time—

"—we were already with you," The big one confirmed, nodding slowly. "Exactly right." He grinned, the expression spreading across his face much the way the sun crept across a cliff. "Just as I said—task complete!"

I have the aishone, Kagiri thought, stunned by this revelation. They've been reduced to nothing but dust after all these centuries, and I've been breathing them in since I entered this cursed place.

They're here with me now, visible to me, because I've been swallowing them, been choking on them, been crying and sneezing and coughing them, for hours now. Maybe even days. He had never had such an intense experience with aishone before, but then he had never absorbed so much all at once, either.

And, with his particular gifts, what he'd taken into himself could last him for a very long time. Maybe even for the rest of his life.

But only if he had a life left.

Grimacing, Kagiri placed his hands flat on the floor. Then, with a grunt and groan and a yowl like a wounded cat, he pushed himself to his feet. He swayed a second there, nearly toppling over, but managed to stumble forward a few steps and place a hand on the wall to steady himself. He was reeling a little, and his vision swam, but he was still standing!

"Yes!" the first woman cheered. All of them had followed him over. "Good job! Now down the stairs you go!"

"You can do it!" the deep-voiced mountain agreed. "We believe in you!"

"Yes, keep going," the other man, the first one to speak, added. He was as broad as the mountain but not as tall, with a strong, somewhat stern face. "We are with you."

This time, Kagiri believed him. He could actually feel the aishone working within him now that he thought about it, effecting his balance and his reflexes, adjusting every move he made. Even as he staggered toward the stairs, dizzy from hunger and thirst and fatigue, he found himself marveling at his new grace. It was like the warrior aishone he'd taken when they'd faced those bandits, only magnified a thousandfold.

If he made it out of here alive, he would be able to teach those merchants and their hired guards a thing or two!

He tripped his way down the stairs, nearly falling several times but catching himself against the rough stone of the wall, tearing the skin of his hands in the process but at least keeping his feet. Several times he blinked and the walls and floor became younger, cleaner, more colorful and elegant, as if he were seeing the way this tower had one looked. Which was probably exactly the case, he reminded himself. He must be seeing the way this strange building had looked back when his five ghostly companions had walked its halls. He had never experienced memories and knowledge from aishone before—that was usually the province of women alone—but given these remains' age, and the sheer quantity he must have unwittingly ingested, he was not surprised to learn that his reactions now far exceeded the normal experience.

Still lost in these thoughts, he made his way back down through that strange smaller room and the first flight of stairs, and eventually found himself marching woodenly toward a dark, distant shape that soon resolved into a tall rectangle of dark stone.

The front door.

Kagiri threw himself against the portal, but of course it did not budge. "Let me out!" he cried, his voice cracking as he pounded on the door until his fists throbbed with pain. "Please, let me out." The last of his strength used up, he collapsed on the floor, forehead pressed against the cool stone of the door, and wept, though his body barely contained enough moisture to generate diminutive tears. "Let me out."

His eyes were fluttering shut, despite the intermittent shouts of his occasional entourage, when he heard noises from the door's other side. Then he felt the heavy stone slab shift before him and begin sliding open. With a sigh of relief, Kagiri leaned in, putting more of his weight on the door, and as it opened he fell forward, catching a glimpse of sunlight and concerned faces and a face full of cool, fresh air right before his consciousness fled into the warm, welcoming dark.

CHAPTER TWENTY-TWO

Noniki had lost track of the days or the distance. He had no idea how far he had traveled since he had fled the site of his brother's death, running headlong from that blighted tower as if somehow he could leave behind the guilt that haunted his every breath and thought. He knew that he must have gone at least some distance, since he was sure that some days and nights had passed, but he could not recall how many—he simply ran until he could not run anymore, then walked, then stumbled until he finally collapsed where he fell and slept until whenever he woke, at which point he would drag himself back to his feet and force his aching limbs into motion once more. His clothes, which had been so fine and new when the merchants had gifted them to him, were now tattered and torn and filthy, as bedraggled as his hair from spending untold days out in wind and sun and rain and occasionally being dragged across rock and mud and sand and dirt. His sandals had been ripped to shreds and fallen from his feet, which were now blackened and bloody and would no doubt have hurt immensely if at some point they had not gone numb. He could not remember the last time he had eaten, and his stomach had at first sent shooting pains throughout his middle but those had since faded to a dull ache. He had not drunk anything either, at least not deliberately, but he had been caught in enough downpours that water had soaked into him and no doubt some had trickled down his throat at some point during those times. At least he had enough energy to keep going, and that was really all that mattered to him, to put as much distance between himself and the Tawasiri as he could manage before he eventually dropped and could not convince himself to move again.

A part of Noniki wondered why he hadn't just stayed, if death had become his only intention. But if he had died near that tower, there would have been the chance of becoming an akatai himself—and he couldn't bear the thought that he might then have found Kagiri's ghost as well, and been forced to deal with that constant reminder of his complicity in his brother's death for all eternity.

Another part howled at him for betraying his promise, of course. He had sworn to Kagiri, right before he left, that he would live in his brother's honor, yet here he was, barely living at all and fully expecting not to live much longer at all. How was that keeping Kagiri's name and memory alive? How was it fulfilling that promise? But Noniki's pain was still too raw, his guilt too suffocating, for him to think clearly about this matter.

All he could do for now was run.

He had passed out of the mountains and into a series of hills when, stumbling along one evening near sunset, he heard voices. They were the first human sounds he had heard since leaving the Tawasiri, and Noniki was at once both repelled and fascinated. The idea of conversing with other people again sent a hungry thrill racing through him, but he also felt that his sins would be carved upon his forehead, and that those people would see his crimes there and recoil, screaming. Plus there was that voice, the dark one that told him how much he needed to suffer, that admonished him further, saying that no one decent would ever want to be near him again, much less speak to him, and that he should not wish for them to, because granting himself the comfort of companionship, however briefly, was disrespecting his brother and the death Noniki's actions had forced upon him.

In the end, however, the choice turned out to not be his to make. Noniki was cresting a steep hill, struggling with the question as he went, and so focused in setting one foot after the other along the rough, rocky, shifting ground that he failed to register just how close those voices had become—until he reached the hill's summit and glanced up to find himself staring a group of women in the face. He froze, caught like a robber in the night, one foot still half raised, and stared at the strangers.

There were four of them in all, and they ranged in age, he noted, from close to his own age to wizened like a tree that has seen several centuries of harsh weather. All of them wore robes, thin and tattered, but far more striking was that all four also wore pale, unbleached cloths tied across their faces, covering all of their features like translucent shrouds. But those cloths told Noniki exactly who they were, and his heart clenched.

Somehow he had stumbled across an enclave of the burahone.

"Who goes there?" one of the women, a stout one who sounded like she could have been someone's stern mother if not for the cloth, demanded. She had her head up, shifting this way and that like a dog scenting the breeze in search of a hare or a bird. "Who are you, that you carry so little within you?"

Her sharp voice broke Noniki from his paralysis, and he bowed. "I am sorry, mother," he answered, giving her the same mark of respect as any elder woman from his own village. "I am merely passing through." His voice tumbled out from between his cracked lips like boulders struck loose in an avalanche, rough and grating and constantly shifting.

"You are young," another of the women, possibly also middle-aged but much leaner, declared. She was scenting for him as well. "And you have not tasted aishone in some time. The last was a soldier, yes?"

"Yes," Noniki agreed, though it made his skin crawl. He had heard of the Bone Blind before, of course, but never had he met one, nor had he ever hoped to, even though some nobles went to great lengths and considerable expense to do exactly that. But then, Noniki did not have aishone he wished examined and memories he wished sampled, so the women's legendary abilities to read aishone even from a distance were wasted upon him.

It was nice to speak to someone again, anyone, even hermit women driven mad by their aitachi. That was why they wore the shrouds, Noniki knew. Even a stray particle of relic bone could set the burahone down a deep spiral into madness, as the memories and knowledge contained therein overwhelmed them. They lived away from other people and covered their faces, to avoid even the chance of contact with aishone. The reason they covered their eyes, however, that was far more frightening—they covered those because their sight had become so overwhelmed by visions that they could no longer bear to look upon the real world directly, claiming that its stark reality was too harsh after the beauty of the ancient world they saw reflected in the bones. So they shunned sight altogether and blocked their taste and smell, relying upon only their hearing and their aitachi to navigate their surroundings.

And now he had just blundered right into them.

Still, the one woman had been right. He had no relic bones on him, and had not touched one since the bandit encounter, weeks ago. In fact, given his recent decision to never use aishone again, Noniki decided that he might be one of the less harmful people the burahone could ever hope to meet. They didn't have to worry about him carrying relic bones with him!

Yet even that was evidently not enough, as all four women began to wail at once. Their voices wove in and out of each other's, rising and falling in some sort of ancient, arcane melody—or in a ritual Noniki did not understand and did not wish to. Then the oldest of the Bone Blind, the wizened old crone, stepped forward, extending one thin, wrinkled arm to point a long finger right at him.

"Your brother!" she cried out. "He suffers so! The ghosts seek to devour him whole, yet are forced to divide him between them. He will go mad from the struggle!"

"Yet even in his pain, his every breath threatens to shake the world," the fourth, who by her rich, vibrant voice seemed to be the youngest, proclaimed. "And his footsteps press upon the very air." She raised her face to the darkening sky. "Though he dies, five other rise in his place, and their coming will reshape everything about us." She shuddered suddenly. "Unless the hunger devours them as well, and returns them to their previous stature as nothing more than angry, impotent spirits, desperate to have any impact upon the living—even if that impact is only done by causing pain and suffering among those who could otherwise have been their followers."

Noniki gaped at her. "I don't understand," he admitted, his head throbbing even from trying to follow those cryptic utterances. "He suffers? From five hungry spirits?" But, unfortunately, once the words had fully sunk in they made all too much sense. Kagiri had been forced into that haunted tower, after all, where aishone were said to litter the very ground but also prove deadly to the unwary. And the most likely reason for that was akatai. The ghosts of whomever had died in that tower must have remained trapped within, feasting upon anyone foolish enough to venture inside. And their latest victim had been his poor, hapless brother—and should have been him.

"You will bear a different fate," the oldest croaked out, shaking her finger at him. "Already the bones cry out for you, but you pay no heed. The past will claim you instead, rising up from within if it cannot smother from without. But either way, you will walk the path of those who came before you, long before, and have since become naught but dust."

That one Noniki truly did not understand, but it didn't matter. He had already heard more than enough. With a sob he turned away from the strange quartet, shoving past their robed forms and charging down the hill on the other side. But there he saw the settlement the four burahone must have come from, a small cluster of rough huts between which milled several more women whose faces were similarly shielded.

And each and every one of them turned to stare at him as soon as he came into view.

"The bones cry out!" one called, and others took up the call. "They hunger for you and feast upon your brother! The bones demand a restoration! Answer the bones!" The women rushed toward him, honing in unerringly despite the cloths blocking their mundane sight, and soon he found himself surrounded by the strangely shrouded figures, all of them shrieking portions of the same message, making the same demand. The shouts became so loud Noniki clapped both hands over his ears, trying to shut them out, but still the words penetrated deep into his brain.

"Shut up!" he screamed at them. "Leave me alone!" Gulping for air, he ran as fast as he could, driving right through the women in order to pass out the other side that much more quickly. They fell away readily enough, their bodies evidently as frail as their atachi was strong, and did not attempt to follow him but instead merely turned where they were and continued to shout their odd warning from there. Noniki was glad the women did not pursue him, and he took the opportunity to put more distance between himself and them while he could. But even when he found himself climbing the next hill, he could still hear the Bone Blind's cries, and their strange curse-like exhortations followed him for many leagues, deep into the night.

CHAPTER TWENTY-THREE

Seikoku was in good humor. Her visit to Madam Akari had gone as well as she could have hoped—the senkousa had been happy to see her, as always, and had offered what Seikoku thought to be a reasonable price for the aishone she'd offered, at least considering their questionable provenance. She had taken the offer without bothering to haggle, and the senkousa had handed her the small pouch heavy with coin right then and there. Now Seikoku was on her way back home, and the day was still relatively young.

She was so pleased with the results of her recent late-night excursion that she was perhaps not paying as much attention as she should have. Which was why she stumbled directly into the path of a large, heavyset man with ostentatiously elegant clothing and an equally self-important air.

"Out of my way!" he bellowed down at her, shouldering Seikoku aside. For most people the rough, rude treatment would have bowled them clean off their feet. She merely twisted, letting much of his force slide past her, and took half a step back so that he was able to squeeze by on the bustling street. But her eyes narrowed, and she watched him go as he pushed and shoved and cursed and commanded his way through the afternoon crowd.

If there was one thing Seikoku hated, it was a bully.

In an instant, she had pivoted on her heel and was darting back through the throng, following the wide swath of embroidered satin that marked the man's back. She caught up to him with relative ease, and then deliberately bumped up against him, slamming into him as if she'd just stumbled forward.

"Oy!" he shouted, startled. But Seikoku was not large enough or heavy enough to really sway the man's bulk, so instead she essentially bounced off him, only to pick herself back up an instant later.

By that time, he had already stopped and rounded on her.

"Watch where you're going, you little tramp!" he shouted, glaring down at her. One of his hands darted automatically to his neck, clutching something that hung down in front there, but he seemed satisfied with whatever he found because, with only an additional scowl, he turned after a second and continued along his way.

This time Seikoku did not follow. Instead she stood still, letting the crowd swirl in about her like a soothing, protective fog, as the man soon disappeared from view.

Only after he'd vanished completely did she allow herself to smile. But that smile broke into a full grin when she patted the small but heavy pouch tucked into her own larger bag. The pouch that had not been there a few seconds before.

He would realize it was missing eventually, of course. And he might even guess that Seikoku had been involved in its disappearance. But of course she would be long gone from this part of the market before he ever thought of that. And it was unlikely that he would come looking, regardless.

Because she had been careful not to let her quick fingers wander anywhere near his precious aishone, much as she might wish she had relieved such an obnoxious person of his greatest treasure.

But no, instead she'd merely helped herself to his money.

And now? Now she fully intended to spend the money, all of it, as quickly as possible.

The market had several established areas, each with its own specialty. Seikoku turned away from the segments dedicated to clothing, tools, and household items and headed instead for the southwest corner, which focused on food. Once there she headed straight for a particular stall, one where she knew the proprietor.

"Ah, Mistress Keiko!" Hintaro called out when he saw her, lifting a hand in greeting. Even though he had known her for several years, and she considered him a good acquaintance who occasionally bordered on actually being a friend, he still only knew her by the false name she had given when they'd first met—a name she maintained here in the market and nowhere else, just as she used different names in other parts of town. Very few people ever earned the right to know Seikoku by her real name.

Why, then, the little voice inside her head snidely inquired, did you so freely bestow it upon some strange boy you just stumbled across one night—in the graveyard, of all places?

Silence, Seikoku hissed at that portion of her self. Through sheer force of will she banished the voice from her mind, and along with it all thoughts of that boy, Noniki, who kept cropping up again and again, and usually at the most inopportune times. He was an aberration, she insisted to herself. An anomaly. A brief leave from her senses, and one that she had long since recovered from. Thankfully, she had not seen or heard of or from him since. But the baker was watching her and starting to look puzzled as to why it was taking her so long to respond to his cheerful welcome.

"Good day, Master Hintaro," she replied, dipping into a graceful bow as she answered to the fake name she had given the man upon their first meeting. "I hope it finds you well."

"Well enough," the merchant agreed. "Now, what can I do for you?" He gestured behind him at his wares, which were arranged in barrels and baskets and even trays.

She thought for a few seconds, running through options and lists and prices. Then, finally, she opened her mouth and placed her order. It was a large one, moreso than usual, and this time she definitely saw Hintaro's eyes widen. To his credit, however, the merchant never once asked how such a young woman could all of a sudden acquire the funds to purchase such an order.

Instead he simply nodded and began tossing the items she requested into a basket he cradled with one arm, as protective as a mother with her baby.

"You will eat well tonight, I hope?" the bulky merchant asked as he gathered item after item. "And, it appears, for many moons to come!"

"I will eat well, yes, thank you," Seikoku replied, touched by his obvious concern. One of the reasons why she liked him— that, his fair prices, and the fact that more than once she had seen him defend a complete stranger from attacks by men of greater stature who seemed to think that their higher rank gave them the right to mistreat and abuse others who had been here for just as long, if not longer. When he had finished collecting her order she tossed him the new pouch, and watched as he emptied the contents into his wide, fleshy hand. She was pleased to see that her initial assessment based on sound alone had been accurate— among the burnished red tint of bronze she also spotted several flashes of silver, and more than a few bursts of gleaming gold as well. The amount proved more than enough to purchase the entire order, and Seikoku accepted back the significantly lighter pouch with her change already within. Then, tucking the pouch into her belt, she hoisted the bags with her purchases and headed out of the market.

It was a while longer before she reached her home, of course. That was in part due to the circuitous route she took as a matter of course and in part because her home was far from the center of town. That was fine, though—she'd always preferred safety and protection to ease of access. Out this far she could be sure that no one had followed her from the market, and easily mark all those who were walking past along such quieter streets.

But finally Seikoku was standing outside a rickety two-story building that had probably been a warehouse before it had been judged too unstable to remain in use. Then it had been chopped up, doors and bathrooms and kitchens added to each compartment, and placed on the market again. Only now it was a series of small homes instead.

And one of those homes was hers.

Picking her way up the stairs, which had been crumbling for years, she reached the peeling front door and, after running her fingers along its worn, pitting frame, found a recessed area and pressed her fingers to that before pushing against it at the edges.

With a faint click, the door unlocked, and another gentle touch eased it open.

Seikoku's apartment was on the second floor, but she did not head up the worn old steps right away. Instead she went to the first door on the left and knocked.

"What?" a crotchety voice demanded from behind the still-sturdy door.

"Mother Pidiri?" Seikoku called out, reaching into one of her bags and extracting a loaf of bread and a hunk of cheese. "I've brought food for you and your grandson." Nothing happened for a second; then the door clicked before creaking open. A wizened hand emerged, open and grasping, and Seikoku extended the food, which it latched onto. Then it disappeared again, and the door slammed shut once more.

Not offended, Seikoku turned away. But before she could even take a step the door had been flung back open, and a small, wiry form had hurtled through the gap and leaped upon her.

"Koko!" her attacker screamed, thin arms wrapping around her waist in a steel-tight grip.

"Hello, Noru," Seikoku replied, laughing as she hugged him back before gently prying herself out of his arms. She reached down and tousled the boy's dark, ragged hair. "How are you today?"

"Good," he answered, beaming up at her with a mouth only partially full of teeth. "I lost another one!" he cried, pointing to a new space in the upper row.

"So I see," she agreed, schooling herself to hide the pang she felt. Noru was of an age when he should be losing his baby teeth, it was true, but she knew part of the reason so many of his teeth were falling out was not just from growth but from malnourishment. His grandmother did the best she could, of course, but she was an old woman who only did cleaning and sewing when she could find work, and even with making sure he ate first, more often than not the boy went hungry.

Which was why Seikoku made sure to share her food with them whenever she could.

"I need to go," she told the boy now, patting him on the cheek to take any sting out of the words. "But maybe some time soon you can show me your newest drawings, okay?" That cheered him up immediately—despite his youth Noru was already a talented artist, and his shabby little home was filled with his sketches. As was Seikoku's. With another quick hug and a promise to stop by again soon, she said good-bye to him and continued on her way.

Which only meant as far as the next door, where Boriki the baker lived with his wife and their three little girls. And then the door past that, which was the home of Madame Tiriyoi the fanmaker and her son and daughter. And so on. At each door Seikoku stopped to say hello—and to share some of the food she had brought. By the time she climbed the stairs to the second floor, she had depleted the first of her bags. The second bag was emptied before she was halfway down the hall, and by the time she had unlocked and opened her own door she had only enough food left to last herself a few days, a week at most.

With a sigh, she sank down onto the low futon that served as both couch and bed in her modest room. She still had the money she'd received from Madam Akari, which would serve to provide another grocery order similar in size to this last one. After that, however, she would back down to scraping by—and all of her neighbors would be back to begging, stealing, and starving. Especially the children.

Which meant it was time for her to plan another job.

Chapter Twenty-four

"Yes?" the man at the desk did not even bother to glance up from the parchment upon which he was inscribing tiny, careful marks. Thickly built, with a wide, fleshy face and a tiny, neat beard, he wore gleaming satin robes and an embroidered cap. Jeweled rings shone on most of his fingers, and more gems flashed from his earlobes.

"Apologies, Master Eijiri," the man who'd led her in called out, his voice respectfully low but loud enough to cover the expanse of polished tile floor between them. "But this young lady has come seeking a job."

"We have no openings," Master Eijiri replied, pausing only enough to wave his free hand at them both. "Tell her to try her luck somewhere else."

"Oh, I would, great Master," Chimehara declared, stepping to the side so that she was no longer hidden behind her guide. "But everyone knows that, of all the merchant houses, House Chohu is by far the greatest at procuring and selling precious stones, and I see little point in working for anyone but the best." She timed her bow perfectly, so that, when the master merchant's eyes did finally turn her way, he caught sight of her just as she was straightening up, so that his first view of her was her lustrous black hair, then the high expanse of her forehead, ending in her slender, arching brows and then her large, brilliant green eyes, opened to exactly the right degree of awe mingled with determination. It was a look she had perfected for just such an occasion, and she could tell from his sharp intake that her efforts had not been wasted.

"Well," the master stated, closing his mouth after a second and then drawing himself up straighter. "Of course, House Chohu is certainly the greatest house in the Empire when it comes to gems, that is very true." He sucked in his stomach and puffed out his chest, as Chimehara tried her hardest not to laugh. "And I can hardly fault anyone for wishing to work here. But"—and here a hint of wise self-protection intruded upon the gleam of lust that had filled his eyes a second before—"because we are such an expert house and so highly regarded, we cannot accept just anyone into our employ. Only those who prove their worth can earn the right to join our establishment."

"Of course." Chimehara bowed again. "That is all I ask for, great master, a chance to prove my worth and earn such a place." She smiled, her shyest, sweetest smile, and laughed inside as he flushed. Sometimes men were just too easy.

"Then we must put you to the test," Master Eijiri declared, setting his quill and parchment aside and rising to his feet, and Chimehara could only hope that he did not realize he had just licked his lips in the process. She would far rather believe he was not aware what a caricature he was, what a perfectly ridiculous demonstration of lust and avarice.

Not that it would affect her plans much one way or the other.

"What is your name, my dear?" he inquired as he crossed the floor toward her, waving away her escort.

"Chimehara, sir," she answered, bowing again. She had considered using a false name but had decided not to bother. She had no real history for anyone to tie her to anyway, and none of those who knew about her past indiscretions still breathed to whisper a word of them, so why not use her proper name and not have to worry about forgetting herself and making people suspicious of her?

"Chimehara." From his lips, her name sounded somewhere between a prayer and an entreaty, and also vaguely obscene, but she ignored all that, focusing on his eyes and his face and his voice instead. Those were what would tell him his intentions, which thus far had been all about lust but now had shifted to half that and half greed. "Do you know anything of gems, my dear?" he asked, stroking his beard with long, immaculately manicured fingers.

"Some," she admitted, conjuring a look of old sorrow. "My grandfather worked with gems, until illness robbed his fingers of their dexterity. His son, my father, had no interest in the trade, and sold the shop as soon as it fell to him, but I grew up hearing my grandfather's stories." She wiped a hand quickly across her eyes. "After he died, my father wanted to simply sell his aitachi, but Grandfather's will specified that I receive them instead. I was the only one in the family who shared his interests, and therefore the only one he could count on to continue in his footsteps."

"Ah, very good, very good," Master Eijiri whispered. "Then perhaps a demonstration is in order?"

"Of course." Chimehara smiled and produced a small but full pouch from behind the sash at her waist. From that she extracted a bone fragment the size of her fingernail, which she raised to her lips. Slowly, deliberately, she bit through the relic bone, then quickly chewed and swallowed the portion that had been in her mouth. Instantly she felt knowledge pour into her, filling in never-realized gaps in her mind the same way water filled in the spaces between uneven stone, seeping into each and every crevice to build a dizzying array of knowledge where before she had possessed none.

"All right," she declared after that strange feeling had passed. She returned the rest of the bone to her pouch and tucked that back away, then turned to face Master Eijiri again. "I am ready."

The merchant nodded and gestured for her to follow as he headed for a small door near the back of the room. That door proved to lead to only a small cabinet, from which he extracted a rolled-up silken pouch. Setting this down upon a long table, Master Eijiri carefully unrolled the pouch, revealing a row of small, glittering objects. Then he stepped aside and motioned for Chimehara to approach the objects.

"Before you are eight pearls," he informed her, his voice clear and soft and now entirely business. "Sort them in order from least valuable to most valuable, and be prepared to explain why that is." He folded his hands together and waited for her to proceed.

Chimehara nodded and took his place at the table. Starting with the first pearl, she carefully lifted the small, delicate globe and examined its luster, color, shape, surface, and size. She used her eyes but also her fingertips, her cheek, even her tongue, which she extended to taste the tiny sphere. And for perhaps the first time since she had grown into an awareness of who she was and what gifts she possessed, Chimehara did not even consider the reaction the man watching might have to the erotic image of such a beautiful young woman touching the tip of her tongue to an equally lovely pearl. Instead she was entirely focused upon the task at hand, all of her attention taken by these eight specimens arrayed before her.

The first one or two she was able to sort with ease. The next few required only a little more thought, but each pearl became more difficult to judge, as the master had no doubt intended. As she went, swapping gems about each time to accommodate the new information she was amassing, she was careful to keep her hands in view at all times, and to keep her sleeves pushed up so there could be no concerns about her trying to make off with one or more of the cultured gems.

The last two pearls were by far the hardest, and Chimehara considered them carefully a long time, swapping their positions more than once. But finally she looked up and bowed, stepping away from the table. 'Here you are, Master Eijiri," she told him. "From least to best." And she held herself still, awaiting his verdict as he once again approached the table.

"Hm," was all he said as he paced its length, casting a well-honed eye down the row. He stopped twice to peer at the gems more closely before moving on, each time choosing not to ask anything or to make any other observation. Until he reached the last pair. Then he turned and studied the young woman in front of him instead of the pearls. "Explain this choice," he insisted, the command clear in his tone and his gaze.

Chimehara couldn't help it—she gulped a little. But she quickly steadied herself, lifted her chin, and replied in a clear, firm voice. "The black pearl is beautiful," she replied, "and perfect in size and shape. Its luster has been artificially enhanced, however." She held up her right hand, the first two fingers extended. "The surface is unusually slick to the touch, presumably from some sort of oil that has been added to temporarily increase its reflective qualities. Fish oil, I would guess, since that smell would be dismissed as a natural one for a pearl. But with repeated handling the pearl would lose its glossy coat, and the customer would be dissatisfied." She lowered her hands and continued. "The blue pearl, though slightly less reflective, is entirely natural, and I judged its rarer color and medium luster to be more than a match for the black pearl's unenhanced qualities."

Master Eijiri nodded once, briskly, giving no indication of whether he agreed with her assessment. Instead he studied her with that same blankly professional look—right before he smiled.

"Well done," the master merchant declared, his face creasing into a pleased little smile. "You have gotten the order exactly correct. And I agree with you about the black pearl—such a trick is unworthy of any decent merchant house, much less Chohu.

Furthermore, I could tell from the processes you used that you are indeed knowledgeable about gems and their properties. Clearly your grandfather was a wise and learned man indeed." And he bowed in her general direction.

"Thank you, sir," she replied, returning the bow. "I am honored by your praise, as he would have been." Then she waited.

"Your skills are certainly valuable. Unfortunately, we do not have any openings for traders just now," Master Eijiri continued after a moment. "I am sorry." He did genuinely appear to be so, but that didn't change his answer as he started to turn away.

"Wait, please!" she cried out, stopping him mid-motion. "I realize that, in a house such as this, even the most talented must start at the very bottom. Surely there is some task available, some job that no one else wishes to take on? I only wish to be of service and to prove myself to be of value to you and to this house."

The merchant considered a second, and she could see his coldly rational business sense warring with his more primal desires. Finally he sighed. "I could perhaps find work for you in one of the counting rooms," he offered slowly. "It is very nearly menial labor, but from there you could eventually rise up to a higher position, one more befitting your skills."

Chimehara let out the breath she had been holding and was embarrassed to discover she would not need to feign tears of gratitude. "Thank you," she managed, bowing deeply even as she dashed a hand forward to blot her eyes. "I am grateful for this opportunity."

And she was. Even though it had cost half the trader aitachi just to get her foot in the door here, now she had a legitimate job within the merchant house. Soon enough, if she played her cards right, she would begin to rise through the house's ranks. In the meantime, at least she would have some money, a respectable job, and hopefully a place to sleep. After that, all she needed was time and perseverance. She was young, after all, and smart, and pretty, and more than willing to use all of those traits and more to her advantage.

And each step upward would grant her more resources, more power, more authority, and more of a chance to climb toward her ultimate goal—

The palace itself.

For now, however, she merely smiled quietly to herself and let a servant show her to a different room, where after only a short wait the merchant house's domestic manager arrived to explain to Chimehara her new duties, her new pay, and the living arrangements available to those who could not afford or for some reason did not wish for a place of their own. Since she had nothing of value or personal significance outside of the clothes she wore, the money secreted inside her sash, the remaining scrap of aitachi, and her knife, Chimehara was more than happy to be led to a small sleeping cell after that, given a plain gray kitoro for everyday use and a glossy black kitoro for special occasions— both with the house's crest embroidered upon them—shown where the house's junior members took their meals, and then wished good luck and sent to the counting floor to begin her new career.

All in all, she considered it to be an excellent start.

CHAPTER TWENTY-FIVE

Noniki stumbled and nearly fell. He caught himself at the last second, tearing more skin off the hand that had blocked his descent, but barely noticed—by now he was so covered in scratches and cuts and bruises that his whole body was battered to the point that every movement hurt, anywhere from an ache to a sharp, searing pain, all of it melding together into a solid fog of exhausted agony. He also had so much dirt and mud caked onto him that the only places his flesh was even visible was where he had shredded that protective coating, creating an odd patchwork of red against a backdrop of brown and black. His hunger had long since faded to a dull ache, his thirst was simply a haze that clouded his every thought and movement, nothing more. He could barely remember his own name now, let alone the brother he had left behind. Yet still he staggered on.

A sharp crack cut through the haze enough to make him lift his head. Light flashed across the sky, revealing a harsh scattering of scrub brush spread across rocky ground, slanting up at a mild slope toward a surprisingly jagged peak a short distance away. Noniki heard a second rumble, and then a loud rush as the sky crashed down on top of him.

The weight of the sudden rain was like an attack by a thousand spears, the thick, heavy droplets slamming across his head, back, and shoulders, stabbing through the dirt to pound his flesh, each impact sending him reeling and all of them at once enough to nearly drive him to the ground. Noniki let out a screech, the sound escaping from his parched throat against his will, the first sound he had made in days or even weeks, since his encounter with the Bone Blind. To emerge so abruptly from the fog in which he'd lived for so long, into such a jarring environment, was enough to leave him dazed, never mind the confusion caused by the rain itself. He turned this way and that, searching desperately for some form of shelter from the onslaught, but there was nothing here, only rocks and dirt and scrub brush, and the brush was too stunted and scrawny to offer any protection, and grasping for it only left his hands even more abraded.

Turning away, Noniki half fell, half ran up the slope, some dim portion of his brain thinking that perhaps he could rise above the storm, or duck below the slope and shelter in its overhang, but when he had reached the peak he only found himself more exposed to the elements, an easy target for the wind that lashed him with water like a madman wielding a braided whip with deadly accuracy, lacerating his flesh with every blow. Noniki stumbled, twisting and raising his arms to shield his face, and his back foot slipped off the peak, finding nothing but air to support it. He toppled, then, howling in pain as he struck the steeper, sharper rocks on the other side, curling instinctively into a ball to protect himself as he rolled and tumbled and bashed his way downhill. Finally he struck the bottom, slamming against the ground there and exploding out of his huddle to lay sprawled out in the mud, face up to the rain that continued to batter him but now too weak and dizzy to care.

The water was striking him too hard and too fast for him to fully lose consciousness, but it seemed that his mind slipped away despite that, because the next thing Noniki knew it was daylight again, and the sun shone down on him from a clear blue sky, warming him and drying the mud into which he had sunk.

He stretched, causing a chorus of protests from his joints and muscles and a cascade of pops and a shower of small flecks as the mud shattered and scattered from each limb he tugged free. After a minute he puled himself up into a sitting position, though doing so awoke fresh agony from his back and sides. From there he was able to drag first one leg free and then the other, and finally he pushed himself to his feet. Standing straight for what felt like the first time in weeks or months, Noniki sighed and took a deep breath—

—and quickly doubled over, nearly dropping back to his knees as a deep, racking cough burst from his chest. The motion wrung from him what little energy he had managed to retain, leaving him tottering and weak as a kitten, and at first he thought it had rained again before realizing that he was only feeling his own sweat standing out across his cheeks and forehead. He coughed again, and again, each one wrenched loose from somewhere deep inside, each one leaving him weaker than before, his vision starting to strobe and his breath whistling through his nose and throat. Sweat was soaking through his rags, causing them to cling to his body, and he had begun to shake as well, then to shiver as a chill wormed its way into his limbs, sapping what little strength and heat remained.

Dimly Noniki knew that if he fell down again he would never be able to stand back up. He would die here, once and for all, his ghost either haunting this plain or simply disappearing along with all his hopes and dreams. And Kagiri's spirit would then be lost as well. It was that last thought that finally motivated him enough to lift one leaden foot and set it down ahead of him, and then do the same with the other. Another step, and another, and he was plodding forward again, shivering and shaking but at least with his head clear for the first time in ages.

He continued on that way for the rest of the day, the sun climbing higher and higher until it beat down upon him mercilessly. The intense sunlight was drying his sweat as fast as it formed, leaving his skin and clothes dry but his body shaking and exhausted, the last of its reserves finally emptied.

Then Noniki's foot caught on a rock, twisting sideways with a sharp stab of pain, and he toppled to the ground, the rocks digging into his arms and shoulders and sides, the air bursting out of his mouth along with another series of sharp, grating coughs. Afterward he lay there, unable to move again, unable to think beyond the need to breathe properly. Dark spots now lingered in his vision, grim harbingers of the fate awaiting him, but try as he might Noniki just could not muster the strength to continue. Instead he lay there, gasping for air, eyes clouding, thoughts collapsing into an incoherent jumble of images and old sensations, and waited for the end to come.

What arrived instead, with no more sound than a swish of air and a muffled thump, was a pair of legs clad in sandals that laced up to just below the knee. Noniki could do nothing except stare as those legs flexed, a shadow falling across him only to be replaced by a dark figure that contemplated him solemnly and silently, as unmoving in its new position as if it were a statue.

Then the figure spoke.

"Why are you here?" the man asked, his voice a harsh, guttural intonation that shredded the fragile peace of the day. "Speak!"

Noniki tried, opening his mouth to respond, but only a thin, high wisp of sound emerged. Rolling his eyes he tried again, advancing to a brief, sharp keening, but as it was still unintelligible he failed to see how that was much of an improvement. It appeared that his strange audience disagreed, however, because the man rose to his feet at once, the legs then hurrying quickly away and leaving Noniki once more to his own solitary misery.

Until those same legs returned, bringing three additional sets trotting along behind.

When four sets of hands reached down from all sides to pull Noniki out of the ground, he screamed once, from a mix of pain and relief, before he surrendered at last to the temporary blindness and bliss of unconsciousness.

His last clear thought was that at least he would be clean, or nearly so, when he finally succumbed to the inevitable.

"Kagiri!" Noniki bolted upright, the scream still tearing from his throat, grief welling up inside of him and threatening to strangle him from the inside. But a hand stopped him before he managed to sit up fully, and gently but firmly eased him back down onto his back.

"Slowly," a deep voice cautioned, and Noniki blinked up at the unfamiliar face peering down at him. The man beside him was tall and lean, with sharp features and dark, alert eyes. His head was completely shaved, only the barest dark shadow remaining across his pate, and he wore a short, belted jacket of rough, dark fabric over loose ponmei of the same shade. His skin was deeply tanned, and about his neck hung a string of wooden beads ending in what looked like a small aishone pouch, except that it had been split completely open.

"Who—?" Noniki started, then his eyes registered the walls behind the man and widened. "Where am I?" he amended instead.

Because he was surrounded by bones.

And not in the same way as when he'd buried himself beneath a body back in that crypt in Ginzai. The wall behind the man was actually built from bones, it seemed, leg bones and arm bones and rib bones all piled haphazardly one atop the other, sticking out of mortar like someone had used a graveyard for the basis of that binding agent. At first glance Noniki thought that it was simply a macabre design scheme, walls decorated and carved to simulate the valuable aishone, but if so the artist involved had been both exceedingly talented and extremely prolific, since the motif was carried around all the walls and no two bones seemed exactly alike. But who would destroy bones in such a way, and so many of them? Because the bones were clearly too integral to the walls to ever be chipped free and used properly. It was such an excessive destruction of wealth, such a bold repudiation of the Relicant Way, that Noniki could only stare, struggling to comprehend it.

The man smiled, the surprisingly sunny break in his fierce demeanor recapturing Noniki's attention. "You are in the Ikibanichari, the Castle of Many Spirits," he explained, his harsh voice contrasting with his kind words and the warm amusement in his eyes. "And I am Brother Yamaki, of the Hakara Ikibanichi."

Noniki frowned. "The Brothers of Many Spirits? I don't understand. I've never heard of you." Though, admittedly, his knowledge of the world beyond his home village had been sadly lacking until their mother's death had freed him and Kagiri to venture forth to seek their fortunes.

Kagiri! Thoughts of his brother once more overwhelmed him, and Noniki closed his eyes, giving in to his grief. But with his eyes closed he was once again cloistered within that hedge, watching through the bramble as the merchants and guards clubbed his brother and threw him into that dark tower. Opening his eyes seemed preferable, so he once again studied his host and their strange setting. Now Noniki could see that they were in a small but high-ceilinged room, and judging by the view out of the high, arched window they were some ways up from the ground as well.

"You are in one of our meditation rooms," Brother Yamaki informed him, correctly interpreting his questioning gaze. "We often use these rooms to rest and recover from bouts, so we thought it the most appropriate place for you to heal."

"Heal?" Noniki frowned. "From what?" But then, all in a flash, the memories returned—the storm, the hill, falling down the slope, laying in the mud, hands lifting him free. "You saved me," he stated slowly.

Yamaki nodded. "Our brothers found you while out searching for a few sheep who had strayed." Again humor creased his sharp face. "You were a larger, wilder beast than they expected to find. They carried you back here and remanded you to my care. You have slept for a full day, and then half again." His lips actually parted in a grin. "We also took the liberty of removing your mud—I hope that you were not saving it for some future occasion."

"What?" Noniki was still bleary from sleeping so long, and from his trials and travails before that, and it took him a second to realize the stern-looking man was teasing him. "No, that's fine, thank you," he finally managed. "I'm sorry to have put you to such trouble." He shuddered as he recalled the state he had been in, only now noticing that his hair had also been trimmed and the scraggly starts of a beard shaved away. His old clothes were gone as well, replaced with attire similar to that of his host, clean and cool and rough-spun but soft and comfortable.

Yamaki waved away the apology. "Not at all," he insisted, and sounded sincere. "We are happy to offer aid to any who come to us, for we are all kindred spirits in this world." The statement carried the formalized cadence of a phrase often uttered, and Noniki realized that the Hakara Ikibanichi must be some sort of religious order. He wondered briefly what they were about, but found himself still too tired and too stunned by recent events to spend any real time considering it. Besides, the man was still speaking. "You did not have any major injuries, fortunately. But many surface abrasions, plus you were severely dehydrated and malnourished. With time, rest, and food, however, I predict you will recover fully."

"Thank you." Noniki tried to sit up again, and again the man—monk?—prevented it. "Once I'm able to walk, I'll be on my way," Noniki declared as pointedly as he could manage. "I don't want to trouble you any further."

"Nonsense," he was told, in the tone his mother had used when he was small and insisted he could swim the river unaided when he could barely even manage to float yet. "We will tend to you until we judge you well enough to travel, and then you may leave, but not before." For just a second he caught a glimpse of the man's fiercer nature, strong and stern, before it once again vanished behind the thin veneer of gentle concern, but it was clear that he was not gong to be going anywhere until this man and his brothers allowed it. With a sigh, Noniki resigned himself to a long, enforced stay where he would be nursed back to health, whether he liked it or not.

CHAPTER TWENTY-SIX

Kagiri awoke to the feeling of being shaken like a rag doll. It was not a situation he had faced since before he had come into his full height, and the part of his brain that had already regained alertness noted that he did not enjoy it any more now than he did then. The rest of him was still easing its way back into the world, however, and for the moment he judged it both easier and more prudent to allow such manhandling while he ascertained its origins and intent.

"Where. Are. The. Aishone?" a voice demanded, each word uttered slowly and ponderously in time with another shake. The voice sounded familiar, and Kagiri was sure he had heard it before, but for the moment at least he could not place it. Nor did he deign to answer a question administered so rudely, so he continued to stay limp, with his eyes closed.

"He's not answering," the same voice pointed out, though clearly this observation was meant for someone else since Kagiri already knew what he was or was not doing. Sure enough, someone else responded to that statement a moment later.

"Shake him again," the new voice insisted. "We have to know." This voice, calm and clear and deceptively mild, Kagiri recognized at once. It belonged to Kishin Narai, the head of the group of merchants who had brought him and his brother all the way from Ginzei.

The same man who had ordered him to be clubbed and tossed into the Tawasiri to search that haunted tower for aishone, even if doing so cost Kagiri his very life.

Now that he had placed that speaker, Kagiri was able to recall the owner of the other voice, and of the large, heavy hands holding him in the air like a plaything, his feet dangling several inches off the ground. Those belonged to Gento, the largest of the merchant's guards, a veritable giant of a man, powerful but slow-moving, with voice and mind to match. That meant that he was back outside the tower, Kagiri realized. He had done it. He had gone in and made it back out alive.

So far.

Having ascertained that much, he decided it was time to ensure his survival. Blinking slowly, and twitching a little to add verisimilitude, he finally cracked one eye open enough to peer up at Gento's broad, heavy-featured face. "Water?" he managed to croak out, and the dry, disused quality of his voice served only to underline the need for such succor.

The guard frowned, then turned away from his captive. Kagiri did not hear a reply, but a second later he was lowered so that his feet finally touched the ground again, and then the hands that had held him unclamped from his shoulders.

He promptly collapsed in a heap, right there in the dirt.

"Bones!" someone cursed, and there was an explosion of motion nearby and several people charged him. Two of those skidded to a stop at his side and proved to be Shizu Yokori ad Eien Kawatai, two more of the merchants. The former checked

Kagiri's pulse, pressing two fingers to the side of his neck, while the latter peeled back his eyelid and peered inside.

"Weak, but intact," Mistress Yokori judged after a second, removing her hand from his throat, and Master Kawatai nodded agreement.

"Here is some water," the dim-witted merchant announced, pressing a waterskin to Kagiri's lips. "Drink."

Kagiri did so—and nearly spit the first mouthful back up, as his bone-dry mouth and throat rebelled, clenching against the sudden return of moisture after so long without. Only by gulping convulsively and coughing several times did he manage to keep the water down at all, and by the time it had cleared his throat there were only a few droplets left, falling into his stomach like an empty bucket dropped into a long-drained well. The next gulp further irrigated his throat, however, and he swallowed more easily this time, a little more liquid reaching his stomach. By the third mouthful he was able to finally let water settle into his gut, easing the cramping there that he had been too busy to even register before.

"Good, good," Mistress Oritano declared, observing the proceedings from a short distance away. The heavyset merchant beamed. "We are very relieved to find you so well, young master," she stated cheerfully. "When you suddenly banged on the door, we feared the worst."

What, that I had barred the door forever so that you could never get to the treasures within, Kagiri thought but wisely did not say. Despite her warm demeanor, the kindly attentions the other merchants were displaying, he had not forgotten the rough method in which he was being questioned when he woke up just moments ago—or the callous way he had been deposited in the tower in the first place.

For now, however, he simply sat and drank the water Master Kawatai forced upon him, turning his head away after a second to make the flow cease and give him a chance to catch his breath.

"Then, when we did open the door and find you there," Mistress Oritano continued with all the relish of recounting a favorite tale, "we were torn between confusion and delight. Because, you see, every known attempt to breach the Tawasiri before this has met only with death and madness. Yet here you were, starved but not raving. Which meant that either you had stayed by the door the whole time and only pretended to go anywhere—"

"—or you somehow explored the inside and returned with your mind intact when no one else ever has," Mistress Yokori finished for her with her typical sharp, smirking grin.

That last part was certainly news to Kagiri, and he stopped to consider this new tidbit of information for a bit. He had known from their initial meeting that this task was thought to be dangerous, little better than a suicide mission. But he had thought that simply entering was as far as anyone had ever gotten. Now he knew that others had probably tromped those same long flights of stairs as he had, and perhaps even reached that same antechamber—but if so, none of them had ever made it back down and out alive and intact. What made him so special?

"It is indeed an impressive feat." Master Narai had stepped closer as well, and stood just behind Mistress Yokori, hands behind his back, face benign but eyes cold and intent as they bore down upon Kagiri. "Now tell us, if you please—what did you find within the Tawasiri?"

"Nothing but dust," Kagiri croaked in reply, though his voice was clearer and stronger than it had been at first. "Anything that had been in there—and anyone—is long since gone." He frowned and shifted his body, the motion slight enough to all but go unnoticed even though it eased him into a better position, his limbs less splayed, his center of balance properly placed, his hands now loose on his knees instead of supporting his weight behind him.

"Dust?" Master Masute repeated, remaining back behind Narai and the others. He sneered, the expression pulling at his gaunt cheeks. "You expect us to believe that? No one has removed anything from that tower in all the years since it fell into disuse—the bones must be there!"

"There are no bones," Kagiri insisted, shaking his head slowly despite feeling more of his strength return. "I can only assume you have already searched me and found none—do you think I would have left them all inside if I had found any, knowing that their retrieval was the only reason you had brought me here? Or let me out?"

"Perhaps you hoped to sneak back in later and bring them out in secret, for yourself," Kawatai argued, though from his frown and his quizzical tone he had already dismissed that notion as unlikely.

"I am telling you, there are no bones left," Kagiri repeated. "Only dust remains." He tried to push himself up off the ground, levering himself to his feet, but suddenly Gento was there above him, and the guard raised one massive foot, forcing Kagiri back down like he was slowly, torturously squishing a bug. Kagiri chose not to resist, but did take advantage of the moment to adjust his seat further, so that he was now cross-legged, forearms on his knees, hands hanging clear.

"If that is true," Master Narai stated slowly, stroking his chin, "then despite your unprecedented escape from the tower itself this entire expedition is a failure. And you, young Kagiri, have no further value to us." He nodded once, sharply, and Gento moved in with a grin, Joshi appearing at the big guard's shoulder and shifting a few feet over to cut off any chance of escape.

"I think you are being a bit too hasty in your conclusions," Kagiri protested, raising his hands over his face as the big, burly guard hefted his spear and then jabbed its base down at his skull—

—and, as the weapon's butt leaped toward him, Kagiri suddenly burst into motion.

Lunging upward with both hands, he grasped the spear's end and tugged down and to the right, jerking the weapon from Gento's unprepared grip. The spear's base slammed into the ground beside Kagiri's knee, and he used the force of the impact to launch himself to his feet, pushing off against the spear and dropping it with his left hand, only to swing the polearm down across his own body and latch onto it again with his second hand just below the tip. A step back with his left foot, a pivot with his right, and he jammed the spear's end forward between Gento's legs, swiping the spear sideways hard enough to take the big guard's legs out from under him and dump the man on his rear in the dirt. Then Kagiri leaned against the spear, both hands cradling it to his chest, and grinned.

The entire sequence had happened so quickly the merchants were still drawing in breath to gasp in surprise.

"How——?" Masute started, but both Yokori and Kawatai cut him off with a single whispered word:

"Gensaiba!"

Though he could not recall ever having heard that word before, Kagiri knew it now, and he nodded. "Yes," he agreed, his voice still dry but growing stronger by the second. "The Gensaiba. They are nothing but dust now—and that dust is in me." He tipped his head at Gento, who had slowly regained his feet and was shaking his head with the confused look of someone who knows he has been beaten but has yet to understand how. "I am Gensaiba now."

The others all turned toward Narai, who as usual had watched calmly the whole while. Finally the lead merchant smiled. "Then you have done well," he pronounced, and everyone relaxed as the need for conflict abated. "We are well pleased, Kagiri." Stepping forward, he clapped a hand to Kagiri's shoulder. "This is the first step toward great deeds, I know. And we are proud to have you with us."

I am sure you are, Kagiri agreed silently, handing the spear back to Gento with an apologetic shrug. Who would not want the Gensaiba, the legendary "living blades," at your beck and call? They once served the Matekai, after all, before the fabled wizards vanished during the Schism, and now their fabled martial talent has resurfaced, but in the hands of your sworn servant? Who would not rejoice at that—and plot ways to use such skill to their advantage?

But other voices were answering within him now as well, voices that had lain quiet at first but which were gaining strength even as he did, growing louder and more distracting with every second. Except that at the moment each of them was asking the exact same thing:

How can you be sure, you merchants, that those master warriors will accept your rule, when they once served the Matekai themselves?

And what will you do if they decide that you are not worthy of their aid?

CHAPTER TWENTY-SEVEN

"Hold!"

The shouted command came from up ahead, and Shizumi's head rose sharply as sleep left her. They had been riding, her and the bantao she'd chosen to bring along, leaving the rest of her shotao behind under Akino's command to finish dealing with the defeated Fyushans, and she had been half-dozing in the saddle, an old warriors' trick that let her catch up on sleep without slowing their progress. Now she glanced about, taking in their surroundings and reorienting herself even as she flexed her fingers in their gloves and her toes in their boots, shifting her legs and rear to restore feeling and some limberness there as well.

They were in the mountains, she saw at once. Since they had crossed the Zinyang River a few days before, she knew they were still in Hochiro, which meant they were still making their way through the northern portion of that province before reaching its barren southern plains. The peaks here were not severe, being lower and more spaced out than up in Korito, well on their way to sinking into mere hills, but for now they were still steep enough and tall enough to make threading between them far easier than attempting to scale each one in turn. The vegetation had begun to rise even as the mountains sank, transforming from brush and bramble to actual trees, and now she found that they were actually in at least a small stretch of forest, the handsome trunks rearing up on either side of their horses and sturdy branches waving well above their heads, emerald leaves spreading wide to dapple both them and the ground with shaded patches between the sunlight. It was beautiful, actually, and when she took a deep breath she inhaled mingled scents of pine and cypress with jasmine, very different from the bamboo of the lowlands and the coasts or the banzai and flowers of the heights.

She had not forgotten the shout that had awakened her, however, and so Shizumi quickly turned her attention to that outcry and its source. And, upon spying the situation, her mind immediately screamed a single word:

Ambush!

It had been cunningly designed, she saw. A single tree had been chopped down so that it ran straight across the path, but the break had been placed some six feet up the trunk, leaving the obstruction just high enough that even for a tall horse and an experienced rider it would be an extremely risky jump. The tree itself was thicker around than a large man, impossible to lift without at least a half dozen hands, though Shizumi would not have been surprised if the architects of this little plan had a block and tackle tucked away somewhere nearby so that they could raise and lower the shattered trunk with only a few people. The path here was narrow enough that you could not fit more than three horses across at once, with the trees close enough on either side to prevent escape in that way—but far enough apart to allow easy attack by any archers hidden within the woods, which would give most people pause.

Not to mention the one bowman already visible, perched on a thick bough just to the side and at roughly head height, on the far side of the downed tree.

Or his friends now melting out of the forest on either side, clubs and knives in hand.

"Hands away from any weapons, or you get a shaft through the chest," the archer warned, tugging his bowstring back to prove the point. The bow looked handmade to Shizumi's seasoned eye, but that did not mean it wouldn't fire, and the arrow certainly appeared straight enough to fly true, and its chiseled stone head would be more than enough to pierce cloth and flesh. She cursed the decision to pack away armor for the trek, but knew it couldn't have been avoided—wearing full gear might have been comforting in a fight but it would have slowed them down in every other way, and they hadn't been expecting any trouble. After all, who would be foolish enough to interfere with a bantao of Honjofu riding with a clear purpose?

Evidently, the answer was—these men.

"You must be joking," Shizumi declared, sitting tall in her saddle and nudging her horse forward. "Do you have any idea who we are?" She didn't really expect to be able to brazen her way past this little group, but figured it was worth a try. Besides, it gave her an excuse to ride a little closer to the action, and a way to stall while she considered her option.

She saw at once that these bandits—that was what she assumed they were, though they had yet to demand money—had made a few potentially lethal mistakes.

The first was not their fault, really. After all, the tree they'd selected was big enough, heavy enough, and high enough to require a half dozen men to move it.

They could never have predicted or planned for Geniji.

The Honjofu currently stood stock still, her beefy arms still clasped all the way around the tree trunk just above the break. Dairamu and Masai stood beside her, one on either side, both with hatchets still in hand. Reiko and Nori stood by the tree's far

215

end, at the top of the trunk, their hands splayed against its rough bark, and Shizumi saw at once how it had happened:

She and her bantao had come across the downed trunk and assumed it had been struck by lightning or simply rotted. Deciding not to wake her for such a trivial matter, Geniji and Isano had taken charge. Geniji had tasked Dairamu and Masai with chopping the broken segment completely free while she supported its weight and Reiko and Nori held the other end. Then they would simply lower the separated trunk to the ground and walk their horses over it.

That was what the bandits had been waiting for, of course, but they must have hoped to catch the entire party dismounted and struggling to shift the heavy wood. Instead they'd panicked upon seeing Geniji hefting half the weight all on her own, and had shown themselves while the other two still had hatchets out.

And of course Isano and Shizumi herself were still mounted.

That had been the first mistake. The second was that, from the way they were moving and checking each other's location, the bandits only numbered six themselves, an even match for Shizumi's group in terms of bodies but not in weapons or training.

And they only had the one bow.

"You're Honjofu," the archer replied, bringing her attention back to him. He shrugged, though she noted that his bow and the arrow nocked to it did not waver in the slightest. So he had some experience, at least. Pity. "I don't really care." He grinned, showing stained, staggered teeth. "Bones, that actually makes this easier." His chuckle was dry and raspy. "It's not like you'll ever admit to being bested by a band of scraggly outlaws, right?"

Shizumi nodded sharply. "That would be correct," she agreed slowly, stopping her horse now that she was only a single length from the trunk. "If you bested us." She allowed herself an answering smile, the sharp, nasty one she'd practiced in the polished edge of her blade. "But I don't see that happening." Then, ignoring the archer's sputtered surprise, she turned her attention to her largest, most dependable soldier. "Geniji," she said softly, making sure to hold the other woman's eyes, "whatever you do, don't drop that tree." Her wink was barely a twitch, but she saw from the way her frequent companion stiffened that she had received the signal.

"Yes, sir!" Geniji replied, grinning back. "You got it."

"Now see here—" the archer finally managed, but Shizumi cut him off with a single raised hand.

"You have one chance," she warned in her fiercest tone. "Drop the bow now, back away, and leave us be, and we will let you go. Do not and"—she shrugged—"on your own heads be it."

"Are you mad?" the bowman declared, eyes wide and face red. "I have a bow aimed at your heart!"

"Then you had best use it," Shizumi suggested, taking a deep breath and readying herself. "Now!"

And, kicking her horse sharply in its sides, she launched herself forward.

Geniji took the cue as intended. With a mighty "Hai!" the big soldier not only dropped the trunk but heaved it to her left— toward Shizumi.

And the bandits clustered, disbelieving, on that side.

Masai was there as well, but he slid nimbly forward, using the remains of the still-planted trunk as shelter from the massive club rushing his way. And, since he still had his hatchet in hand, it was a simple matter for him to also turn and thwack the nearest bandit across the back of the head with the flat of the blade as he moved.

Unfortunately for the man he struck, he dropped right in the path of the tree, and was still just conscious enough to scream as it crushed him between its weight and the hard, rocky ground.

Three of the other bandits were taken completely by surprise and swept from their feet by the tree that suddenly came hurtling toward them, hitting the ground with thuds and cries and groans and not getting back up. The last man had been near the far end and was able to fling himself back to avoid being crushed— but that put him right next to Reiko, who simply reached out, grabbed the man's head in his large, capable hands, and gave a quick twist. The bandit crumpled like wadded-up paper, eyes going blank, his neck broken.

Which left only the archer himself.

Shizumi was already focused on him. She had crouched down, hugging herself close to her horse's neck as he burst into a run, his muscles bunching and then uncoiling as he leaped the tree, clearing its falling length with ease.

The bowman fired.

He was a decent shot, she suspected. But the attack with the tree had startled him badly, as had her sudden charge. And it was one thing to aim at another person, but something altogether different to actually shoot them in cold blood. Nor was it anything like killing a deer or a rabbit, not when you had just been speaking to this person mere seconds before.

His shot went wild. Shizumi had her nihono unsheathed and raised already, and struck the arrow out of the air anyway.

Then she was across the gap and straightened, arm extended, the edge of her blade stopping just shy of the man's throat.

"Drop it," she ordered, and he did, the bow falling from his hands to clatter to the ground below.

"That," Shizumi told him, her tone light but the words still rushed from the excitement zinging through her, leaving her taut as a stretched bowstring herself, "is the first smart thing you've done today." Then she smiled, tight-lipped and, she suspected, a little wild. "Now jump."

That made him stare. "What?"

She angled her sword away from his neck just long enough to point with it at the ground below. "Jump."

"It's ten feet down!" he protested. She didn't bother to answer, or to repeat herself again. Instead she just waited. And, finally, he gulped, nodded—carefully—and brought his one leg up so he could swing it over the bough to join his other.

Then, taking a deep breath and squeezing his eyes shut, he pushed himself forward and slid off the limb, toward the ground.

"Aah!" the cry escaped his lips when he hit, landing hard on his hip and one arm. "Bones!" But he clamped down on the pain, shutting up the second Shizumi nudged her horse forward so that his lead hoof just brushed the man's leg.

"That will remind you not to try this again," she instructed. Sheathing her sword, she gestured for her bantao to mount up, and in under a minute they were all back in the saddle and riding past the men. At least two of whom would never awaken, and some of the others would carry permanent marks from this failed encounter.

They were not the only ones to risk damage, however. As soon as the path had curved enough for the scene of the attempted ambush to disappear from view, Geniji rounded on Shizumi.

"What in the name of the First Emperor were you thinking?" the big soldier demanded, completely ignoring protocol and rank in her rage. "You rode straight at an archer with an arrow aimed at your heart!"

"I didn't think he'd be able to fire straight," Shizumi explained as calmly as she could. She did not reprimand Geniji for her breach—those Honjofu who'd served with her knew that Shizumi did not stand on ceremony, especially when out of combat, as long as no nobles were around. She wanted her soldiers to be able to express themselves freely.

Though perhaps not this freely. "That was too big a gamble," Geniji insisted now. She shook her head. "If he had, you'd be dead right now."

Shizumi shrugged. "I judged it an acceptable risk." And she had. She was not surprised, however, when her bodyguard's brow lowered, her eyes narrowing suspiciously.

"You?" she asked. "Or an ancestor?" All around them, the other Honjofu pretended not to be listening in, but all of them held their breath.

"An ancestor, of course," Shizumi replied. "My great-uncle, in fact." She smiled. "I palmed aishone when I rode closer, used the motion to distract him—and you, apparently."

Geniji nodded, still clearly annoyed but at least slightly mollified by the answer. "Well, don't play that fast and loose again," she demanded. "At least, not without me next to you."

"I'll do my best," Shizumi promised, which seemed to satisfy the big soldier—for now.

But, as Geniji turned away, Isano caught Shizumi's eye.

And shook his head, ever so slightly.

Of course he had noticed, she told herself, just managing to swallow a curse before it slipped free. He'd been right beside her, also on horseback, the whole time. And he had the sharpest eyes of the group.

Still, when she shrugged he merely arched an eyebrow. Evidently he was less concerned than Geniji with the idea that his commander had been relying upon her own tactical sense rather than that of some mythical ancestor.

Shizumi filed that information away. There might be a time when it came in useful.

But, as she did, something else occurred to her. The one thing that had been truly out of place in the entire attack, because it had been glaringly absent—

Those bandits hadn't demanded their money, because they'd never gotten the chance. But they hadn't required the soldiers' aishone either—because they couldn't have used them anyway.

None of the men had been wearing much more than cast-offs and rags, and not a one of them had shown an aishone pouch.

They had all been Untouched.

Which melted the last of Shizumi's lingering anger toward them and turned her sympathy toward pity. Not because Mukanichi were so despicable, but because she could understand their desperation only too well.

Indeed, if not for a lucky break or two, she could easily have been one of them.

That gave her something to think about, and she barely noticed as the mile slid past beneath her horse's hooves, her Honjofu tightly placed around her and alert for any additional danger as they galloped down out of the mountains and onto the plains.

CHAPTER TWENTY-EIGHT

"Um, excuse me? Miss?"

Chimehara had deliberately affected not to notice his approach but had kept at her task, which involved examining beads of jade, rejecting any that did not meet the house standards for clarity and color, and counting those that did. Now she paused in her work, making a small note of her current count before turning toward the man who had interrupted her.

"Yes?" she asked, then let her eyes go wide with feigned surprise which she knew only drew attention to their size and color. "Oh, Master Nagoi!" she said with a quick little gasp, her hand fluttering to her face—and, not incidentally, drawing his gaze to her bow-shaped lips.

"Oh, uh, sorry to startle you, miss," the gangly young merchant managed to stammer out, his face already turning red.

"I know you must be terribly busy, what with all of those to get through." He indicated the open cask by her elbow, which was filled almost to overflowing. Jade beads were one of the cheapest and most common ornaments available, which meant that House Chohu moved them in great quantities but made very little money on each strand and so did not wish to waste the time of any traders by forcing them to the incredibly tedious task of providing quality-control for the inexpensive gemstones. A brand-new worker, however, was the perfect employee to hand such a thankless task.

And Chimehara had accepted it with a smile, even as she groaned inside.

She had known she would wind up with such low-level jobs when she'd begged for the position. And it would only be by accepting each task cheerfully and performing them quickly, admirably, and without complaint that she would ever be able to advance beyond these menial level.

Or at least, that was how any normal person would think.

But Chimehara already knew that she was far from normal.

The first thing she had done, after landing the job, was to ingratiate herself with the household staff. That was going to be invaluable—they knew everything that went on throughout the house, who was in trouble, who was on the rise, who was sleeping with whom, who was skimming money, who was sleeping late. And a few smiles here and there, a few thank yous, a few times holding the door or helping to hoist a heavy basket, was enough to earn her an extra helping at dinner, an extra pillow for her bed, help sewing up any tears in her kitoros, and a knowing glance away if she was running late in the morning.

It also meant she basically had the run of the place, with the exception of the vaults—those were off-limits to all but the senior merchants and their personal guards. But that was fine. For now.

Because it wasn't the row upon row of precious gems or the stack upon stack of coin Chimehara was interested in right now.

No, her second goal had been to familiarize herself with the merchant house's layout. There were many nooks and crannies that the regular workers never even saw and the merchants completely ignored, but those who had to clean the place knew every one. And they were only too happy to share those little hiding spots with such a nice, sweet girl.

Then Chimehara had moved on to the next step—learning everything she could about her new housemates.

Master Eijiri, for example, kept a young mistress in a "counting room" near the back of the house. Ostensibly she was a junior merchant, but all she really did was make herself pretty and wait for the house's ruling member to pay her his nightly visit—and sometimes his mid-day one as well. That was good to know, but not terribly useful—Eijiri was a noble, so the practice of keeping a mistress was nothing scandalous, and he did not let her presence interfere with his work.

Besides, his private chambers were within the merchant house's walled compound. That did not help Chimehara any with the plan she'd devised. She was looking for a merchant, preferably a junior one, who lived off-site.

Master Nagoi was perfect.

He was young, not much older than her, and still unmarried. Which, given his lanky, awkward frame, long nose, small eyes, big ears, and large, splayed teeth, was not that much of a surprise. Some men were powerful enough, important enough, rich enough to get away with an unattractive face and an unappealing frame. As a minor member of House Chohu who had barely advanced beyond the novice level himself, Nagoi was not one of those. He could be a catch some day, if he ever managed to work his way up to at least mid-level within the house, but even then his own personal wealth would be limited. Unless you were the head of the house or at least one of its senior traders, you could not enter significant agreements on the house's behalf, so that also limited his influence.

But he was still several steps above Chimehara's current status. And he had privacy, which would be useful.

Catching his eye had been simple enough. Though her gray kitoro was standard-issue, she had long since learned how to modify her clothing to her best advantage. The ever-helpful staff had happily provided her with needle and thread, and Chimehara had stayed up late her first night there, taking the silk in a little here, letting it out a little there. The result was a kitoro that, while still proper, rode just a little higher on her hip, exposing more of her shapely legs; tied a bit more snug around her waist, highlighting her curves; and sat just a little farther out on her collarbone, displaying her graceful neck—and just enough of her cleavage to make any man wish for more. She had tested the garment's effect on a few of the workers, and their stammers and bulging eyes and red faces told her that her alterations had worked perfectly.

After that she'd simply made a point of walking past Master Nagoi a few times a day. Slowly. At least once each day, she would glance in his direction and smile shyly before quickly looking away.

By the third day, he was deliberately crossing her path as well.

By the sixth day, he had started coming down to the counting room, supposedly to check up on work being done there or to double-check some tally or other, but each time he had placed himself where he could stare at her from a distance. She had pretended not to notice, and had waited patiently for him to gather enough courage to approach her.

That day had finally come.

But now, having spoken to her, the poor young man simply stood and stared. Sweat beaded his upper lip, and his eyes were starting to look a little wild. Partially to spare him but also to cut short her own frustration, Chimehara bowed—which of course gave him a perfect glance down the front of her kitoro. "Did you require something, Master Nagoi?" she asked sweetly when she'd straightened back up, not acknowledging the way his eyes lingered on her chest.

"Hm?" He started and tore his eyes from her bust, focusing quickly and a little desperately on her face. It was almost sweet. "Oh, no, Miss—" he foundered, but she quickly came to his aid.

"Chimehara, sir." She smiled at him.

"Yes, Chimehara, of course." She had to fight not to laugh as he straightened, visibly working to gather his dignity around him like a tattered cloak. "Well, Miss Chimehara, I know that you are new here, and wanted to welcome you to House Chohu."

"Oh, thank you," she gushed back, clasping both hands to her chest. "Everyone here has been so nice; I'm just so grateful for the opportunity!"

"Of course, of course." His eyes had followed her hands, and he probably did not even realize when he licked his lips. Then he flicked his gaze back to hers. "Well, I was thinking that, perhaps you and I—that is, I wondered if you might—I mean—" His courage failed him again, but this time she could not help, only stand there patiently and wait. It would not do to seem too forward, after all.

At least, not yet.

Finally he managed to stammer out, "I was hoping to take you to dinner. To celebrate your arrival." The words came out in a rush, aimed as much at his feet as at her, and the last few were all but inaudible, but still Chimehara beamed.

"Oh, that is so sweet of you!" she assured him. "Thank you! I would love that!" The warmth in her words brought his eyes back up, and he smiled back in response to her sunny expression, the enthusiastic response helping him recover from his embarrassment.

"Excellent!" he told her, affecting something like cheer himself. "Tonight, then? We could meet at the front gate after the close of day." The compound had a large brass gong in the center of the main courtyard, and struck it to mark certain key hours, including the start of the work day and its close.

"I will be there," Chimehara promised, fluttering her lashes and peering up at him through them. "I'm looking forward to it."

She glanced quickly back at the jade beads, and fortunately the young man took the hint.

"I'll let you get back to your task," he promised hurriedly. "I will see you tonight." And he departed quickly, all but tripping over himself in his glee.

Chimehara watched him go, and did not have to fake her good mood. Everything was going exactly according to plan. And if the night went as well as the day, she would be one step closer to her goal.

She intended to do everything in her power to make sure that happened.

The restaurant was beautiful. Master Nagoi had clearly chosen it to impress, and despite herself Chimehara was. It didn't help that she had never actually eaten at any sort of dining establishment before. Back in Suranmui, she had mostly gotten by on scraps she had begged or stolen. Until she'd matured enough to attract attention, that is. Then she had eaten far better, as men young and old had brought her food to curry favor. But even so, the best she could hope for was a fresh pot of soup or a thick slick of roast meat. Her first night at House Chohu she had nearly wept when the cooks had presented her with a tray loaded with rice, vegetables, meat, and gravy. It was more food than she had ever had at one time, and they had given it to her without a second thought!

And now this place! With its velvet curtains separating the booths, and its carved wooden screens, and its tasseled pillows atop each seat, its sumptuous silk tablecloth edged in tiny beads so that each time she shifted her legs a small swishing sound like a soft rain erupted, its soft light emanating from painted paper lanterns, it was easily the most elaborate, most elegant, most luxurious place she had ever seen.

And the food!

They had brought out pickled radish first, sliced so thin you could read through it. Then a soup, the delicate broth swimming with tiny mushrooms and equally delicate shrimp amid cellophane noodles practically invisible to the eye and delightfully slippery on the throat. Now the main course had arrived, and it was a whole roast duck the waiter was expertly carving, flipping the paper-thin slices onto a neatly spread stack on a gold-edged plate.

Nagoi was studying her closely, and for once Chimehara did not have to fake her reactions. Her astonished delight was completely genuine, and judging by his satisfied smile that was exactly the reaction he had been hoping for.

And no doubt he expected her to be appropriately grateful afterward, as well.

That was fine, though. That part she could play easily. She had certainly done so enough times in the past. Only, back then it had been as much for survival as anything else.

Now it was to further her plan.

"This place is amazing!" she burst out, leaning forward in her seat, arms resting on the table in front of her—and her kitoro deliberately draping open just a little more, providing a deeper glimpse inside. She wore a hosode, of course, but it was of sheer white silk and just a little too small, so that her breasts visibly strained against the shimmering material.

The eyes of the poor young man across from her nearly popped out of his head.

The waiter had finished carving now, and, using the same knife and a long-tined fork, deftly unfolded a circular wrap and slid several slices onto its center, dusting the whole with droplets from a small ewer of some dark sauce before folding the whole thing into a neat package and transferring that unerringly to her plate. He repeated this until each of them had five of the tidy little rolls before them, then bowed and retreated.

"Try it," Nagoi suggested with the eager air of a little boy desperate to share a secret delight. Chimehara did so, and could not keep back another gasp as the first bite exploded into her mouth, coating her tongue with the greasy richness of the duck meat, the soothing earthiness of the wrap, and a salty, thick, surprisingly spicy flavor that had to be the sauce. She had never tasted anything like it, and it was amazing. She just wanted to curl up inside the complex mix of flavors and never leave.

The laughter erupting from the man across the table drew her back to herself, and the present. "I thought you might like it," he told her. "It's Yatamaran duck, with spicy plum sauce."

"It's amazing," she admitted, quickly grabbing at a napkin as drool threatened to spill from her mouth. Fortunately, he seemed to find that charming, and smiled indulgently at her. "Thank you. This is also so incredible."

"You're most welcome," Nagoi assured her, more relaxed and self-assured than she had ever seen him. The way he lifted one of the rolls to his mouth, expertly tilting it up so that he was able to bite into it without any of the sauce spilling, showed that he had dined upon food of this type before, if not in this particular establishment. "So, tell me about yourself," he asked after swallowing that bite. "How did you come to join us at House Chohu? I am sure I'd remember if I'd ever seen you anywhere around before." The fact that he managed not to leer too badly as he said that was almost admirable.

Chimehara launched into the story she'd carefully rehearsed, a more elaborate version of the one she'd sketched out for Master Eijiri when they'd first met—about the small trading house her great-grandfather had founded, how her grandfather had continued it but her father had shown no interest and had sold it off as soon as the property fell to him, how she had inherited some of her grandfather's precious aishone and had chosen to follow in his footsteps instead of merely selling them, how she had chosen House Chohu as the place to try because it had the best reputation for gems, which was her grandfather had loved as well. Nagoi listened, rapt, though she knew that was partially because he was so busy drinking in the sight of her lips and her cheeks and her eyes and the rest of her. But he did seem genuinely engaged in her story, and asked a few questions about her history, her family, details like that.

Fortunately, she had come prepared. And she had always been good at making details up on the spot, anyway.

They ate while they talked, with her turning the conversation back to him several times as well, both to appear equally interested and to give herself a chance to breathe. Besides, people like to talk about themselves, and she doubted the hapless Nagoi got much opportunity. Especially to a pretty girl who was hanging on his every word.

She wanted to give him every opportunity to enjoy the experience.

After they had finished their duck, and the creamy white rice pudding that followed it, delicately spiced with cinnamon and cardamom, and were sipping jasmine tea from small cups of deliberately mismatched glaze, she posed the question she had been waiting all evening to ask: "I don't ever see you at night," she started, eyes dropping demurely downward. "Do you sleep in the inner wing?" The outer wing housed the servants, the staff, and the lower workers like herself. The inner wing was for more senior traders and merchants.

As she'd hoped, her companion flushed but also puffed up, looking extremely pleased as he replied, "No, I actually live outside the compound. I have my own place."

She treated him to her best "astonished and impressed" face. "You do? Wow. I didn't even know you could do that!" And she coiled a strand of hair around her fingers, then tucked the tip between her lips, making sure his attention was on her mouth as she took a deep breath and, in her deepest, huskiest whisper, added: "Can I see it?"

"Um—" It was clear from his shock that he had never even considered such a request. At least, not on their first evening out together. But Chimehara had waited long enough—she was done being patient. Fortunately, after gulping several times, he nodded spasmodically. "Sure! Yes! I mean, of course!" He nearly toppled backward, he was in such a hurry to get to his feet, and then he was digging in his purse for a handful of coins that he tossed down on the table before reaching for her hand. He stopped himself then, and took a deep breath before more gently offering her assistance. "Shall we?"

"Certainly." She gave him a warm smile as she rose to her feet, dabbing delicately at her lips with the napkin one last time before leaving it folded across her empty plate. Then she bit her lip, the perfect picture of nervous indecision, which gave him the courage to lead her from the restaurant and down the street.

But inside, she was practically singing.

"It's not much to look at, I'm afraid," Nagoi insisted as he slid the door open and gestured her inside. "But it's clean, and its private, and it's all mine." He followed her in and shut the door again before locating a lantern and lighting it so that they could both see their surroundings.

Perhaps it wasn't much compared to House Chohu's massive compound, but it was certainly far nicer than any home Chimehara had ever seen. The floor mats were finely woven and smooth to the touch, the walls were clean white plaster, the door frames were handsome circles of dark, polished wood around sliding doors whose crossbeams were a similar hue, and a smaller circle framed a window that actually looked out, not onto a street, but toward Atsani above, with its walls of palest yellow like fresh butter. The room they were in now was clearly a sitting room and led into a small kitchen area, which meant the second door must lead to a bedchamber, presumably with a small bathroom beyond. The furnishings were simple but clean, clearly the belongings of a young man with decent taste but limited funds who was not here often enough to dirty the cushions or mats much.

It was perfect.

"How ever did you manage to get them to let you out of the compound, though?" she asked, turning back to her host and— apparently accidentally—letting the front of her kitoro slide open just a little, so that the smooth edge of its collar snagged against the rise of her breast. "They don't own this place, do they?" Her hand had slipped into her sash and extracted a tube of lip gloss, which she applied now, a single quick swipe of vivid blue across first the upper and then the lower atop the scarlet gloss she already wore there.

"Oh, no!" he protested, eyes glued to her chest, all pretense of politeness driven away by the lust she had been stoking since she'd first set her sights on him. "I do! It's not even rented—I inherited money from my family when I came of age, and I put all of it into this place. I own it outright."

"Do you, now?" She took a slow, deliberate step forward, stopping only when she was so close each breath caused her clothing to rustle against his own, and peered up at him, tilting her head to one side so he could admire her eyes and still ogle her cleavage at the same time. "That is impressive!"

Then she rose up on her tiptoes and kissed him, pressing her whole body against his while her lips hungrily sought his. He was forced to throw his arms around her just to maintain his balance, but after a second they tightened, squeezing her to him while his mouth responded to hers.

"Oh, Chimehara," he managed to moan when she at last let him pull back to catch his breath.

"Yes?" she asked softly, smiling.

"Oh," he said again, but this time with more confusion than wonder. He repeated the sound again, now truly surprised, his eyes nearly bursting free as his face paled. "Chim … e … hara," he managed to gasp out, before his arms slid away from her and he stumbled backward, falling onto his rear on the floor. "What?"

"It's called yadi-oribuno," she explained, crouching at his side. From the same pouch she extracted a small cloth, which she used to wipe her mouth clean, and then his, before wrapping it around the gloss and shoving the small bundle back away. "Devil's helm. An apt name, don't you think? It's very poisonous, especially when absorbed somewhere sensitive." She tapped him on the chin. "Such as the lips." She pouted. "You should have been more careful who you kissed, hm?"

"Why?" Nagoi asked, already struggling to manage even that short question. He was sweating now, droplets springing up across his forehead, cheeks, and arms, and perspiration was soaking through his kitoro as well.

"I'm sorry," Chimehara told him. "It wasn't anything personal. But I need to advance, and the only way to do that was by creating an opening." She glanced appreciatively around the room they occupied. "Having a private place from which to work and plan made you too good to pass up." Leaning forward, she treated him to another long, lingering look at her chest straining against her shirt, as she kissed him gently on the forehead. "Don't worry," she promised, sitting back. 'It will be over soon." The old woman she had bought the poison from had assured her that a single dose could kill in seconds, and that it would look like the victim had simply suffocated or had his heart fail.

This time Chimehara did allow herself to hum out loud, as she sat there and watched the young man die. She was already working out exactly how she would dispose of his body, making it look like he had simply collapsed and fallen down some stairs in the process. The rest of her was appraising her new home, deciding what changes she would enact to make it more distinctly her own.

Yes, everything was proceeding according to plan.

It was a shame she could never go back to that restaurant again, lest they remember seeing her with Nagoi. The food truly had been astounding.

CHAPTER TWENTY-NINE

Seikoku stared up at the fence and frowned. This was not going to be easy.

She was on the dirt road behind the cemetery, the same place where she had entered before—and exited, far too quickly and empty-handed, with an unexpected companion at her heels. She ignored all thoughts of him and concentrated on her former route instead.

Unfortunately, as she'd noticed before, the bannin were not entirely brainless. They had somehow figured out that she had used the old beech tree for entry, or at least that it might be possible, and had taken steps to prevent that from happening again. They had sheared away all of its branches that extended past the perimeter wall, chopping boughs with wild abandon and leaving the road bereft of its former shade—and her without a way in.

Or so they thought.

Because most woodcutters were used to merely felling trees at their base. But the cemetery was sacred, its trees ancient, and the town elders must have been concerned that their ancestors' spirits would be displeased with denuding their resting place even though the elders chopped up those same ancestors' bones and sold them without the slightest compunction. As a result, they had left the tree trunks intact, and all of the branches within the graveyard, only severing those limbs that extended past it.

And only as high up as they could comfortably reach.

The bough she had used before this had been only some ten feet or so off the ground, and had hung well out into the road. That was gone now, but the tree itself still rose a good thirty feet or more. And its trunk was only a few feet past the wall, close enough that if she had dared to thrust her arm between the iron rails she might have been able to brush her fingertips against its rough bark.

Not that the bannin would let her get that close.

Still, if she could make it to the tree somehow, she would be fine. Once there she could shimmy her way down the trunk to the ground and then flit through the graveyard, free as a windblown leaf.

It was reaching the tree that was the problem. But she had that part worked out.

She hoped.

Glancing around again, Seikoku once more considered distances and angles and obstacles. Yes, it should work.

All she needed was to wait until nightfall.

And for the First Emperor, who sometimes took pity on fools, to favor her with a bit of luck.

The night was dark and cool, thick with moisture and murky from the fog that seemed to be taking full advantage of the moonless sky to spread its tendrils into every shadow.

Exactly as Seikoku had hoped.

She watched the bannin stomp along, spear resting on his shoulder, club swinging at his hip, and waited only until he had just drawn past her before rising to her feet and bouncing slightly to restore the feeling there. She had been crouched down for enough time that her legs had gone stiff, and she would need all of her agility for this next feat.

Swiveling to the side, she leaned down and hoisted the coil she had lugged along with her. The rope was woven silk, lightweight and strong, and, undyed, it bore a soft brown hue like lightly tanned skin—perfect to disappear into the fog. One end she had fashioned into a simple loop, glad that some of her own aishone had come from an ancient sail maker who had known all sorts of knots so that Seikoku had been able to effortlessly fashion a slipknot.

Unfortunately, she did not have any ancestors who had been experts at rope-tossing. That she would just have to manage on her own.

Peering out into the night, Seikoku gauged the distance. Then, holding the coil in one hand and the loop in the other, she swung her arm a few times, testing the weight. Finally, when she thought she had it right, she pulled her arm back and then hurled it forward, releasing the loop from her grip at the top of her arc. It sailed out into the mist, all but disappearing in the fog as she played out coil after coil so that it could travel unhindered, watching as it soared across the gap—

—and hit the top of the fence, nearly snagging on one of the spikes there.

Bones! Gritting her teeth, Seikoku quickly tugged the loop back, recoiling the rope as she went. Fortunately it had not caught, nor had it made a sound when it struck. This was why she had waited until the guard had passed, though. The chance of noticing a rope flying overhead on such a night, with such poor visibility, was slim at best, but she had chosen not to risk it.

Of course, that also meant she only had until the next guard appeared to actually succeed at her toss.

She tried again, but a stray gust of wind blew the rope off-course, diverting it just enough that it did clear the fence but struck only empty air beyond. Quickly she pulled it back and prepared to try again.

The sound of something tapping nearby alerted her, however, and she ducked back down just as the next bannin appeared, emerging from the mist like a phantom formed out of its shroud, slowly taking on form and substance as he approached.

Once he was past, Seikoku rose and tried again. But this time she was too rushed, and her toss fell short, not even reaching the fence. She hauled the rope back again, and forced herself to close her eyes and take a slow, deep breath. She had to get this right!

This time, the rope sailed true. It cleared the fence, dropping down a few feet beyond those sharp spikes—

—and its loop settled over what had been a cluster of branches protruding from the trunk but was now only a clump of hacked and gnarled wood, useless for climbing across.

But perfect for anchoring a rope line.

A quick, sharp tug and the loop tightened around the clump. Seikoku tested it, yanking on it once and then again, but it held firm. Perfect.

The other end she tied around the chimney beside her, glad that whoever owned this house had sprung for the luxury of a proper fireplace. Another bannin appeared just as she was securing that side, but marched past without ever noticing.

Then, trying to settle her racing heart a bit, Seikoku grabbed the rope in both hands and slid beneath it. She wrapped her legs around it as well, crossing them at the ankles, and began to crawl her way across the gap as quickly as she dared. Branches she could simply walk along, but the rope was far too thin and too slick for that, so crawling was safer. Plus this way she would not be as noticeable.

Both of which were good things when you were some thirty or more feet off the ground.

That was what she had noticed when she studied the area earlier. Though they had cut back the tree's branches, they had not lopped off the tree top itself, so that still rose well above the height of the fence. As did the buildings on the other side of the road. All she had to do was tie a rope from one to the other and she could cross unseen, right over the guards' heads and the fence top both.

It had sounded a lot easier—and quicker, and safer—in her head.

She was only two-thirds of the way across when she heard the next guard approaching. Seikoku froze, clinging tightly to her rope, and hoped that he would not look up—or, if he did, that the pale clothing she had deliberately chosen would help mask her within the fog.

Whether it was because of that or because he didn't even raise her head she had no idea, but the bannin passed right below her and kept going without pause.

She didn't breathe in again until he had gone.

As she approached the fence, Seikoku saw that she had judged well. Several feet separated her back from those sharp spikes, so she was able to breach the perimeter with ease. And once she'd reached the tree it was a simple matter to drop down—after she'd pried her gloved fingers from their deathgrip on the rope—using the remains of branches as footholds and handholds.

Soon enough her feet lightly touched the ground, and she straightened, allowing herself a single brief sigh of relief.

She had made it back in! She had not been entirely sure she could, not after the last time. But here she was.

And they had increased the security outside the fence but left only the same old patrols within, which meant she already knew their patterns—and could evade them at will.

Patting the rough bark of the tree affectionately, she moved away from it, making no noise as she strode through the leaf-strewn graveyard like a ghost. The guards made no effort to hide themselves—they relied upon intimidation more than stealth, scaring off any would-be thieves—which just made it easier for her to steer clear each time they approached.

The largest, oldest, most significant mausoleums were at the center of the graveyard, right alongside the river. Those would be the most heavily guarded, since they contained the bones of former town elders and master craftsmen. For that reason Seikoku avoided those, turning instead and making her way toward a row of smaller, less lavish crypts closer to the outer wall but not so close that her movements would be visible to the guards on the other side of the fence. The crypts were all locked, of course, and the town elders and the senior guard held the only keys, but Seikoku had long since figured out how to get around that particular obstacle. Extracting a pair of slender but strong metal rods from her hair, she bent and inserted them into the lock of the nearest crypt. One of her aishone was from a lock maker, and she had learned how to assemble—and therefore disable or otherwise trick—a variety of locks from him. That relic bone was almost gone by now, of course, but Seikoku had constructed a few fake locks out of cheap materials and used those to practice on until she could pick a lock even without the bones' help. That paid off now, as it took her only a few seconds of fiddling before the lock clicked softly and the door shifted ever so slightly as the bolt holding it in place retracted.

Next Seikoku returned the rods to her hair and pulled a small skin from her sash. This she squeezed, administering droplets from it where the door's hinges would be. They were on the inside of the crypt, of course, but once she slid the door open the fish oil would drip down onto them and make them move more easily, and more quietly. Sure enough, after she'd finished and gave the door a gentle shove, it swung open a few inches with only the faintest of groans, a sound easily swallowed up by the mist and the breeze that stirred it.

Sliding into the crypt, Seikoku paused to let her eyes adjust to the dark interior. After a few seconds she could make out the low pallets carved into the stone on either side, and smiled as she stepped over to the nearest. The body stretched out upon it had been reduced to bones now, though shreds of its burial clothes still clung here and there and a smattering of hair still graced its skull. Its empty sockets seemed to peer up at her as she moved in closer, drawing her knife and reaching for its hand—

And then she stopped.

A face had just flashed up from her memory. A handsome face, with wide, bright eyes and a strong, broad mouth.

A face currently twisted into a rictus of horror and disgust.

"You're koshitsu!" the face from her memory accused. He looked so dismayed, so astonished—and so disappointed.

Not for the first time and probably not for the last, Seikoku cursed his name.

"So what if I am?" she whispered, but the memory shook its head. And, after a second, she found that she had lowered her hand, the knife blade still unsullied, the body before her still intact.

Damn you, Noniki! she cried in her head. What have you done to me?

Because she couldn't do it.

Oh, she could still steal from people like that trader, she was sure. They had already removed the bones from their resting places, had bought them or traded for them, and all she was doing was taking the aishone from them. But for the first time Seikoku found that she could not bring herself to desecrate a body that lay as yet untouched. Every time she tried, she saw Noniki's face again, and his disapproval. It was wrong to disturb the dead, she could practically hear him say. That's not your ancestor, you have no right to his bones, leave him alone. Let him rest in peace.

And somehow that remonstrance was stronger than her desire. It stopped her cold.

Finally, with a sigh and another muffled curse, she sheathed the knife again. And then crept back out of the crypt, locking it behind her. Shaking her head, Seikoku crept back to the tree, scaled it, and took hold of the rope. She couldn't simply slide back across—if she did, someone would eventually discover it hanging there, and then they would probably cut down the trees completely, making it impossible to ever get back in again.

Not that it looked like she'd be coming back, at this rate, but she wanted to at least keep her options open.

So instead she loosened the loop and tugged it free. Then she climbed up as high as she could go, dragging the rope with her. Once she was near the tree's peak, Seikoku waited for the latest guard to pass, took a deep breath—

And jumped.

Her leap carried her forward, past the fence top spikes. As her weight carried her down toward the ground, the rope pulled taut and then swiveled, swinging her down and across the road.

Just as it neared its lowest point, she let go.

The drop to the dirt was only a few feet, and she landed lightly, keeping her feet. Instantly she was up again and sprinting across the rest of the road to the building she'd climbed earlier. It took her only a few minutes to repeat that ascent, and soon she was standing on the roof once more, reeling in the rope. She coiled it quickly over her shoulder, untying it from the chimney as well, and then snuck back down to the ground and moved away from the entire graveyard area as rapidly as she dared.

Grumbling under her breath the entire way.

Seikoku had been a thief all her life, since she'd been old enough to sneak a roll or a pear off a street cart or pocket a coin someone left carelessly on a counter. It was simply how she survived. This was the first time she had ever not been able to take something—and she didn't like it.

But she suspected that, wherever he was, Noniki would approve. That thought warmed her slightly, even as she reminded herself that such warm approbation would do nothing to put food in her belly. But she also knew that she would never be able to steal aishone from the graveyard again.

She would just have to find another way.

CHAPTER THIRTY

"Your Imperial Majesty!"

Hibikitsu's head sprang up at the shout, which was followed closely by the ringing clatter of the throneroom's polished outer door slamming against the carved column beside it. The man running toward him wore standard-issue army gear, now mud-spattered and stained, and the emperor's hand went to his sword, remembering the recent incident in his study with that supposed servant, but then he recognized the approaching figure and relaxed, his fingers unclenching from the hilt. He remained leaning forward, however, perched on the edge of his seat as the runner continued at full speed across the inlaid tiles of the floor, his studded boots tearing away tiny chips with each step. Finally he skidded to a stop just shy of the dais, and immediately dropped to his knees, chest heaving for air.

"Apologies for my unseemly haste, Imperial Majesty," the man declared between gasps. "Esteemed Rojiri," he added, glancing up as if noticing the assemblage of astonished councilors for the first time. "But this could not wait."

Amani Denbi was already sputtering, of course. "This is an outrage!" she insisted, her silvery bun quivering atop her head as if her very hair somehow shared her anger. "We are in the middle of a very serious discussion regarding the fate of the empire itself! We cannot be interrupted by some mere lackey in a hurry!"

Hibikitsu spoke before she had a chance to gather her fury about her further. "Itamon is a valued member of my household guard," he explained, "a gunso who has more than earned his rank through not only acts of valor but great personal loyalty." He let a hint of steel creep into his voice. "I have every confidence that he would never have interrupted our conversation if the matter were not truly one of great importance."

Taking the hint, Denbi bowed to him. "Of course, your Imperial Majesty," she replied, smoothing any sign of irritation from her face and scrubbing it from her voice as well. "We all serve at your pleasure."

"Good." That settled, Hibikitsu returned his full attention to the weary lieutenant, gesturing for the man to rise. "What news, Itamon?" he asked, granting the soldier permission to speak.

"We have just received word, Your Imperial Majesty," Itamon answered, bowing deeply even as he spoke. He had recovered from his run but was still sweaty and dirty, a fact that clearly annoyed Denbi, much to Hibikitsu's secret delight. "The Tawasiri has been breached!"

"What?" That had the emperor on his feet, his hand once more going to Kosshiki's wrapped handle. "How is that possible?" His grandfather had been the first emperor to place guards around the supposedly haunted and certainly ill-fated old tower, and Hibikitsu's father had maintained that protective cordon, as had he.

He guessed at the answer even before Itamon's face twisted into an angry scowl. "Your guards were slaughtered, sire," he answered shortly. "Their bodies were only discovered this morning, when their relief arrived and found the tower unguarded. It appears that they were killed and tossed over the cliff, but one fell against the rocks and became wedged in there, which allowed the new guards to spot him and learn of his fate." His scowl deepened. "The seals on the tower door are also gone, and the stoop shows signs of recent use. Someone has been within."

"Bones!" Hibikitsu slammed his hand down on the throne's arm, though the impact produced only a dull thud rather than the loud crash he would have liked. "Do we know who, yet?" There was a standing decree, also from his grandfather's time, that the Tower of Ghosts was forbidden to all, on the emperor's direct orders. To violate that commandment was punishable by death—but only if you were caught.

Sure enough, the sergeant shook his head. "Whoever it was left no signs of their presence beyond a few footsteps and areas that had clearly been swept clean," he reported. "The guards scouted the immediate area but then returned to their posts at the tower door. They dispatched a bird at once, however, and I rushed here as soon as I had received it." He bowed again.

The emperor frowned. "Yes, you did well," he assured the soldier, whose broad face showed his obvious relief. It was no small thing to interrupt a meeting of the emperor and his Rojiri, after all. In more difficult times, with more volatile rulers, men had died for less. "Muster a shotao to pursue—have them ride to the Tawasiri and then out from there, looking for any sign of our intruders." He pounded his fist into his other hand. "Whoever did this, I want them found—and dealt with."

"Of course, sire." Itamon bowed again and then backed up, retreating toward the main doors with far less speed than he had arrived. He remained facing Hibikitsu the entire time, as was proper.

But before he could reach the doors they were flung open again, and a second soldier appeared. This was no mere gunso, however, but Maniko Kohori herself. Skirting the retreating sergeant with only a raised eyebrow to indicate her curiosity, she entered and hurried toward the throne, not running but moving at a brisk pace.

"Another interruption?" Denbi muttered loudly. "What now, a question about what tea to serve at lunch?" Kohori spared the councilor only a quick, dismissive glance. There was no love lost between the two mature women, and they had clashed before over their emperor's safety, availability, and attention. Sunao Tadazi was bristling as well—like Fujibuki Haro, Kohiri was a Taikoro, a Lord Commander, and answered directly to the emperor rather than the Lord General, which he no doubt took as a personal offense. But Kohori ignored the slighted noble altogether as she wove her way expertly through the crowd of Rojiri, stopping where Itamon had stood only a moment before and bowing deeply.

"My apologies, Your Imperial Majesty," she intoned, "but I have grave news." She paused only long enough to receive his nod before continuing, "I have just received a report from our patrol up in Korito. They are under attack."

Hibikitsu bared his teeth in a grimace. "Fyushu again?" he asked, a hiss escaping his clenched teeth when she nodded. "Ah, I had thought the failure of their latest raid would have taught them better."

"This is no mere raid, sire," the commander of his household guard replied. "It appears that may have been a feint to test our defenses. The report states that this is a full tyodao, at the very least." Her brows lowered as she announced, "This is a full-scale invasion."

"What?" Etsuya Kenshin burst out. "That is insane! They would never be so foolish!" His heavy jowls shook with his vehemence.

"Clearly they are that foolish, and more," Hibikitsu replied dryly, the councilor's furor serving to abate his, at least temporarily. He stroked his chin as he thought out loud. "They must be met with a show of force, obviously, and pushed back— no, beaten back, crushed so badly they will never dare such an attempt again."

For once, it appeared that his senior councilor agreed with him. "Good," Denbi stated crisply. "I agree. Fyushu has evidently forgotten to fear Rimbaku's might. They must be reminded of that, immediately."

The emperor located Tadazi in the crowd "What is the current disposition of my generals?" he asked the Lord General. "Where are my taisho?"

The aged military leader bowed. "Taisho Atsumi is in Bezenkai, overseeing the placement of the new guard forts along the southern coast," he replied, showing that whatever flaws he possessed the man did at least know where his subordinates were and what they were doing. "Taisho Daishin is in Tatsuma, training new troops. Taisho Masagi is in Obanari, inspecting the patrols there." He grimaced, the emotion flickering across his face for only a second as he continued, "Taisho Noboru is here in Awaihinshi, recovering from a recent injury."

"A war wound?" Hibikitsu asked, trying to picture the portly noble in a fight.

The Lord General shook his head ever so slightly. "A fall from his horse while touring a plum orchard," he answered. Which made far more sense, given Noboru's love of sweets.

"What about Ryori?" Hibikitsu inquired, but again the old noble replied in the negative.

"Retired," he reminded the young emperor. "You have yet to appoint a replacement."

"Ah, yes." Now he remembered—Taisho Ryori had been the oldest of his generals, and the woman had done valiant service for many years but now her eyesight was failing and her back was bad and her legs hurt when she sat a horse and so she had asked to be retired so that she might spend the rest of her days with her grandchildren. Hibikitsu had acquiesced, of course, and had meant to promote one of her Issa to replace her, since Tadazi had deferred the responsibility to him, but evidently he had not remembered to do so yet. He didn't even consider sending Tadazi for a second—the old noble would beg off anyway, citing his advanced age as an excuse for being unable to take the field, but in all honesty Hibikitsu couldn't imagine the pompous old fool out there leading troops into battle anyway.

There were always the Honjofu to consider, but unfortunately they were not well placed to be useful in this matter. "Fujibuki Haro is in Nariyari, dealing with a bandit infestation there," he recalled aloud. "And Misataki Shizumi is no doubt there with him, since he is hardly capable of taking effective military action without her." A few of the councilors gasped to hear the Lord Commander so maligned, but Hibikitsu ignored them.

"Send word to Daishin," he ordered now. "Have him gather as many men as possible and take sail to Tabichi at once, then to Korito to stop the Fyushan advance." Watane Yatahei was nearby, and Hibikitsu focused on the stout gray-haired noble. "Have your ships ready to carry them across," he instructed, and his Lord Admiral nodded quickly. He was far less of a fool than his army counterpart, and when it came to water battles Hibikitsu was happy to leave those in Yatahei's capable hands. This was different, however.

He frowned, though, as he considered his current plan. Taisho Daishin was a decent soldier but he was a stolid leader at best, good at following orders but not very clever at devising them himself. If he was left in charge of driving back the Fyushans he would resort to tried-and-true strategies every time—and any halfway decent commander on the other side would find holes in those tactics and tear them to shreds.

If Shizumi had been more available, Hibikitsu would have sent her up to Korito to assist Daishin—or even to take charge herself, though she was only a commoner and he knew promoting her like that, even just for the length of the battle, would incite near-revolt among his Rojiri and the other nobles. Especially since the Honjofu and the Aiashe rarely mixed. The point was moot, however, since she was either in or on her way to Nariyari already, and would not be able to reverse course in time.

Which, Hibikitsu decided, left only one option.

"Saddle my horse and assemble my Honjofu," he instructed Kohori. "I ride for Korito at once."

That elicited a collective gasp from the assembled nobles. "You, sire?" Denbai managed, her lined face paling. "You intend to lead the army yourself?"

"Yes, me," he snapped, his mind already working out various details and annoyed at being pulled back to the present. "Someone has to take charge, someone who is still young enough to take the field and can actually think on his feet, and that isn't Taisho Daishin. I will command, and he will follow—which is what he's best at."

"But who will manage the empire in your absence?" There was no mistaking the gleam in his most senior Rojiri's eye.

Hibikitsu considered that question seriously, ignoring his irritation with her obvious power play in order to think about the matter only from the empire's perspective. "You and the other Rojiri will see to any matters of policy and governance," he stated finally, quickly adding, "though you will not enact any new legislation or issue any decrees without my express approval. You are to maintain the empire as it stands, nothing more." Then he grinned down at the old woman. "I will be leaving Taikoro Kohiri here as well, to maintain the safety and security of the palace and its occupants. She will also be guarding the throne room and my study—you will use your council rooms for your meetings, as per usual." He could tell how disappointed Denbi was—no doubt she had hoped to perch on the throne herself or at least set a chair beside it, and he was happy to be able to quash that dream, at least. How sad that this was one of the greatest pleasures in his life! The Rojiri bowed, however, and Hibikitsu dismissed them with a wave, returning his thoughts to his upcoming trek.

It was a long way from here to Korito. He could only hope that his soldiers managed to hold the Fyushan forces at bay until he could arrive.

CHAPTER THIRTY-ONE

Noniki was almost glad when Brother Yamaki kicked him out of his room.

And "kicked him out" was only a slight exaggeration. Noniki had been laying across the bed sideways, gasping for air and brushing sweat-slicked hair back out of his eyes—he had been walking around the room, as the monk had instructed him to do twice a day to regain strength and mobility, and felt as wrung out as an old dish towel, and just as useful. The healer-monk had appeared at the door without knocking or announcing himself, as was his wont, and had crossed the space in three long strides, then had kicked Noniki soundly in the shin. "Get up," he commanded.

Noniki pushed himself up on his elbows—a feat in and of itself—and glared at the monk. "I was up," he replied testily. "That's why I'm laying here now."

Brother Yamaki regarded him through narrowed eyes. "Good," the monk declared finally, jerking his head in what might have been an approving nod. "That means you're fit to walk. Do so. Now."

"Are you booting me from the Ikibanichari?" Noniki asked, eyes wide. Though he had been eager to leave when he'd first awakened here, he had to admit that it was nice having a clean place to sleep and hot food to eat and someone else to worry about whether you lived or died. Plus, if his recent exertions were any indication he was in no shape to depart just yet.

Fortunately, the fierce-looking monk shook his head. "No, not out of our home," he answered, those thin lips quirking into the half-smile that often hovered there. "Just out of this room. I have someone in more need of it than you." And with that he reached down, grasped Noniki by the wrist, and hauled him to his feet.

"Oh. Okay." The room spun a little, and Noniki had to grab onto a bedpost to steady himself, but once he had he moved away slightly, straightening. "What happened?"

Brother Yamaki studied him again, peering down that long nose of his. Finally, he replied, "if you are well enough to ask, you are well enough to help." He sounded pleased with this decision, and went to the door, shouting down that his patients should be brought up now. Then he gestured for Noniki to move to the side, by the window, to stay out of the way until needed.

Noniki did as instructed. In the days he had been here, he had learned that Brother Yamaki was an odd mix of kindness and harshness, charity and severity. It was best to do as the monk said right away, and to save any questions for later.

Besides, he could use the extra time to catch his breath properly.

A quartet of monks appeared, two at a time, each pair supporting a man between them. Noniki stared, both because these were the first other monks he had seen since he arrived and also because the men they were half-carrying half-leading were very clearly not Brothers of Many Spirits. These newcomers were eve shaggier than he had been upon his arrival, their clothing just as tattered if not moreso.

And their faces were twisted in grimaces of agony.

"Set him down there," Brother Yamaki instructed to the first pair, who deposited their burden on what had until moments before been Noniki's bed. The room did have several other beds spaced out across the floor—he had been using them for additional support during his exercise, weaving from bedpost to bedpost—and the second set of monks carried their man to one of those others before bowing and awaiting further instruction.

"Fetch me that pitcher, and the pile of cloths beside it," the healer-monk ordered, and it took Noniki a second to realize that the man was staring at him rather than at his fellow monks.

"Who, me?" he asked. "Why me? Why not them?" He turned toward the other monks, but they were already exiting the room.

"They have already done their part," Yamaki answered. "Now it is time for you to do yours." His gaze was as fierce as ever, and Noniki sighed, knowing he would not win this argument. Or probably any with the tall, sharp-featured monk.

"Fine," he grumbled instead, and made his way toward the table his taskmaster had indicated. He wobbled a little but managed to stay upright without having to grab onto anything, and was feeling pleased with himself by the time he'd reached the small table.

Until he tried to lift the heavy earthenware pitcher there and found that he couldn't even budge it.

"Both hands," Yamaki advised behind him, reminding Noniki that he had an audience Biting back a retort, he nodded and added his other hand to the attempt, wrapping both around the pitcher's cool, rough glaze. It took all his strength, but he was able to lift the pitcher just enough to slide it toward him, where he then bent down and hoisted it at the same time. When he straightened back up, it was cradled protectively to his chest like a small cub nestling against its mother's breast.

If he thought he'd receive any sort of praise from the monk for his efforts or his marginal success, Noniki discovered he was sadly mistaken. "Cloths as well," Yamaki reminded, in that absent tone that said he was only barely paying attention. With another grumble, Noniki managed to swipe at and scoop up the pile of cloths stacked neatly beside where the pitcher had been, and clamped those against its base as he turned and slowly, laboriously, made his way back.

Yamaki was already examining the first of the men, who winced and yelped in pain as the tall monk probed his arm with long, tapered fingers. "Broken, to be sure," he announced, reaching for one of the cloths and dipping it in the pitcher so that he could wipe sweat and dirt from the offending limb, which was clearly bent at an odd angle. "I can set it, and it should heal properly, provided you can leave it alone long enough." He sniffed. "What exactly happened here, Ari?"

"We were attacked," the injured man managed to utter through pain-clenched teeth. "Gang of bandits, all of 'em armed." Tears stood out in his eyes, and not just from physical pain, Noniki guessed as the man continued, "They killed Kano and Masa, and Taki died from his injuries this morning while we were dragging him here."

The monk merely nodded, but Noniki couldn't keep quiet. "You were attacked by bandits?" he burst out. "Really?" He stared pointedly at the wounded man's torn cloths and ragged hair. "What, did they steal your clothes, too?"

The man—Ari—bristled at the accusation. "Who the hell are you?" he snarled back, glaring up at Noniki through his mess of sweaty, dirty hair. "You're no monk!"

"He is a guest, as are you," Yamaki explained, his flat tone indicating that this was not a subject for debate. "And, although he lacks tact, he is not wrong in his question." The monk frowned, drawing his heavy brows even down even farther over his sharp, bright eyes. "Tell the truth, Ari. What really happened to you?"

When the man didn't answer, the healer monk sighed and folded his arms across his chest. "I cannot treat you or Jubei without knowing the truth." The fact that he knew the men's names suggested to Noniki that the monk already had a good idea what had really happened, and he suspected the kind-hearted Yamaki would help them regardless, but the threat worked, because after a second Ari sighed and looked away.

"We were the bandits, okay?" he growled. "We were starving, and nobody'd hire us, so we took matters into our own hands. Worked perfect a time or two, but then we made a mistake, trying robbing a band of Honjofu." He scowled. "Their leader was some sort of she-demon, vicious and nasty and lethal with a blade. She and her crew snapped Kano's neck, clubbed Masa, dropped a tree on everyone but me. I was perched in another tree, and she gave me a choice—fall out of it or get run through." He grimaced and indicated his injured arm. "I took the fall. Least this way I'm still alive."

'Through no fault of your own," Yamaki retorted, though he did start cleaning with the cloth again as he continued to lecture the would-be bandit. "What were you thinking, going up against Honjofu? You know that you can always come here and we will feed you."

"We didn't need no handouts!" Ari protested, all evidence to the contrary. "We just needed to earn the money ourselves." He was actively crying now, the tears carving rivulets through the dirt on his cheeks, and Noniki looked away.

He felt a pang of sympathy for the man. Yes, turning bandit had been dumb, and trying it against Honjofu nearly suicidal— but was that really any worse than breaking into a graveyard to steal aishone? Noniki knew what it was to be desperate, and really he and Kagiri had had food and shelter and some pay, at least. This man and his friends apparently had nothing.

Including aishone pouches, he suddenly realized. "You're Mukanichi," he exclaimed. "Aren't you?" Which explained why no one would hire the man and his friends.

"Yeah, so?" Ari snarled, tears drying up as he glared at Noniki again. "What about it?"

"Nothing," Noniki replied, holding up both hands. "Just—I hadn't realized."

The failed bandit continued to scowl at him but must have seen that Noniki really hadn't meant offense, because finally he sighed and slumped against the headboard.

"You have no idea what it's like," Ari stated, his tone as hollow as his gaze—or his cheeks. "Nobody'll hire you, nobody'll help you, hell, most people won't even look at you!" His eyes flicked to Brother Yamaki, who had stayed silent during this exchange. "Except the Brothers, of course."

"We are all kindred spirits in this world," the monk agreed, as he reminded Noniki at least once a day. "The use of aishone merely blinds us to the world around us, and to our connection with our fellow man, which is far more important than drawing upon our past."

Noniki had spoken to the monk enough times now to know that he meant exactly what he said. It wasn't just that the Hakara Ikibanichi didn't believe in using aishone—that was why they wore split-open pouches around their necks, to symbolize their decision never to own or utilize the relic bones. He had once asked Yamaki if he even had aitachi, and the monk had waved the question away. "Whether I do or not is immaterial," he had replied. "Here we make a conscious decision never to rely upon such things. We prefer the present, and the living, to the past and the dead." The monks didn't ignore the past—they built their dead into the walls, after all—but they rejected the notion that it was necessary to draw upon the talents and skills of the dead. Instead they did everything themselves, with no aishone to help them. Yamaki had actually said something about him and his brothers drawing upon each other somehow, like aitachi but with the living, but had clarified that it had less to do with stealing one another's skills and more to do with just supporting each other, drawing emotional strength and reassurance from that sense of your fellow monks all around you.

It was an admirable choice, and one Noniki would have found horrifying just weeks before. Back then, the quest for aishone had meant everything to him.

And it had cost him everything, as well.

Now, as he handed the monk cloth after cloth, taking away the used ones as the healer tended first Ari and then his companion (who had been struck by the falling tree and had several cracked ribs and a great many bruises and a large knot on his head but seemed otherwise intact, having only taken a glancing blow), Noniki found himself really thinking about the Brothers' choice for the first time. Here was an entire little community that had chosen to reject the Relicant Way in its entirety—and still functioned. Not just survived, in fact, but thrived. True, they had no luxuries, no wealth, no power, but the monks clearly did not care about such things. Yamaki and now the other four he'd seen were all obviously fit and healthy, they had solid clothes and good food and a sturdy home. And they had each other.

If Noniki had been less focused on finding aishone, he and Kagiri would still have each other, as well.

He had already turned his back on the Relicant Way, but that had been out of anger and grief, with no real plan except to push back against the pain. Now Noniki started to accept the idea that rejecting aishone might be a genuine alternative—not just giving up and curling up to die but actively choosing a different, maybe harder but still viable path.

When Yamaki had finished caring for the two men, and ordered them both to sleep, he turned to Noniki and indicated the door. "Shall we?" he asked.

Noniki smiled for what felt like the first time since his brother had died. "Yes," he answered, straightening up and pleased to learn that he could now do so without shaking. "I'd like to see more of your home and learn more about how life works here."

CHAPTER THIRTY-TWO

Kagiri shifted in his saddle, tightening his knees as he did. His horse acknowledged the subtle cue by stopping at once, the hooves that were already planted on the ground remaining there as if fixed and the other two dropping down to join them upon the hard-packed dirt of the trail. "Hold," he called out, raising a hand, and around him the merchants and their guards paused.

"What is it?" Mistress Yokori snapped, wheeling her horse about to confront him. "Did you forget something? Your spare sandals? Your comb?"

He ignored her, glancing instead at Narai and then at Joshi. "Men coming," he declared, his voice as calm as if he were discussing what to have for lunch but his body taut as a drawn bowstring. "A score or more. Riding fast down the trail straight toward us. Armed and armored. Soldiers." The last word emerged soaked in disdain, which drew a raised eyebrow from Master Kawatai.

Joshi only scowled. "I don't hear anything," the stocky guard captain growled back, but Kagiri had already switched his attention back to Narai.

"You are sure?" the master merchant asked in that soft voice of his. At Kagiri's nod, he sighed. "There's no room to duck out of the way," he mused aloud, stroking his chin, "and if we go back we'll just wind up back at the Tawasiri. Which must be where they're headed, since this road leads there and nowhere else. What would you suggest we do?"

"We keep going," Joshi replied, banging a mailed fist against his chest. "The road is clear, I tell you!"

But Kagiri cocked his head to the side, like a curious bird, and the guard captain quieted down. "You will wait here," he answered after a second. "I will deal with them."

"What, alone?" Mistress Oritano scoffed, but the mocking smile slid from her face as Kagiri glanced her way.

"Yes," he confirmed, then nudged his horse forward and looked down at Joshi. "Sword," he ordered, holding out one hand. "Bow and quiver." He held out the other.

The guard turned to his employer, who nodded. "Give them to him," Narai agreed. "We must put our faith in young Master Kagiri now and trust that the aishone he absorbed will show him a way past this dilemma."

"There is only one way past it," Kagiri answered, accepting the weapons the guard thrust at him with a short nod that conveyed exactly how barely adequate they were. "And that is straight through it."

Then, still using only his knees, he angled his horse past Joshi and into motion, cantering away from the small party he had become part of. He could feel them staring at him as he went but put that out of his mind so that he could better concentrate on the task at hand.

It was a shotao, he was sure of it. Twenty to thirty men, most of them mere foot soldiers, but with a handful of mounted officers to lead them. A unit that size would have two or more gunso and a shosu or even a chuisu in charge. Those would be his primary target.

Pulling up short, he readied the bow. It was a passable tool, lacking elegance but competent enough as long as he did not draw back too far and crack the limbs. Sticking the sword through his belt for now, he drew an arrow and nocked it, sighting down its length. Straight enough, and he could compensate for the very slight bend and the damage to one of its fletchings. He gathered himself, bow partially drawn, arm extended but lowered, left eye closed, breathing slow and steady, and waited.

After he had demonstrated some of his new prowess, Narai and the other merchants had ordered the guards to pack up and get them underway as soon as possible. Kagiri had not understood the rush—not at first.

But, as he waited for the others to gather their gear, he had paced around the small clearing before the tower. And in doing so, he had noticed a few things.

Like the way the ground bore a faint overlapping series of circles, like a lizard's scales—or like someone had swept the area clean of any tracks before they'd arrived.

Like the tattered scraps still clinging to both sides of the tower's door frame, as if some form of paper or ribbon had been stretched across it until recently—and had then been forcibly removed and stripped away as completely as possible.

Like the waterskin he found off near the bramble, caught between its lowest branches and its roots where no one would easily find it, a rough-skinned, sturdy piece not that different from the ones Joshi and his men carried—but not the same as them, either.

Like the dark streaks atop a few of the rocks that jutted up at the clearing's edge, blocking the way to the bigger, nastier rocks that lurked below, just waiting for anyone foolish enough to leap out past the barrier. Dark streaks that he knew could only be dried blood, and less than a week old since it had not yet begun to flake off.

All of that, and his remembering that Narai had sent Joshi and his men ahead "to scout" before the rest of them approached the Tawasiri, told him everything he needed to know.

The merchants had warned him and his brother that the Tower of Ghosts was haunted.

They hadn't said anything about it being restricted.

Or guarded.

Kagiri was guessing that the men racing toward him were more guards like the first ones, the ones Joshi and his crew had killed. Judging by their speed, these approaching soldiers already knew their friends were dead.

And they knew that anyone they ran into on this road had to be coming from that tower, which made them—and him—the parties responsible for whatever had happened.

That meant there was no point trying to reason with these soldiers. They already knew enough of the facts to want him dead.

All he could do now was take them out before they took him out.

He did not foresee that posing a problem.

A minute passed and then the first two soldiers jogged into view. Another pair was right behind them, and then another and another and another. Kagiri counted twelve pairs, which confirmed his original assessment. Twenty-four soldiers—and four on horseback, with better armor and better weapons than the men around them.

As soon as all four of them were in sight, he raised the bow, sighted down the arrow, and released, letting the bowstring go at the same time as he exhaled. It was as if he thought the added wind would somehow grant his shot that much more speed.

His first shot was already streaking toward the soldiers as he drew the next arrow, nocked it, pulled it back, and fired a second time. He managed to release two more before chaos erupted from the platoon arrayed against him. Two of the mounted figures reared back and flew off their saddles, one with a feathered shaft clean through one eye and the other with an arrow in the chest. A third rider had been struck in the shoulder but had managed to stay seated and conscious, and was now screaming orders at the soldiers around her. The fourth arrow had missed completely, and the man Kagiri had been targeting with it now drew his sword and waved it in the air, shouting down at his men to follow him.

Obviously his first goal was to remove that officer. Kagiri slung the bow over his head and across his chest and reached for his sword even as he urged his horse forward. The blade he'd been given was shorter and straighter than he preferred, heavier and clumsier than a proper sword, but its edge was good and its balance decent. It would have to do. Raising the blade, he charged toward the troop, which already milled about, confused at the sudden attack upon its officers and the absence of any threat beyond this lone young man racing toward them.

By the time the first few soldiers realized their mistake, it was too late.

Kagiri's horse barreled into them, its bulk knocking men aside. His sword flashed out, slicing through helmet strap, toughened leather collar, and abraded flesh all at once, a trail of blood spraying out behind it from where it had just cut through a man's neck, continuing on even as that first soldier dropped, then looping back to strike on his other side, clearing a space around his charge—which was aimed straight at that uninjured officer.

The same officer who retained enough presence of mind to halt his own horse, tighten his grip upon his blade, and block Kagiri's first strike, a blow that otherwise would have removed his head. Kagiri recovered and pulled back a fraction, reversing his blade's direction and striking from the other side, but again the officer anticipated his blow and parried it. Then Kagiri swung his sword up and, gripping the handle in both hands, brought it whistling straight down—but then tugged up with his off hand, twisting the sword so that it struck from the side instead.

And the officer was caught unawares, his sword raised over his own head to block the original blow and unable to pull back in time.

The sword caught the man in the temple, and although its blade was not narrow enough or sharp enough to cut through the skull, still it opened a long, deep gash that wept a curtain of blood down across the warrior's face, blinding him. He reflexively lowered his sword to wipe the blood away—and Kagiri took advantage of that pause to stab forward, spearing his blade clean through the other man's throat right at the point where his armored coat's lapels overlapped and angling downward to sever the spine as well. The officer only managed a faint, surprised gurgle before he stiffened and then tipped sideways, and Kagiri only just succeeded in extracting his blade in time to clear the body before it fell.

That left only one officer, the one he had wounded in the shoulder. The same one who was desperately trying to rally her troops around her.

Several men got in Kagiri's way as he approached her, but he hissed in his horse's ear and it lashed out, its heavy hooves striking men to either side and forcing the rest back away to a safe distance. Kagiri closed the distance between himself and his remaining opponent quickly, halting his horse within arm's reach of her. The woman glared at him, and he found himself responding with a sunny smile and an arched brow more appropriate to a dance hall than a battlefield.

"Who are you?" she demanded, her sword thrusting for his throat. The attempt was weak, since she could only put one arm into it—her other hung loose at her side, blood streaming down from where his arrow still pierced it. He knocked her thrust aside with the base of his own blade but did not retaliate. Not yet. "What do you want?" the officer continued. "Why did you attack us?" Then her eyes narrowed. "You were at the Tawasiri," she guessed aloud, her pale gray eyes alight with curiosity and perhaps a bit of dread. "That's how you did all this. The aishone you took from there, you used it!"

He couldn't help it—he laughed in her face. "Aishone?" he asked playfully. "Is that all you can think to say? Maybe I'm just really that good." He winked at her and had to parry another attack in response, this one aimed for that same eye. "Now, that's not very nice," he protested, pouting. "I'm trying to be friendly here!"

"You killed my gunso," she snarled at him. "And several of my soldiers, too. How is that friendly?"

"Well, I didn't say I was friendly toward them," Kagiri pointed out. She swung at him again and he sighed, knocking her sword aside hard enough that he knew the shock must have traveled up her arm, making her entire side quiver. "You don't have to do this," he assured her. "Just order your men to retreat and don't look back and I'll let you and all of them live."

She glared at him. "I serve the emperor," she replied stiffly, straightening in her saddle. "He has commanded me to retake the Tower of Ghosts, and to apprehend or dispatch any who may have unlawfully gained entry to that cursed place. I intend to carry out my orders."

He sighed. "I understand," he promised her. "I do. And I respect that. And I'm sorry."

She barely had time to start as his sword leapt toward her, and her own blade was only halfway up by the time his bit clean through her neck, blood gouting out as he tore the sword free again. She was still staring at him with rapidly dulling eyes as she toppled from the saddle, her choked gasps growing fainter by the second.

Now Kagiri wheeled his horse around in a circle. "I have killed all of your officers," he shouted, waving his sword above his head. "In the time it would take most men to eat a plum. They had more training than you, better weapons than you, and they had horses." He bared his teeth like a wild dog. "Just think, then, what I will do to you."

The soldiers stared at him. None of them made a move, not even the few within easy reach. Kagiri laughed, the sound short and sharp like a dog barking.

"Run away, you fools!" he bellowed, leaning back and tapping his horse in the sides so that it reared up, forelegs kicking wildly in the air before thudding back down to the ground. "Run, if you want to live!"

That did it. The soldiers broke and fled, many of them dropping their weapons in their haste. A few found the courage to stand and fight, but after Kagiri rode two of them down and lopped the head off another, even those hardy few surrendered to their fear and took off after their fellows. Kagiri watched them go, then wiped his sword on the commanding officer's saddle blanket, sheathed it, and turned to go.

But before he had even touched his heels to his horse's side, he thought of something, and stopped.

Yes, that would be worthwhile, he decided, as he slipped his leg over the side and slid down.

Besides, he had time.

"What happened?" Master Masute demanded when Kagiri returned to them. "Are they still right behind you?" The merchant's sharp eyes flicked over the young man before him. "And what are you wearing?"

"The soldiers?" Kagiri answered with a slight frown. Then he grinned and shook his head. "No, they're long gone. We won't have to worry about them anymore."

"What do you mean?" Mistress Yokori asked. "Gone where?"

He shrugged. "Scattered to whatever towns and villages are around here, I'd imagine. Except for the dead ones, of course. Those are right where I left them."

Joshi was eyeing him. "You took their armor," he stated, studying Kagiri's new attire. "Some of it, anyways."

"They weren't using it anymore," Kagiri agreed. "And I felt naked, riding without it."

He had ignored the common soldiers, of course, and focused on the four officers. The woman, unfortunately, had been far too small for him to even consider any of her armor, which was a shame since hers had been of the highest quality. And one of her two gunsos had been a short, stocky man, built more like Noniki than him. The other two had been decently sized, however, and that short one had feet roughly the same size as Kagiri's own, so he had pulled armored boots from this one and gauntlets from that one and breastplate and greaves from another and a helmet from the first one again. He had taken all four nihono, even though the woman's was too small and light for him and one of the men's was such poor quality it must have been bashed out by a common blacksmith.

Still, they were trophies, and he was loathe to leave them behind.

The other two nihono he had thrust through his belt, one on either side, and now he returned the chokoto to Joshi. The guard merely nodded as he accepted the weapon back.

Narai was staring at Kagiri in that quiet way of his. "How many of them were there?" he asked now, stroking his chin.

"Two dozen, plus the officers," Kagiri replied.

"And how many did you leave alive?" the merchant asked.

Kagiri had to consider that one carefully. "Perhaps eighteen," he answered finally. "Of the regular soldiers. None of the officers."

"So you, all alone, killed at least six soldiers and four officers," Narai clarified. At Kagiri's nod, the merchant's face sagged ever so slightly, shock flitting across his features before he mastered himself. "Who are you?" he muttered, the question barely a whisper.

But Kagiri heard it nonetheless. "I am Gensaiba," he replied tersely, turning his horse sharply and cantering a short distance away.

Only once he was sure they could not see his face did he squeeze his eyes shut, his jaw bunching from the effort to keep it clenched.

Because that had not been the answer he had almost uttered.

Instead, a name had nearly sprung from his lips: "Onyoku Jeizen." And another: "Geido Shinen." And Shito Kibi, Bushiki

Kenin, Komu Setsui, and Nikiyu Sinchu. All of them clamoring to be heard, to be let out.

This wasn't aitachi. This was different. When he swallowed an aishone, he gained the talents and skills of that person, feeling them in his muscles like they were his own. But he didn't hear that person's thoughts. He didn't feel their emotions. He didn't become them. Even women, from what he knew, only gained the dead's knowledge and experience. This wasn't like that. This was as if those six ancient warriors had somehow been transplanted directly into his skull, as if they had come back to life within him. And they weren't fading. They weren't going away. They were all still here.

All of them trapped within him, fighting for control.

Kagiri had been a passenger in his own body the entirety of the recent battle. He had been forced to watch and listen in awed horror as first one and then another of the Gensaiba took charge of his limbs and his mouth, moving him this way and that like he was a giant puppet and they the puppeteers.

He had control again now, but for how long?

And what would happen when one of them grew strong enough to overpower him for good?

EPILOGUE

Far behind the confused Kagiri and his awed but thrilled entourage, the tower known as the Tawasiri stood as it had for centuries, its glossy black surface reflecting the rays of the setting sun and scattering those beams before it so that dancing spots of light played across the plateau at its feet. The sea roared as it slammed up against the cliffs below, repeatedly dashing itself on those jagged rocks, and birds cawed as they spun overhead, but otherwise the twilight was silent.

Until the tower's door flew open with such force that it was torn clear off its hinges, the heavy metal panel soaring across the plateau and landing with a resounding clatter upon the dirt and rock of the road beyond.

The birds fled, screeching in terror. Even the waves seemed to subside, subdued by the force of that sudden ejection.

And into this new quiet something pulled itself free of the tower door, struggling through that narrow portal and expanding rapidly once it was clear.

It had no true form, no substance, no color. If anything, it was the absence of those things, a ripple in the air that somehow leeched brilliance from the water and the sky and the rocks, leaving them wan and listless in its wake. Its shadow or its self or some combination of the two brushed against a corner of the scrub brush that bordered the small clearing, and where it touched the vegetation withered and died, drained of life and left white and shriveled. That contact seemed to energize the strange force, and it gathered itself, then took to the air. With no more substance than a cloud, it floated away from the tower that had been its prison for so long, but it did not drift aimlessly. It had purpose, and direction, and it gathered speed as it went.

In its wake, it left a swathe of washed-out devastation. Plants shriveled. Animals did as well, shrinking in on themselves like they had wasted away from hunger, leaving only pale, desiccated copies of themselves behind.

And with each new death, the thing grew stronger. Its shadow took on more depth, more shadow.

More substance.

And, deep within it, the colors it had stolen swirled and roiled, twisting and writhing as if struggling to break free.

On the strange, silent force traveled. Trees decayed as it passed over them. Birds wheeled about and raced away, those who were too slow gasping and plummeting in its wake. Animals that were too slow or feeble to evade its grasp stumbled and fell, looking as if they had starved for weeks by the time they hit the ground.

Then two figures appeared on the horizon. Two young men, barely more than boys, trudging together down the road.

The thing seemed to sense them. It shifted course, and zoomed straight toward them.

When it passed over their heads, the two boys glanced up and gasped. Their skin, already pale, turned the color of new bone. Their hair, an inky black, surrendered its color as well, fading instantly to an ashy gray. And their eyes filled with swirls of white and gray, the pale dance leaving no room for anything else in their blank gazes.

Ibaru turned to Iraku. "I am hungry, brother," he stated, his words soft but somehow piercing.

"As am I," his brother agreed. He turned, looking the way the force had headed, his strange new eyes somehow seeing the nearly invisible entity. "Come," he stated, and turned, facing the blighted path it had created.

Beside him, his brother nodded. And together, arm in arm, they followed the force that had transformed them—and, they hoped, would soon transform all of Rimbaku.

The Silent Change had come. And it would not be stopped until all the world had been changed by its dark, hungry touch.

END OF BOOK ONE

GLOSSARY

Aiashe: "foot bone," a foot soldier in Rimbaku's army

Aikaye: "sea bone," a sailor-warrior in Rimbaku's navy

Aishone: relic bones

Aitachi: The Relicant Touch, the ability to absorb ancestral memories, skills, and knowledge by touching or consuming objects or people from the past

Akatai: family or household demons; malevolent ancestral spirits

Awaihinshi: The City of Polished Light, the marble capital of Rimbaku. Divided into six tiers (one for each level of the soul), with a shanty town/slum (Suranmui) at the bottom outside the walls and the emperor's palace at the top. Each tier has an outer wall of a different shade of marble, growing lighter in shade witch each height, from black to white. The tiers are:

- One: Aihiri, the Imperial compound at the very top. Walls of purest white marble.

- Two: Atsani, where the Daijin and other important nobles live. Walls of palest yellow.

- Three: Motohiri, where the most influential merchants and the minor nobles live. Walls of peach.

- Four: Sakiriti, mid- to lesser merchants and the most important artisans. Walls of the hue of cherry blossoms (a pale rose).

- Five: Bejinuri. Other artisans and craftsmen. Walls of pale violet (red wisteria).

- Six: Mazihini, laborers and other menials. The walls surrounding this level are pale blue like water, and the outer walls of the city as a whole.

Bannin: guards, watchmen

Bezenkai: a southern province

Burahone: the Bone Blind. These women's aitachi is so strong they are constantly overwhelmed by memories and knowledge, drawing it from the very elements around them.

Chohu: a prosperous merchant house specializing in gemstones

Chokoto: a straight-edged sword with a ring pommel

Chosinichi: A "reservoir," someone who can hold absorbed skills for a long time

Daijin: imperial ministers

Dojo Kuge: aristocratic bureaucrats

Fyushu: a rival nation to Rimbaku's north, constantly testing the borders.

Gensaiba: "Living blades," legendary warriors of mythic ability

Ginzai: the nearest large town to the brothers' home

Hakara Ikibanichi: the Brothers of Many Spirits, a monastic order

Happoa Kappua: "The Foamy Cup." A tavern in Ginzai

Honjofu: Bone warrior, Rimbaku's elite military unit

Honteno: "Emperor's bones," the Rimbaku Imperial Guard

Hosode: an undershirt, usually plain and unbleached and typically of silk.

Jigekugi: lesser bureaucrats, the lowest rank of nobility

Jubanichi: The "perfect touch"—someone who absorbs quickly and holds for a long time

Kaemusei: "the Silent Change" or "The Silent," a magical being of limitless hunger

Kampaki: acting imperial regents

Katacho: the most common nihono

Kenroichi: A solid touch, someone who can absorb decently and hold it decently

Kindichi: bosses or kings

Kitoro: a silk outer garment, like a wide-sleeved robe, usually decorated.

Koshitsu: a graverobber

Matekai: a wizard

Menatu: a warrior's face mask, made of metal and hooked onto or tied to the helmet.

Mukanichi: An "untouched," someone who can't really absorb at all, the lowest of all people

Muraito: A larger town or small city not far from Ginzai

Naritaba: a pole weapon, a wooden or metal shaft with a curved single-edge blade at the end. The blades were forged in the same way as nihono. Often used by mounted warriors, and by women warriors.

Nafti: a fruit, round and juicy, with mottled green and gold skin and crisp white flesh.

Nihono: a long sword with a curved blade, the most common bladed weapon in Rimbaku

Nodacho: a longer nihono

Ponmei: loose cotton pants with a drawstring tie and tapered ankles.

Rimbaku: "land made barren from cursed magic," the land after the Schism

Ritakhou: "land rich with blessed magic," the land before the Schism

Rojiri: counselors to the emperor

Senkuniki: ancestral spirits—typically akatai are considered the darker, more malevolent ancestral spirits, while senkuniki are those more inclined toward benevolence

Senkousa: a Bone Reader. These women have strong aitachi and can actually "read" aishone, telling what memories and knowledge and skills each bones possesses.

Shugiri daimyo: grand nobles, closest to the emperor in status and power

Shugodiri: lesser nobles

Sokuichi: A "crude touch" or "rough touch," someone who doesn't absorb easily and needs a lot of material to absorb anything

Suponichi: A "sponge," someone who absorbs quickly

Takotsu Hakara: Home of Brotherhood, the mountain monastery of the Hakara Ikibanichi

Tawasiri: the Tower of Ghosts, an ancient tower at the southeast tip of Rimbaku, long since abandoned and believed to be haunted. Originally the meeting place of the matekai of Ritakhou.

Tokimichi: A "flutter touch," someone who can't hold the absorbed skills for long

Tsukifuko: the Moon of Lawlessness, a month during which no rules or laws apply

Tsurogo: a double-edged nihono

Zinyang River: the "Central River," the large river that runs east-west across Rimbaku right through the center of Chibiri, separating Hochiro and Saruto to the south from Obanari and Yunigiri to the north.

*

Rimbaku is divided into four regions: Kitini (north), Chibiri (central), Miniri (south), and Shitimi (island)

Within each region are two or more provinces. They are as follows:

Kitini:

- Tabichi (northwest region, bordering Fyushu above and the ocean to the west)

- Korito (northeast region, bordering Fyushu above and Yatamaro to the east)

Chibiri:

- Yunigiri (northwest, bordering the ocean)

- Obanari (northeast, bordering Yatamaro to the east)

- Hochiro (southern band, bordering Yatamaro to the east)

- Saruto (the capital region, with the ocean on one side and the southern band on the other)

Miniri:

- Bezenkai (southwest, bordering the ocean)
- Nariyari (southeast, bordering Higinasi to the west)

Shitimi:

- Iwikaru (the northern island)
- Tatsuma (the southern island)

Rimbaku is roughly 1200 miles wide by 2000 miles long, or 2,400,000 square miles (somewhere between China and India in size).

*

Military groupings, smallest to largest:
Bantao = Squad (4-10)
Shotao = Platoon or troop (2-4 squads, 16-40)
Chotao = Company (2-4 platoons, 60-160)
Dantao = Battalion (4-6 companies, 300-900)
Reitao = Regiment (2-4 battalions, 600-2000)
Tyodao = Brigade (3-6 battalions, 1000-3000)
Sudao = Division (3 or more brigades or regiments, 3k-6k)
Gaodao = Corps (2 or more divisions, 25-50k)
Gyunao = Army (2 or more corps, 100k-150k)
Gyunshadao = Army Group (2 or more armies)
Chukogao = Regional Theater (the entire military force in a region)
Sanseidao = Front (the entire military force in a war)

Military ranks:
Sotaisho: commander-in-chief, usually the Emperor himself
Karo: military governor

Dogenriku: Lord General, the field marshal (in charge of tactics, fills in for the Emperor on the battlefield if he is not present)
Taisho: general
Issa: colonel
Chusa: lieutenant colonel
Shosa: major
Taisu: captain
Chuisu: lieutenant
Shosu: junior lieutenant
Gunso: Sergeant
Gocho: Corporal

Naval ranks:
Dogenkaishu: Lord Admiral
Kagono: admiral
Kagusho: vice-admiral
Daiso: captain
Kumigashi: commander
Kogashiri: lieutenant commander
Chudai: lieutenant

Special units:
Taikoro: Lord Commander, in charge of an entire elite force (like the Honjofu or the Honteno)
Chuisu: lieutenant, can command a chotao
Gunso: sergeant, can command a shotao
Gocho: corporal, can command a bantao